Praise for *Jesus's Bro*

"*Jesus's Brother James* is a novel about finding faith and friendship in the strangest of places. Set in our crazy times of constantly pinging iPhones and anxiety brought on by need-it-now workplace demands, Jesus's not-so-famous brother silently communicates with four struggling, lonely people who need a heavy shot of ageless compassion and empathy. Timothy Reinhardt is witty and observant, steeping the pages of *Jesus's Brother James* in gallows humor while never breaking his stride in delivering a subtle manifesto on the dangers of modern life. However fantastic the situations, you know the truth of these characters and will recognize their choices as ones you may have taken in your own life."

—Alice Osborn, Author of *Heroes without Capes*

"*Jesus's Brother James* is delightful! Clearly drawn characters with surprising depth take us on a crash course of hilarious and poignant events while they search for answers but end up finding themselves."

—Steven Roten, Director of Theater at Meredith College

"Tim Reinhardt's dark, satisfying sense of humor propels *Jesus's Brother James* in directions the reader never sees coming. It's a wild, wicked journey, full of offbeat characters and moments of joy and madness. Definitely well worth the trip."

—Don Vaughan, Founder of Triangle Association of Freelancers

"Many of us who spent 12 years at Catholic school stay at home Sunday mornings. Yet, we still root for Notre Dame Saturday afternoons. Tim Reinhardt captures that dichotomy perfectly in Father Coady, a priest who uses his collar as a badge, a shield, and a magnet. *Jesus's Brother James* shows us there's a lot going on under the average cassock."

—Bob Langford, Writer/Producer

To my friends, Wendel and Mike.

Wendel, the first teacher who inspired me to write.

Mike, a dear friend—always. Life doesn't always give you
a chance to say goodbye.

www.mascotbooks.com

Jesus's Brother James

For more information, please contact:
Mascot Books
620 Herndon Parkway, Suite 320
Herndon, VA 20170
info@mascotbooks.com

Library of Congress Control Number: 2018907659

CPSIA Code: PRFRE1218A
ISBN-13: 978-1-68401-966-3

Printed in Canada

Jesus's Brother James

Timothy Reinhardt

Chapter 1
Mike

It's hard to believe this little phallus-shaped thing can kill somebody.
Mike chuckled as he fumbled the bullet into the chamber of his gun.

Examining the shiny, smooth copper casing of the bullet, Mike considered the fatal process of this small object if it were to propel out of the barrel, slice through the air, and smash into its target. Rolling it back and forth across the lines in his palm, Mike gazed at the primer below the casing.

Reading the engraving, "Remington 12 Peters," Mike pondered the holiness of a different Peter: St. Peter. Images of his blood, bone fragments, and damaged organs overwhelmed him with feelings of guilt, angst, and nausea. Bending over, Mike tried to vomit, but he only managed to expel air. His body shook as he tasted bitter bile. He needed more alcohol to wash away the unpleasantness.

Trying to distract himself from those unnerving thoughts, Mike squeezed his large round frame between a car seat and the back of the passenger seat as he worked to dislodge a sippy cup handle from underneath one of them.

His thick fingers pushed through crusty bananas hardened to the plastic at the bottom of the seat's mount. The decaying food stunk, but the smell did not deter him. After a few tugs, he pulled the cup free. Mike examined the smiley silver face of Thomas the Tank Engine. The cheery face annoyed him, so Mike frantically scratched through Thomas's face with the bottom of one of his bullets. He sighed with relief when the smile was no longer recognizable. "Thomas, he's the cheeky one." Mike softly sang the *Thomas* theme song lyrics, which had been branded into his memory. *I won't have to listen to that anymore.*

The thought of no longer listening to children's songs saddened Mike. He examined the cup. The child's mug had fancy compartments, one holding fish crackers and the other holding Honey Nut Cheerios. Mike chanted *eeny, meeny, miny, moe* to determine which snack to devour. The Cheerios were the winner.

As he chomped down on a handful of stale Cheerios, he felt as though the recently deformed face on the cup was mocking him. He laughed, trying to shake the idea that a cup could intimidate him. Mike popped the clear top and emptied the moldy liquid onto the pavement, replacing it with El Dorado rum. Hesitating for a moment, Mike pondered the level of microorganisms residing in the filthy cup. He shrugged, deciding that he preferred to drink from the cup instead of straight from the bottle; plus, he reasoned alcohol would kill most everything.

Mike sucked hard on the sippy cup, which took time due to the small opening at the top of the cup, requiring several deep breaths. *How the fuck do kids drink from these fucking things?*

Frustrated, Mike snapped the top off and tossed it on the floor and chugged the rum. He shook from the effects of the alcohol as though he had wandered outside naked in the bitter cold. Mike gulped a second-long swig. He peered around the crumb-covered minivan, pondering how it could get so dirty after only two years.

He considered how he had arrived here at this place in his life. He reached into his back pocket, took out his wallet, and retrieved a letter. Delicately, he opened the letter and perused the contents with care. Mike's fingertips felt the wrinkles of the old paper, which he had held so many times. Although the letter contained good news from many years ago of his acceptance into the architecture program at Cal Poly San Luis Obispo, it brought Mike intense melancholy. He did not want to read it again. With the delicacy of a master chef, he folded the letter and gingerly placed it back into his wallet and refilled his sippy cup.

If only I had the chance to do it all over again.

Gazing down at his soft middle-aged frame he sighed, as though the poor condition of his body symbolized the state of his entire existence. Running his hairy fingers over the small bumps on his bald spot, he recalled how he had won "Best Hair" in his senior year of high school. Memories of various young girls vying for a ride from school in his Porsche flashed through his mind.

The memory caused his saggy face to brighten as he visualized his license plate, *E-TKT*, which represented the most exciting ride at the local amusement park. He pictured racing on back roads with his girlfriend screeching with pleasure as they sped around curves. The memory evaporated and the sight of his wife's old-looking, filthy minivan returned. Mike thumped his fists into the back of the seat, attempting to crush the depressing thought of his coming suicide.

Anger came much easier to him now. Always a good-natured person, the sharp of edges of life had punctured Mike's childhood optimism. This hard lesson started after high school. Mike, trapped by his need to constantly maintain his late uncle's Porsche 911, spent too much time in his low-paying job instead of focusing on his community college classes. His dream of becoming an architect promptly drifted away from his future.

The idea completely died when he took a permanent position with a mobile device company. Being smart and technically savvy, Mike quickly became a regional manager. For a nineteen-year-old, the job paid well. The excitement lasted for a few years. It wasn't until four months into his first marriage, when his new bride started pricing homes, that Mike realized the low ceiling of his potential income earnings had practical implications.

In the next decade, Mike managed to get divorced and remarried, while never switching jobs or moving higher up the corporate ladder. He also realized that the lack of a college degree plateaued him in his current role. He felt trapped, and his life, like a rapid stream on a stationary stone, started to erode his pleasant personality. Like a reversal of Oscar Wilde's character Dorian Gray, Mike kept the beautiful portrait of himself hidden from public, and he only displayed to people the worn, beaten aspect of his face. After brief attempts at changing his life, including several self-help books on positive thinking and seminars on starting a new career, Mike decided it was easier to simply justify his negative thoughts.

Life is brutally unfair, he concluded. His brain became a fertile area for toxic thoughts, rendering and exploring nefarious ideas, hoping some crazy act would transport him out of his soulless prison. Gathering data from numerous hours of watching documentaries, Mike snickered at anyone who attempted to tell him life was good. He purchased a "Life is Good" shirt and put a red slash through it. Whether it was a nature show about life in the Serengeti, a narrative on children with cancer, or a biography of Teddy Roosevelt, Frank Lloyd Wright, or Bette Davis, they all contained pain, suffering, and death. Mike finally concluded that whether you were a former president or a wildebeest, death came to you, and often in an unceremonious way.

As Mike drank, he fingered a new Bible his wife had been carrying with her. *Never opened*. Mike laughed. *Figures!*

Feeling superstitious, Mike decided he would try to use the holy book to predict his future. Holding the book up perpendicular to the floor, he dropped it to let fate determine which page and possible verse would dictate his future. The Bible dropped and fell open to Matthew 13:55. Mike read aloud, "Isn't this the carpenter's son? Isn't his mother's name Mary, and aren't his brothers James, Joseph, Simon, and Judas?" *Shit, that didn't help.*

Mike held up the book a second time and dropped it once more. Mike smiled as he read the second verse, "They have rebelled against their God. They will fall by the sword; their little ones will be dashed to the ground, their pregnant women ripped open." *Even the Bible is brutally unfair.* He felt vindicated.

On his phone, Mike opened YouTube and opened a bookmarked show on black holes. He watched a scientist describe how a black hole would eventually engulf Earth. Images of every person, structure, and element pulverized into tiny particles and spat out across the universe made Mike chuckle.

For some viewers, this daunting fact could have caused consternation. For Mike, the concept soothed him. Every flaw, mistake, and embarrassing moment would be demolished beyond recognition. No matter what action he took, whether a huge success or a miserable failure, it all ended in the same place.

Mike smiled at the thought. *In the vastness of history and space, who gives a shit about what the fuck I do?*

The pleasantness faded. Mike gazed to the dark sky and pondered if someone was watching him. He felt so alone. He clung to the hope that somewhere, a set of sympathetic eyes peered at him. He waited for a signal. He looked, but saw nothing. He listened, but only heard crickets. He put his chin high in the sky and felt a breeze tickle his cheeks. He concluded that there was no one there.

Mike downed one more sippy cup of rum. He snapped the cartridge into the chamber and released the safety. He aimed the gun into the darkness and imagined the damage a bullet would do. He got out of the minivan. He stood erect, pounded his chest three times, and let out a guttural yelp. He felt ready.

Jesus's Brother James

Chapter 2
Amber and Paul

"You're not going to be back tonight from New York for my birthday?" gasped Amber into her cell phone. "Are you serious?"

Amber, gripping the phone, moved it away from her ear in disgust. Paul's last-minute cancelation did not surprise her. After all, he consistently did whatever he wanted, but his absence *on her actual birthday* pissed her off. She took deep breaths, trying to remain calm as she attempted to think of a cutting retort.

While her mind filled with anger, nothing came to her. Earlier that week, she had fantasized about reigniting their fading courtship. Amber, a ferociously independent career woman, did not usually stress about relationships, but Paul's indifference dented even her robust pride.

"Sweetie, how many times in my life will I get the chance to meet Garry Kasparov?" replied Paul.

Amber put the phone away from her ear to let Paul's imploring tone drift off. She despised any form of begging, especially when people pleaded with her for any form of forgiveness. She once threw a coffee mug through her television when a politician trotted his pathetic family out to apologize for his sexual indiscretions. The sight of a wife having to endure public humiliation through no fault of her own enraged her. She tapped her phone on the bathroom counter, hoping the banging would pierce Paul's ear.

"Amber, that tapping is killing me," Paul said.

"If only that were true," Amber responded dryly, loud enough for Paul to hear.

"Amber, I'm really sorry I'm missing your party, but this is such a great opportunity. Kasparov is a world chess champion and a major dissident voice against Putin. Do you know how many followers he has on Twitter?"

"I can guarantee you I look better naked," Amber scoffed.

"Amber," was all Paul could stammer, realizing that the introduction of sex into a conversation translated into a checkmate for Amber. "You understand, right?"

Amber did understand, but Paul did what he wanted without permission, regret, or indecision. Like adventure seekers who climb the highest mountains or who brave Class V rapids, Paul sought excitement by identifying famous people, tracking them down, and building a relationship with them.

She admired that daring spirit. Paul had used his tried-and-true technique when he courted her. After meeting her at a friend's party, Paul tracked her down and convinced her to accept his invitation for a first date. He did not simply get her number, but researched her favorite restaurant, bought her favorite flowers, and came prepared to discuss her favorite author, Jane Austen, which was not normally an author that grown men read. Amber had never been so impressed.

Today, however, she did not admire Paul's tenacity as she only felt slighted. Although Amber never imagined herself settling down for a domestic life, she recently started to become insecure. Daily, female friends bombarded her with the question, "Are you ever going to have kids?" She felt like a contestant on a million-dollar game show, pondering the ultimate final question. She knew the answer was no, but wavered as her bio clock ticked down to zero.

"Amber, I picked up something that's going to make you scream," Paul claimed, sweetening his voice as much as he could.

"I just really wanted you to be here," she started, but stopped herself as she detected the sound of a pathetic beggar in her voice. Changing her tone, she scoffed, "I can have a good time without you." The sound of car horns blaring from Paul's end of the line saved her.

"What was that?" Paul yelled. "It's hard to hear you through the street noise."

"Can you call me back when you're someplace quiet?"

"Sure, I'll call you tomorrow and let you know how the meeting with Garry went. Have a great time at your party."

"Tomorrow?" Amber asked as Paul hung up the phone.

In New York, Paul checked Google Maps for the exact location of the restaurant where he'd be meeting Garry Kasparov. Tonight's meeting validated Paul's life turning point, which he had made five years earlier. After college, Paul gave up his dream of being a photojournalist to take a corporate sales position for a blue-chip stock company.

At first, the pay allowed Paul to buy things he could never afford in college, but after more than five years, Paul had a small mental breakdown as the soulless monotony of corporate life wore on him. Endless meetings pushing drugs to condescending physicians seemed like a worthless job. After all, medicines have mountains of clinical data to support their efficacy. Why did doctors need sales representatives with no science backgrounds to entice them?

Wanting to escape, he took a job teaching English in the southern Russian city of Stavropol. On the plane flying from New York to Moscow, Paul felt liberated. Like an addict feeling the rush of a narcotic, Paul became hooked to the rush of adrenaline produced from his fearless audacity.

My time in Stavropol! Paul exclaimed to himself. *That'll be my icebreaker to Kasparov. He'll love it.*

Paul took out a small notebook, stopping in the middle of the sidewalk, forcing people to move around him as they walked. He quickly jotted down all the interesting people he had met in Stavropol years before: the chemist trying to start a pharmaceutical manufacturing site, the old teacher whose daughter Svetlana had moved to the U.S. to marry, and the film director who had made movies during the fighting between Georgian rebels and Russian forces. Paul pushed so hard on the pen it made his fingertips ache. The excitement made him giddy. Paul slapped the notepad with anticipation.

Garry's going to love those topics, Paul said to himself. *I just need to get him started. Then let him talk about whatever he wants.*

A recent casual conversation on a flight from Los Angeles to Raleigh with a CEO of a small consulting firm birthed this potential meeting. The CEO mentioned that Kasparov had wanted to speak at corporate team-building functions.

Paul seized on this angle, figured he could become Kasparov's "agent," and took a few weeks of intensive Russian classes to brush up on his rusty language skills. He called up his former colleagues to understand how they hired speakers and also read several Kasparov biographies so he could ask the right questions. Paul formulated a prepared sentence around leaving corporate America for a job in Russia during the fighting in Georgia.

As he dashed though the crowded sidewalk, his phone vibrated. Amber. He looked at the phone with disappointment. *This is why I'll never get married. She would have me fly back to Raleigh for a silly birthday party instead of meeting someone who shapes world events.*

Paul clicked the ignore button, but gave his phone a long stare. Amber's sudden neediness surprised him. Paul loved her independence, her drive, and her emphasis on her career. Although he did not want it for himself, Amber's lifestyle proved a good match with his goals.

Paul had always avoided women without a career, knowing that they were looking for a benefactor. Being married and trapped with a family represented a living death for Paul. He spent the last seven years spontaneously traveling to remote locations around the world. He spent a year teaching English in Ahmedabad, India; six months in a music program in Freiburg, Germany; and a year working on a vineyard in the Mendoza region of Argentina. He felt none of these things were possible with a serious relationship. Being a corporate widower to Amber seemed a natural fit for him.

Paul thought he met a perfect partner with Amber. She was beautiful, smart, and, best of all, she had trouble leaving the office in the evening. When she did leave her office, she plopped herself in the kitchen to work on urgent projects, never questioning Paul's schedule. Her work addiction allowed Paul ample time to plan his next adventure or last-minute flight to somewhere more interesting.

He had carefully created a system of automatic revenue from a variety of investments and products to subsidize his lifestyle. There was no need for him to be in one place to get paid. When he spent time with Amber, it was quality time. They went to elaborate dinners, weekends in New York, or skiing in Colorado. Not the type to sit around waiting for Paul to entertain her, Amber desired exciting companionship or she wanted to be left alone. Paul loved that.

This new, needy Amber surprised and disappointed him. For a moment, he felt heavy guilt as he sat at the table waiting for his meeting, but then considered the benefit of missing Amber's party.

My absence can be a test. If Amber gets upset with this, it's a sign she wants to get serious, which means it's time to end things.

Then Garry Kasparov arrived, shook his hand, and Paul's concerns for Amber vacated his mind. Garry apologized for being late, due to a last-minute interview on CNN.

Paul sighed with deep satisfaction. "*Nichego*," he said, which meant it was nothing in Russian. Before long the two were in deep conversation about potential speaking engagements and Paul traveling to Russia to speak to dissidents about the aggressive foreign policy of Vladimir Putin.

Amber did not have such a fulfilling night. Although her friends had gathered at their favorite restaurant, Little Hen, in downtown Raleigh, drinking several bottles of wine, she never shook Paul's indifference. She reprimanded herself for caring about his absence. A vicious cycle ensued of Amber thinking of Paul and then Amber berated herself for thinking of Paul.

Rejection? Amber mused as she sipped from her glass of Sancerre. *I've never been ignored so completely.*

Amber was right. From high school, through college and up to the present, no boyfriend had broken up with her. Several suitors had begged her for more time or attention, but no one had ever had the courage to dump her. Amber took their neediness as a sign of weakness and usually quickly ended relationships when the men groveled. She had her sights on succeeding in life and did not want someone holding her back. The worse she treated a man, the more desperate they became to please her.

Paul's independence had been one of his best traits. His looks were average, his personality acceptable, and he dressed too casually for Amber's taste. But Paul gave her the necessary space for her to focus on her sales management career—the same corporate path Paul had discarded.

He never complained about her long hours or work demands, which was important because Amber was on the cusp of becoming a regional manager of her company. Paul served the role of interesting boyfriend at corporate functions. Paul entertained her colleagues with his tales of places he had been, but knew when to allow Amber to take over a conversation.

Why am I concerned about his indifference now? Amber questioned herself.

She searched her memory banks. Amber recalled a recent cocktail party when Paul described his volunteer work in a hospital in Ahmedabad, India, where poor children suffered from various illness long forgotten in the United States.

The story had sparked a memory in Amber, who had entered college with the dream of becoming a doctor—a vision she shelved after an "F" and then a "C" in organic chemistry. The grades had destroyed her perfect grade point average. Amber concluded that she was better off switching her major to business. Paul's story resurrected her dream, making her question her current career.

Although dedicated or almost obsessed with her job, Amber's current position did not fulfill her. She tried to convince herself that her nice salary and benefits made up for the lack of purpose. Her job had become a test of enduring an endless series of mundane tasks, navigating passive-aggressive colleagues vying for her job, and gritting her teeth through the required artificial workplace behavior.

She had no friends at work, did not like her job, and complained constantly about it. Still she focused on her career growth. Her boss's retirement in a couple months meant a chance for promotion. Amber blocked out the negative and rededicated herself, neglecting everything else in her life.

Now, on her thirty-fifth birthday, she glanced at Jennifer, her only friend who didn't go home after dinner. Until tonight, Amber had not concerned herself with all the rejections she had received. Now, she suddenly felt alone. *No, I'm not going to feel sorry for myself.* Amber leaned over to flirt with the young bartender.

"What can I get for you?" he asked.

"Are there any wines you recommend?"

The bartender took out a bottle of Grgich Hills. "This is a Yountville special." He poured her a taste.

"Thank you." Amber smiled.

A young perky waitress called for the bartender. "Excuse me, ma'am," he said as he slid away from Amber and into the waitress's arms.

"Another man who has no problem ignoring me," Amber sighed to Jennifer as she pushed the wine glass away from her. She pulled out her phone and glanced at the Uber app. "I think I might call it a night."

"What?" Jennifer questioned. "Is this about Paul?"

"No," Amber lied.

"You know there are other men in the world," Jennifer stated with a nudge and a head nod to the striking man at the end of the bar. In his thirties, he wore all black: shoes, pants, and shirt. He had a large, square head, with a trim beard and muscular neck and hands, wrapped around a short thick glass of whiskey, no ice. The man met Amber's stare and returned it.

"What, him?"

"Yeah, him," Jennifer responded. "I think he's military. His forearms are covered in tattoos."

"He's probably married."

"There's no ring."

Jesus's Brother James

"I don't hit on men," Amber huffed.

"I never thought of you as passive," Jennifer volleyed back in an insulting tone.

The use of the word "passive" pissed off Amber. She moved from her barstool, adjusted her dress, and strutted down the bar. Her steps, as though she glided on ice skates, allowed her to gracefully accentuate her figure. Several men turned their head to appreciate her movements. Even the absentee bartender watched her move. He followed her and placed a newly poured glass of wine in front of her when she stopped at the end of the bar.

"Why, thank you," Amber stated in a sappy sweet tone. She glanced back to Jennifer with a smile.

Amber leaned against the bar waiting for the man in black to introduce himself, but he said nothing. He had noticed her, but he kept his face forward, glancing at her through the corner of his eyes. Although never turning to face her, he observed her hair, her lips, and looked from her slender ankles up to her firm stomach to her shapely chest. But he said nothing. He couldn't.

Amber slowly sipped at her Chardonnay, allowing the man time to gather his courage, but he still remained silent. Amber peered at Jennifer, who eagerly motioned for Amber to speak with the man. Torn between the foreign activity of initiating a courting conversation and returning to sad thoughts about Paul, Amber decided pull the man from his introverted shell.

"Are you alone tonight?" Amber asked with a soft voice and clever smile. The man, surprised, did not respond, but sipped again from his whiskey. Amber persisted. "Did you come out tonight with someone or are you alone?"

"I am never alone," he stated as his voice fractured from tension. His hand shook with stress, which flattered Amber.

Amber surveyed the man, muscular and hard. She surveyed his thick neck and square jaw, which was dimpled. Although she did not hit on men, she felt a welcome surge of excitement.

The man, flustered by the fact that Amber's question had a sexual connotation, leaned back and reached into his pants pocket. He retrieved a rectangular white piece of plastic, the clerical collar used in the shirt of all priests, and displayed it for Amber to see and placed it on the bar.

"I am never alone because God is always with me," he said in a fractured voice.

After an awkward silence and a few confused glances, he took out a pack of cigarettes, picked up his glass of whiskey, and strolled out into the cool night for a smoke.

Amber picked up the collar and held for Jennifer, who was approaching. "No shit, a priest."

Jennifer delicately touched the plastic as though it were magical. "He's too good looking to be a priest."

Chapter 3
Father Coady

Father Coady fumbled to get a cigarette through the opening of the fresh pack, hoping a series of drags would calm his rattled nerves. An attractive woman making a sexual advance did not unnerve him. Instead, the lust her approach generated bothered him. Coady had been leering at Amber for an inappropriately long time while she chatted with her friend, sipped her wine, and constantly checked her phone.

Amber, dressed in her Elie Tahari business suit, drew his attention as she was unique from all the short-skirted women prancing around the bar. Her eloquent beauty impressed him, but her serious steady scowl captivated him. Father Coady immediately fantasized about laying her on a couch and speaking to her in a way that priests were not allowed to speak to their parishioners.

It's her age, that's it, Coady muttered to himself. *Why do only old people and families go to mass?* Father Coady sipped steadily at his whiskey. *I don't know how to relate with people under fifty.* He sipped again and then corrected himself. *I don't know how to relate anymore.*

Father Coady pictured an endless parade of elderly people eagerly gripping his hand at the end of mass as though a priest's touch might save them from some evil. Sweating in the heat in his long robes, he felt guilty when he yearned to be away from them. They smelled of cheap detergent, moth balls, and outdated colognes, but that wasn't the thing which agitated him.

Their self-centered, myopic, callous view of the world irritated him. Never did any of his parishioners exit the house of worship inspired from his emotional sermons; instead, they always launched into a never-ending series of complaints about their spouses, children, bodies, and society in general. He started referring to them as the Teflon people, or those who never let any of his ideas stick to them.

He often invited everyone to tell him the ways that the mass enriched their spiritual being. He would survey the congregation, anticipating what people would say to him as they left the church. Images of parishioners exposing their souls danced in his head as he listened to the choir singing.

At the door of the church, he'd spin and clasp hands in excitement. After all, this was why he joined the priesthood: to help people on their spiritual journeys. His very first elderly couple slowly waddled toward him. He was ready.

"Mr. and Mrs. Corcoran, how are you doing this fine Sunday morning?" asked Father Coady.

"I'm still living, I guess," Mr. Corcoran dryly replied. "Never get old, Father, never get old."

"I'm afraid I don't have much choice in that," Father Coady replied. "Consider it a blessing to have so many years."

"I take so many medicines," Mr. Corcoran responded without acknowledging Father Coady. "And those damn things give me terrible heartburn. Last night I didn't get any sleep with all the pain."

"What did you think of the homily?" asked Father Coady.

"He slept through it," snapped Mrs. Corcoran. "That's why God structured mass the way he did. By forcing men to change positions every ten minutes. God knows men have a very short attention span."

Jesus's Brother James

"Father, don't believe her—I was just resting my eyes," admitted Mr. Corcoran.

"Come on, Jack, we've got to get to the soccer field for the grandkids. You can get some more sleep at their match," said Mrs. Corcoran.

Not one person that day exited the church and said anything about spirituality. They discussed body ailments, complained about the parking of other parishioners, or condemned politicians for one thing or another, but not one commented on his message. The outcome had shaken Father Coady.

Feeling depressed, he wondered if living too long killed the spirit. During seminary school, he studied a group of Christians called Gnostics. They believed that the spirit was trapped in the body and death brought freedom. Seeing his parishioners that day, he saw validation in the theory that people are prisoners within their own bodies. He did not tell any of his fellow priests, though; Gnostics were officially labeled heretics by the early Catholic Church.

Feeling underutilized in his role in a small-town parish, Father Coady actively campaigned to enlist in the army as a chaplain. After more than a year of work, he succeeded and served in Iraq with the troops. Although often seeing violence and tragedy, Father Coady felt fulfilled during his tour.

He had seen so much with each new day bringing excitement and reward. Complaints about aging bodies were replaced with counseling soldiers who had severe physical and mental agony. And the troops loved him. Dealing with the reality that they could meet God in person at any moment, the soldiers exposed all their authentic fears to him. He in turn gave them real and honest advice. The work fulfilled him.

Ironically, when his tour ended, he felt like a convicted felon being sentenced to an emotional jail when he returned to his parish. At first, he attempted to distract himself, raising money for the troops and other church events, but this felt insufficient. He counseled soldiers, but this proved challenging because many soldiers did not attend church, and if they did, they did not want to speak about their war days. So he quietly led a life of imprisonment, where robotically he performed mass seven times a week in a stoic fashion. Drip, drip, drip, his anger filled within him.

To distract himself from the monotony, he spent evenings at the bar and fantasized he might meet servicemen. When he noticed Amber, he noted her every movement. Her steady drinking, her nervous twitch, and her deep sighs telegraphed to Coady that she was dealing with some serious issues. He wanted to help.

There was more to it than that. He coughed out the bitter taste from his mouth. He took a drag from his cigarette. *Admit it. She is beautiful.*

Immediately his body stiffened with shock from the reality of his own humanness. Since he had been a boy, the idea of sex had bewildered him and this remained constant. The admission that his brain overflowed with sexual content as he watched Amber filled him with complex emotions so intertwined and conflicting that he did not even attempt to understand them. When he studied at Mount St. Alphonsus, he had his first serious discussions about the imposing vow of celibacy. His close friend Peter had broached the conversation with him during a hike along the Hudson River.

"Coady, how do you handle all the sexual thoughts?" Peter asked one day on a stroll through the woods.

At first Coady thought it might be a trick question, but then he saw the pain on Peter's face, and he knew was struggling. "I try to distract myself from those thoughts. If I see a pretty girl, I think of my sister."

"Does that always work?" Peter asked.

"Hardly," laughed Coady. "You know I have thoughts about so many girls and only one sister."

"I hear you," Peter admitted. "So, what do you do when you can't get rid of these pesky thoughts?"

Coady picked up a few pinecones and started tossing them into the river. Like a child not wanting to admit guilt, Coady felt shame admitting his weakness to Peter.

Before Coady could say anything further, Peter blurted, "You know that college student Iliana I offered to tutor in history?"

"Oh, yeah," Coady replied, conjuring up images of a dark-haired Italian beauty who started attending the local parish. Iliana had come from Staten Island to attend the local university, pleasantly surprising the brothers by attending the local church. Most brothers only attended the church when required, but this changed when Iliana routinely started attending Sunday's eleven o'clock mass. Peter's attendance paid further dividends when he agreed to help her with her early American history class.

"Every time I study with her I can't help imagining her naked. I think she is starting to notice. I feel so awful."

"You feel awful. Really?" laughed Coady.

"Coady! I'm being serious. I'm supposed to be the peoples' spiritual guide and all I can think about is the flesh. I'm afraid I'm becoming obsessed with her."

Coady picked up a few more pinecones and continued to toss them into the river. "You know what I do when I get overwhelmed by those types of thoughts?"

"What?" asked Peter with desperation. Coady hesitated as though he was hiding a critical secret. "Come on, Coady, I'm dying here."

Still unsure, Coady muttered in a tone barely audible, "I masturbate in the shower."

"Shower?"

"Yeah, no one can see me and there is no evidence when I am done."

"But they teach us that masturbating is a bad thing."

"Yeah, but isn't it better than doing other things?"

Peter picked up a few pinecones of his own and angrily threw them into the river. "I wish I didn't have all this temptation."

"You know, 'the only way to get rid of temptation is to yield to it.' You know your namesake, St. Peter, was married."

The two laughed at Coady's jest, but Peter did eventually yield to his temptation. Before completing his studies, he left the seminary, married Iliana, and moved to Staten Island. They had five children and Peter taught high school history.

Father Coady snapped his head around as he heard a noise in the alley. A young man and a young woman were romantically wrestling each other against the bar wall. Their arms were getting tangled as he tried to push his hand under the woman's sweater as she tried to unzip his jeans. Although the young man outweighed her by seventy pounds, she won the struggle. As though she possessed a high-powered stun gun, the man froze when he felt her fingers enter his jeans. The man gasped and leaned back against the wall not moving any part of his body. The young woman slapped his hands to let him know that she wanted him to continue his work under her sweater.

Father Coady chuckled to himself as though he were an alien watching a foreign life form. He moved away from the alley to give the couple some privacy even though they were in a public place. As he smoked he put his hand on the cold steel of the streetlight pole. The low temperature ran through his fingers and down his arm, which seemed to help him calm his nerves. As he started to feel more relaxed, he felt a tap on his shoulder. He turned to greet Amber's deep blue eyes. She stood in front of him with a glass of whiskey, no ice.

"I thought you might like another whiskey," Amber said, with a not-so-subtle flirtatious smile.

"Thank you," Coady stammered. surveying her whimsical expression. He could not take his eyes off her full lips, which she had recently recoated with a deep red lipstick.

"You will have to forgive me. I've had way too much to drink." Amber admitted.

Father Coady hesitated as he tried to speak in his calm clerical voice, "That is quite alright. I'm use to forgiving people."

"But it's not okay if I keep having those thoughts now that I know you're a priest," she chuckled. "God, I'm glad the Uber will be here soon." Amber smiled at Coady, opened her lips and mouthed the words "good God" as she surveyed his muscular chest.

Although Amber's continuous flirting flustered him, Coady tried to remain calm. "I can stay here until the car comes, if you like."

"That would be nice. It would give you time to decide."

"Decide what?"

"Decide whether or not you are going to come out with us." Amber laughed and again mouthed the words "good God" to Coady with a smile.

With his clerical voice cracking, Father Coady strained to joke. "Come out with us?" He continued to stare as though she held a gun at his midsection and he feared moving his eyes at all. As they stood in this standoff Coady slowly ran his eyes from her full red lips down to her high heels, recording every image of her in his memory in case they never met again.

Finally, a black Passat pulled up and the Uber driver called out to Amber. Father Coady sighed. "Your car is here."

Just then, Jennifer exited the bar and stopped when she noticed Coady. "Is he coming with us?"

Amber smirked as she stood erect and adjusted her attire. "Come on. It's my birthday."

As though she were seeing a worm squirm on a hook, she grew uncomfortable watching his gawkiness. "I, uh, I," Coady stammered, but did not complete a sentence. Amber smiled one last time and then kissed him gently on the cheek, her hand squeezing his firm midsection. Father Coady gasped from her soft hands.

Moving away from Coady to the car, she straightened her hair, put her finger on the corner of her mouth, and then slid into the car. Coady watched her, happy that temptation had moved away from him, but sad the inspiration of such wrongful thoughts was leaving. The car door closed and he knew such excitement probably would not return for a while. Father Coady gulped the remainder of his whiskey, repeating to himself, *Shower, shower, shower.*

Chapter 4
Dancing with Death

The physical exertion of a long walk slowed his rapid heart rate, and the smell, sight, and touch of Amber faded. Father Coady strolled the dark streets of downtown Raleigh. The faster he walked, the calmer his breathing became. That seemed illogical to Coady, but he quickened his pace all the same. The cool breeze and dark horizon distracted him from the vivid images of Amber. He paused to look at the stars, but had trouble seeing them through the artificial light.

During his service in Iraq, Coady often spent evenings gazing up to the stars when contemplating the complexity of existence. The vastness of space seemed to minimize the personal struggles. Coady had done the same as a child, lying in his backyard, imagining he had Superman's power to leave Earth's gravity.

Coady stood gazing into the dim heavens while retrieving a cigarette from his pocket. As he tilted his head to light it, he noticed Mike stumbling around his minivan with a gun. Coady's immediate reaction, as his pulse increased, was glee.

An adrenaline addict, he moved closer to the armed man. He let out a small, sly smile as though he were a football player entering a stadium. This rush from possible danger excited him; filling him with meaning. Whether this was a criminal or a troubled man did not matter to Coady. All that mattered was the hope to be useful.

Father Coady, filled with this vigor, moved slowly to Mike with purpose. Mike staggered aimlessly in a lopsided circle, muttering unintelligible things to himself. From his slurred speech and labored, lethargic movements, the priest immediately concluded Mike was drunk.

Repeatedly tapping the gun to his forehead as though knocking on a dense door, Mike increased his head-tapping in speed and intensity until he was wincing in pain. Mike plopped down on the floor of the open minivan, putting the gun at his side. He tossed fish crackers into the air, trying to catch them with his mouth. Too drunk to succeed at such a stunt, Mike fell to his knees. The action reminded Coady of a seal, perching his neck stiff in the air for a treat from a trainer.

Mike, so absorbed with catching the fish, did not notice Father Coady's approach. *I can't do anything right*, Mike sighed. He peered at his unused gun, trying to revive his desire for death. Minutes before, Mike had the resolve to pull the trigger and end his life.

He remembered his pain. He recalled his troubles, but each time they came to his mind, they faded when he felt the hard steel and the reality of death. Like an athlete psyching himself before a big match, Mike had jumped up and down, chanting, "Come on, you pussy, you can do this. You can do this. You can do this." He huffed and sighed, "Can't you?"

Tossing the crackers quickly fatigued Mike and he got up and sat back down on the floor of the minivan to catch his breath. He frantically rummaged through the minivan's back sections, looking for something to eat to squelch his sudden hunger.

In the netting on the back of the passenger seat, Mike saw the remnants of a Happy Meal smooshed on top of a copy of the book *Aladdin*. As he retrieved the red flattened cardboard box with its yellow smile, Mike discovered several untouched chicken nuggets and half a bag of stale French fries.

Make your last meal a Happy Meal, Mike chuckled to himself.

Desiring privacy, Mike picked up the gun and squeezed himself into the back seat as he started to devour the French fries. Although stale and cold, Mike consumed the meal as though it was his favorite. He reached over and grabbed some stale Cheerios from the seams in one of the car seats and gobbled them up.

He turned on the video player with the point of his gun, hearing the blaring theme song from *Thomas & Friends.* Mike hated that music. Mike flipped through the DVDs and plucked out *The Incredibles* and started it. Mike did not like kid movies, but he loved this one; after all, it starred a fat middle-aged superhero.

Although Mike chuckled at the amusing cartoon, an intense unpleasant feeling of melancholy blanketed his thoughts. He took out his gun and firmly tapped his forehead until he felt pain, hoping the discomfort would chase them away.

Not wanting to endure more pain, Mike worried his will was disintegrating. With determination, Mike placed the gun in different places on his head, calculating which location guaranteed the greatest possibility of a fatality. His shaking hand and sweat layered forehead betrayed him. He couldn't steady the gun. Afraid he could not end it, Mike wept.

Father Coady, who had been observing Mike's activities, saw a hesitation and Mike lowering his gun and decided this was an excellent time to approach. Prominently displaying his white collar, he cheerfully called to Mike. "How are you doing?"

"That collar doesn't impress me." Mike coughed with disgust.

Father Coady stopped when he heard Mike's tone, deciding on a slower approach. He took out a cigarette, coolly lit it, and asked, "Would you be willing to share a little bit of that drink? It's a bit nippy out here."

Mike waved his gun at him. "Damn religious people always want something. Looking for last rites money?"

Father Coady held the pack of cigarettes in his palm. "How about a cigarette for a drink?" Coady asked, hoping the gesture would display his good intentions.

Mike waved at the cigarette, "No, I don't smoke." Mike looked down at the cup and then handed it to Father Coady.

"Thank you very much." Father Coady took a few short deliberate swigs. "I taste a hint of apples in this."

"Hey, don't drink it all," Mike grimaced and motioned for the cup back and Father Coady complied.

While Mike sucked down the remainder of the alcohol, Father Coady surveyed the inside of the minivan. There were two car seats, various children's picture books, DVDs, and plastic toys in the back. Father Coady's eyes roamed to the front seat littered with empty Doritos bags and crushed Entenmann's coffee cake boxes scattered on the seat and floor. Father Coady's gaze stopped on the rearview mirror and the black rosary beads dangling from it. Someone in the family might be Catholic, although Father Coady had witnessed Mike's aversion to his collar.

"My name is Coady." Father Coady stated, touching a St. Christopher medal attached to one of the children's car seats. "Are you Catholic?"

"My wife believes in that crap. She treats people like shit all week and then goes to you bastards for forgiveness on the weekend. Convenient. And you enable such behavior."

Sensing Mike's desperation, Father Coady decided to display one of his own flaws. "I'm not completely a priest."

"What do you mean?"

"I'm on leave for a bit."

"On leave?" Mike scoffed. "Does that mean you're not going to try and cheer me up?"

"I could try. A priest is doing confessions and his replacement never shows up. So he leans out of the confessional booth and sees a janitor walking by." Father Coady waved his hand as though he was motioning for someone. "'Can you sit here while I take a break?' The janitor is not sure about it, but the priest assures him it's okay and shows him a list with each sin and their corresponding penance. The reluctant janitor finally agreed to do it."

Father Coady took a long drag from his cigarette, monitoring Mike's facial expression to determine his reaction to the joke. Mike, looking like heavily sedated polar bear, sat motionlessly, staring at Coady without expression.

That was a good sign. A catatonic person represented less danger than an angry, animated man. Unfortunately, Mike still held the gun. Father Coady had experienced this type of situation in Iraq with emotional soldiers. Coady had a rule to relax the finger on a trigger before speaking on a serious topic.

Father Coady continued the joke. "A young, pretty woman comes into the booth and confesses to the sin of giving oral sex. The janitor looked through the list and can't find the sin. He checks the list again, and checks it a third time. Starting to panic, the janitor leans out of the booth and notices an altar boy organizing hymnals in the pew."

Father Coady pretended to wave to get the attention of the altar boy. "The janitor calls the boy over to him, 'What does a priest give out for oral sex?' The altar boy looks at the janitor and confidentially replies, 'Two candy bars and a Coke.'" Father Coady looked to Mike, but still saw an expressionless face. He paused knowing the alcohol had dampened Mike's responsiveness; he waited. No smile came. A large grimace covered Mike's face.

"That's awful," Mike exclaimed. "What kind of a priest tells a sick joke like that?"

"Not a very good one," Father Coady admitted.

Mike's agitation with the joke melted upon hearing the holy man admitting that he was not very good. "My name's Mike," Mike said as he reached out his hand to Father Coady. "God sent me a dysfunctional priest. Fitting," Mike said with a chuckle.

Father Coady took a small, empty, smashed McDonald's paper cup, popped it back into its original form, and asked Mike if he could put rum in it. Mike nodded his agreement. Father Coady poured some rum into the cup, but it leaked right onto his pants through a small hole. Father Coady tried to drink it as the liquid dripped all over his hand. Mike laughed for a moment and tossed Father Coady the empty sippy cup.

"Can I ask you a priest kind of question?" Mike asked.

"Sure. Those are my favorite type of questions."

"Where's the best place to shoot yourself?"

Father Coady paused for a long moment, realizing his answer could have a serious impact. Watching Mike clumsily moving the loaded gun all over his body, he now feared an accident as well as an intentional shot. Father Coady tried his hand at psychology.

Assuming Mike was more troubled than evil, Father Coady thought the mention of someone evil committing suicide might illustrate to Mike the negative aspect of suicide. Luckily Father Coady remembered that the most recognizable evil person in the world, Adolf Hitler, shot himself, so he planted the seed into Mike's head.

"Hitler killed himself with a shot to the mouth," Father Coady stated.

"Mouth, huh?" Mike grimaced at the thought of placing the barrel of the gun into his mouth.

Mike opened his mouth and placed the point of the gun underneath his upper lip, stopping when the metal clicked against his teeth. Father Coady sighed, disappointed that the mention of Hitler did not have any impact on Mike. "Yes, Adolf Hitler," Father Coady commented, but Mike was not listening at this point.

Mike focused all his attention on holding the gun steady to stop the barrel from vibrating against his teeth. The gun in the mouth worried Father Coady, afraid the gun could discharge at any moment. The sound of the metal popping against Mike's teeth irritated Coady, like nails on a chalkboard.

"Are you sure this is what you really want?" Father Coady snapped in a tone that sounded more like a statement than a question.

"Fucking priest. 'Is this what you want?' I'm not ordering dinner here, pal." Mike wanted to sound certain about his suicide, but his voice fragmented as though he was entering the early stage of puberty. "It's not what I want. It's all I have left."

"You need to get some rest right now," Father Coady implored. "You're in no condition to shoot yourself."

"Rest?" Mike questioned. "Are you saying I'm going to need to rest up for what comes next?" Mike started to laugh, slowly increased his guffaws as he fully absorbed the absurdity of Father Coady's odd statement. "You're kind of crazy."

"I admitted that I wasn't the best priest," Father Coady commented. "How about we get some coffee and we talk for a little while."

"You're going to try and sober me up a little. You want me to sober up in order to shoot myself?" Mike questioned, still laughing.

"I thought there might be a few things you want to say before the act."

"Say?" Mike tensed, afraid to stop his momentum toward suicide, but longing to leave some testament before his death. "Say? You think I have something to say?"

"When I was in Iraq, some of the soldiers would talk to me in case anything happened. They had me write letters for them to send home. It gave them comfort."

Mike looked at his gun through tears of confusion as images of his head being blown apart returned to his mind. His resolve to end his pain conflicted with the small hope that his life could continue. He looked at Father Coady, for whom he had a sudden and strong fascination. The odd joke, the drinking, the smoking, and the general conversation calmed Mike.

"Comfort?" Mike stated as though the word was foreign to him. "I guess it could also be called relief."

"How about that coffee?"

"You won't try to talk me out of it?"

"I can't make a grown man do something he doesn't want to. Come on, the store is just a few minutes' walk from here."

Mike examined Coady's collar, which didn't sit flush in the shirt. Perhaps Father Coady had flaws just like Mike. Perhaps Coady could provide a reason for him to go on living. And Mike wanted to live. He nodded his head in agreement. "Okay, fine. As long as I can bring my sippy cup."

"You can only bring it if you are going to share."

Chapter 5
Brother James

Father Coady had to continually slow his pace as they trekked to the nearest convenience store. Letting a suicidal man lag behind in the dark frightened Coady. He had tried to engage Mike in a dialogue, but Mike's gasping for breath did not allow Mike to sustain the chat. So in the dark silence, Coady recounted stories about his days in Iraq, which Mike enjoyed.

The tales helped Mike, but it put the priest on edge as he remembered the awfulness of war. A loud popping sound jolted Coady before he realized it was only an NC State student lighting a fire cracker inside a can. Every time he heard the student letting off another fire cracker, Father Coady's body shook with anxiety. He finally motioned to Mike for the rum sippy cup and sipped each time he heard a loud sound.

"Why do people who live in safety and happiness take such pleasure in destructive activities?" Father Coady questioned.

The small old convenient store, packed on this late weekend evening with college students buying dry day-old hot dogs from under the heat lamp to satisfy their late-night munchies, did not calm Coady's nerves. He pushed, in an unpriestly manner, past the group toward the beverage section. The coffee, dark from sitting on the burner for hours, made Coady sigh with joy. Coffee always calmed his nerves. For a moment he forgot Mike, who had stopped to stare at a young, dark-haired female student. Coady peered at Mike and then at the young co-ed, who bore an uncanny resemblance to Amber. Coady stared at her for a long moment, which the girl noticed. She smiled as she formulated a way to draw attention to herself and amuse her friends. The young female student staggered back and forth, trying to steady herself from a high alcohol content, pointing to Coady's collar.

"Bless me, Father, for I have sinned, and I am about to go sin some more," she called as she undid her blouse a button. She burst into laughter, causing her group of drunken girlfriends to shriek in unison with her. The girl high-fived everyone in her clan as they applauded her witty sexual innuendo.

She peered back at Coady, hoping to catch a glimpse of his embarrassment, but Coady stared at her with a strange admiring smile. Coady imagined Amber had channeled herself into this co-ed. The unblinking stare unnerved the young student, so she pushed her friends out of the store to escape Coady.

Father Coady watched the group leave the store howling and returned his attention to his mission, the dark coffee. For a quick moment, the coffee reminded him of cool mornings in the Iraqi desert, when he would share strong coffee with others.

The dawn represented a new day and Coady always hoped for the best. He did not miss Iraq, but he missed the camaraderie. Others often came to him in the morning for advice or to share something, which seemed so infrequent lately. Even with a crowded parish and another priest in the rectory, he constantly felt alone. He shook his head.

Focus, Coady, he snapped at himself. He surveyed the store for Mike. Like a parent in a department store who had lost track of their child, he panicked. Then he discovered Mike sitting on the floor eating a powdered donut. "Mike, pick out anything you want to eat. I will get the coffee."

Mike gave him a thumbs up.

Father Coady snatched two large steel coffee cups, something durable that drunken Mike would not spill, and poured the thick coffee to the brim. Rushing over to the counter, he pulled several crumpled bills from his pocket. Along with the wrinkled money was a note from Amber, which slid across the counter and onto the floor.

A young clerk picked it up and read it: "You are too damn cute to be a priest." She signed it "AM." The clerk returned it to Coady with a smile. Amber must have slipped it into his pocket when she squeezed his midsection before she got into the Uber. Coady smiled and then felt embarrassed when he noticed the clerk staring at him.

"It's a long story," Father Coady explained.

"Do you preach at a church around here?" the young clerk asked, hoping to discover some local gossip.

Father Coady ignored the question, simply shaking his head and gathered Mike off the floor for the return walk. During the walk, Mike found his second wind and launched into a constant chatter about his personal history as though he were dictating his memoirs.

"My troubles all started when I lost my virginity in high school," Mike stated as a simple fact.

"You're feeling guilty because you had pre-marital sex?" Coady asked.

"Hell, no," Mike howled. "It wasn't the sex that was the problem."

"Right."

"It was the partner. I used to hang around this cute, smart girl, but I was so awkward." Father Coady nodded his head. "I was insecure. And she was a straight-A student heading to Harvard." Mike stopped and silently stared into the darkness.

"She was your first?"

"The smart girl, no. I went on a couple dates, but never made a move. No, some slutty girl came onto me at a party and we did it in the hatchback of my old Dodge Charger next to the river. That was that." Mike laughed a sad laugh as though he were joking about the blade on the guillotine waiting to cut off his head. "I never hung around the cute girl anymore. Ever since then it's been one slutty girl after another. It's funny; people call girls easy when they sleep around, but I was the one who went for the easy path."

"Why do you think that's a bad memory?"

"I don't know. I think it would have been better to lose my virginity with someone as inexperienced as me. It would have meant more. She was a cute girl. She was smart." Mike sighed and hesitated.

"Don't stop, continue."

"I should have taken the smart girl to a romantic dinner and bought her flowers. You know. I should have gotten a hotel room or something. It should have been memorable. It would have been special." Mike's with eyes filled with tears. "You know what I mean?"

"Yes."

"How did you lose your virginity?" Mike asked in a serious voice, stopping as they reached the minivan. After a long moment of silence, realizing the inappropriateness of his question to Coady, Mike started to chuckle.

"I really can't comment on that type of question." Coady tipped the coffee cup toward Mike.

"Shit, sorry. What was I thinking?"

"No trouble. I'm sure some priests might have had sex before becoming a priest."

"Maybe you're right. I just wish I was like my brother James. Everything he does is perfect. He is charming, handsome, successful, rich. He always does everything right."

Father Coady chuckled. "That's funny."

"What?"

"Reminds me of another James."

"Who?"

"Jesus's brother James. He picked up the pieces after Jesus was crucified. He started the church in Jerusalem." Mike gave Coady a strange look.

"I didn't know Jesus had a brother."

"Yep. James is mentioned in several gospels and again in the Book of Acts. James was one of the founders of the early church. As a priest, I must call him Jesus's half-brother or cousin because Mary supposedly remained a perpetual virgin."

"You're one weird priest."

"I can't argue with you," Father Coady replied, letting a small amount of annoyance enter his voice feeling Mike was ungrateful.

"Don't get me wrong. I kinda like your weirdness. You're easy to talk to."

Father Coady shook his head, knowing he should not let these negative thoughts cloud his perspective. He surveyed the inside of the old cluttered minivan again for clues to the reason Mike was despondent. The minivan was filthy as though Mike had been living in it for some time. "Don't want to go home?"

"You're interrogating me with questions again." Mike whined and took a long drink. "Do you think I want to live in this goddamn minivan?"

Frustration rose within Father Coady at Mike's sharp tone, so Coady walked away from the minivan, avoiding eye contact with Mike. Coady knew these volatile emotions were not priestly. Love should be patient and kind.

Patience, eternal patience, was a job requirement for his occupation, but he grew frustrated with people like Mike. The man, ready to kill himself, whined about how he lost his virginity. Coady had seen so much real suffering, he could not endure this type of superficial self-loathing. "This is pathetic," mumbled Coady. He took a cigarette out, lit it and looked up at those stars. *Compared to the hardships others have to endure, this is nothing.*

"Maybe I am pathetic. This is my home for now. And maybe I deserve to be living here." Mike, sensing Coady's mood, stated his response in a different softer tone. Mike pointed to a small bed of blankets in the back of the minivan.

"I'm sorry, I should not have said that."

"No, maybe I need tough love."

"What happened?" Father Coady asked, spinning to face Mike, ready to show more empathy.

"I lost my job."

"And?" Father Coady made motion with his hand to signal to Mike that now was the time to reveal everything.

"Corporate downsizing. My boss was looking for synergy targets and I volunteered. I figured I'd take my severance and relax. I didn't like my job anyway. I didn't even tell my wife." Father Coady took out another cigarette. "After four months, the severance ran out and I couldn't find another job. So now I'm stuck with two kids, bills streaming out of my ass, and no way to pay for them."

"Money is a common problem with couples," Father Coady assured him. "What did you finally tell your wife?"

"I didn't."

"You never told your wife?" Father Coady exclaimed in a harsh tone. "She still doesn't know?"

"No, I never told her I lost my job."

"You never told your wife?" Father Coady repeated in disbelief. He never understood domestic relationships, which seemed overflowing with small lies, deceit, and distrust. Marriage, a pillar of the seven holy sacraments, represented nothing hallowed to the majority of his faithful. *Faithful. What a waste of a word for these people.*

Again, Mike sensed Father Coady's disapproval, so he blurted, "I thought she would leave me if she knew I had no job. I also thought she was seeing someone else."

"Now, why would you think such a thing?" Father Coady asked, intentionally easing his tone.

"Catholic upbringing."

"Catholic upbringing?"

"Yeah, even Jesus's parents argued about paternity. Poor Joseph had to believe a spirit knocked up his fiancée!"

Father Coady smiled as Mike's little joke melted the tension. "You've got a very good point there. And if Mary was a perpetual virgin, they never had sex. Joseph did have a lot to endure."

"So the shitshow gets better," Mike continued, changing his tone to flamboyance. "I hacked into my wife's computer to see if she was stashing money. She's always buying Coach shit and I don't give her money. Thought it must have been her parents." Mike tossed the coffee on the ground and picked up the sippy cup of rum. "I'm scanning her hard drive and find pictures of her with some guy."

"Some guy?"

"I can't see faces. Just flesh, dicks, and shit like that. Who the hell takes pictures like that?" Father Coady shrugged. "Isn't that kind of weird? I mean, really strange."

Father Coady put his face close to Mike's. "Are you sure it was your wife in those pictures?"

Mike takes a deep breath. "Why would she keep pictures of other people fucking?"

"You're going to kill yourself. You're going to take away a father from your children. You're going to take away everything you have and everything you will ever have on an assumption?" Father Coady stopped Mike from drinking anything more.

Mike started to cry. "I don't know. I'm all fucked up."

"Give me the keys. I'm driving you home right now." Mike nodded his head, complied, giving Coady the keys.

It did not take long for Father Coady to drive to the outskirts of the city to Mike's house. When they arrived in front of the house, Mike reluctantly stood in his front yard. Father Coady nudged him forward like a father nudging a first-time swimmer toward the deep end of the pool. Mike took several big breaths and started through the freshly dewed lawn.

"Give me the gun," Father Coady gently demanded.

"What if she's with someone?" Mike questioned.

"Do you really want to kill someone?"

"Other than myself, no." Mike started toward the house again, before stopping a second time. "I might want to shoot her though." Mike clutched the gun.

"Trust me, you do not want the gun."

Mike did not immediately relinquish the gun. "I have a right to bear arms."

"Do you want me to go with you?" Father Coady moved forward.

Mike shook his head "no" and placed the gun on the grass.

"Remember. Everything in life happens according to part of God's plan," Father Coady assured him, hoping the mention of God would bring him strength.

Mike nodded his head "yes" and then started for his front door. Father Coady put the gun in his jacket pocket.

Standing in his hallway, Mike pondered how he had arrived at this place. His first marriage had ended before the honeymoon when his new bride commented on the flight to Hawaii that she felt the marriage had been a mistake.

Mike spent his honeymoon intoxicated in Honolulu after his new bride caught an early flight back to North Carolina. He returned home to sign a few legal papers to end his brief marriage, swearing he would never enter the institution again. His fear of marriage lasted until he fell in love with Alyssa a few years later.

Marriage with Alyssa, slightly more successful than the first, made it through the honeymoon. This freshness of the marriage dwindled when Alyssa started making comments about his weight. Long hours in his car for work made his frame round and soft.

Along with subtle comments, she purchased a gym membership and a stationary bike. Her figure stayed firm. She flaunted it in a local play, where she pranced naked with a male co-star throughout the whole production. Mike, although upset, suffered awkwardly and silently through multiple showings.

Mike concluded that only a callous heartless woman would show such disregard for her husband. Leaving her often entered his thoughts, but he did not want to fail once more in love. Being divorced twice before the age of thirty-five seemed to represent a stigma he could not handle. Yet part of him wanted to find Alyssa with someone. That would vindicate his insecurity. It scared Mike that a feeble part of his psyche wanted him to find his wife with another man. As he ambled down the hall, Mike felt like Sisyphus, working hard all day, only to be crushed under a boulder in the evening.

End it? Mike thought to himself. *End my marriage or my life?*

Mike shook with fear realizing he stood at the abyss facing two choices: return to an unhappy marriage or end everything. Neither choice seemed appealing, but that was all he thought he had. The door was ajar. Through the small crack, he peeked in and could see his wife from the waist up, on her stomach, facing the door, lying on top of a pile of pillows. Mike sighed. *I'm so insecure.*

Mike strained to remember the happy memories he had with his wife as he started to open the door wider. He smiled at her face as she lay sideways on the bed. She was pretty. As he admired her long neck, smooth shoulder, and the side of her voluptuous breasts, Mike realized she lay naked. *That's odd.*

Then her body convulsed. His wife levitated, her torso rose, but her head remained on the pillows. She slid forward and then back. Mike, a huge *Exorcist* fan, first thought she was possessed. She started to pant. Then her breathing turned into a steady stream of low guttural moans. Mike's stomach clenched, and then he froze for a moment as his wife's face transformed as her eyes started to roll. She let out a gasp, which turned into a carnal scream.

Mike pushed the door fully open to get a full image of the silhouette of a naked man on his knees thrusting himself into his wife. The man clutched her hips as he pushed back and forth, loudly moaning with each new movement. The man started to moan in an erotic synchronized duet with his wife. Mike's wife grunted faster and faster. At the crescendo she tilted her head up and saw Mike standing transfixed in the doorway.

To Mike's surprise, his wife did not scream with shock or shame, but simply yelled at her lover, "That's it! Don't stop, don't stop!"

Jesus's Brother James

Chapter 6
Stars

The man climaxed, slumped onto Mike's wife's back as she collapsed face-first onto the mattress, like human dominoes. As she glanced up, he thought he saw a coy smile on her face, which infuriated him. Mike roared and charged. The naked lover, shocked, recoiled upright. Mike, upon launching toward the bed, snatched up a lamp and threw it at the man's head. The heavy lamp whizzed past the lover's head through the window behind the bed.

Mike's wife yelled, rolling herself into the comforter to cover her exposed body. Under the cover, she crawled across the bed, like a soldier shimmying under barbed wire hoping to stay out of the line of fire. She slid down behind the far side of the bed, peeking back to watch the fight.

Her lover reached to the floor for his boxers, but froze when he saw Mike above him. Mike's momentum brought both of them crashing down onto the end table. A picture of Mike and his wife from their honeymoon in Costa Rica shattered under the weight of their two large bodies.

The naked lover rolled across the glass and up to his knees, noticing blood flowing from several small cuts on his chest. He plucked out a few slivers embedded in his skin. Mike got his bearings and launched a fresh new assault from behind, slamming the lover's chest back down on the broken glass. The man's testicles felt a piercing pain as they landed on a bed of jagged glass. The lover, acting like King Kong when Fay Wray was taken from him, straightened up, pounded his chest and roared.

The naked lover flung Mike to the other side of the room. With delicate care, he probed his testicle sack, gently probing for any splinters that might have entered his scrotum. Hearing heavy breathing, he detected Mike readying for a third charge. The lover spun to his feet, widening his stance into a defensive position.

Being tall and muscular, the lover easily deflected Mike's drunken rush. After Mike's two punches missed their target, the lover retaliated with an uppercut to Mike's jaw, which knocked Mike from his feet, into the wall, where Mike's right shoulder punched a deep hole into the sheetrock.

Mike pulled his shoulder out from the drywall, which caused a memory board to collapse down on top of his head. Family pictures from Christmases, vacations, and birthdays floated down through the air like confetti at midnight on New Year's Eve.

A photo from a first birthday party flew in front of him, while a butterfly made of macaroni by his nephew landed and stuck in the blood flowing from a cut on his cheek. Mike swatted the photo away and threw the macaroni at the lover, who had scrambled into his boxers.

Mike, feeling physically overmatched, looked for a possible weakness. When the lover slid one leg in his boxers, Mike saw an opening. He charged. The man dropped his underwear and spun out of the way, causing Mike to miss and crash head-first into the dresser. Dazed, Mike fell on his back on the floor. Hoping to restrain Mike, the naked lover jumped on top of Mike's chest, pinning him down.

Mike, stunned from the head blow and the alcohol, looked up to see a raging figure looming next to a broken dresser. His wife's Victoria's Secret lingerie fell from the damaged furniture to his forehead. The silky-smooth undergarments irritated his skin, so he struggled to break free of the lover's grip. As Mike twisted, he felt the tip of the lover's penis, which had not yet been covered by the boxers, right below his bottom lip. The humiliation of having his wife's lover's penis, which had just been inside his wife, resting on his face caused Mike to shriek with fury. His throat croaked from the strain.

Trapped, like a little brother would be under his big brother, Mike desperately twisted, squirmed, and wiggled in a feeble attempt to free himself from the awful position. Realizing he did not possess the strength or skill, Mike pushed his head forward, growled, and sunk his teeth deep onto the man's dick.

The bite caused the man to fall to his side and Mike scurried on all fours through the shattered glass into the hallway. He did not stop crawling until he reached the stairs, where he tumbled down to the first floor. When he gathered himself, he sprinted out of the house, falling across the slippery wet grass before he reached the driveway.

Father Coady, who had been watching the house, listening to the screams, and witnessing the smashing of glass as a lamp soared from the second story window, rushed to assist Mike. "I'm here, I'm here," Father Coady told Mike.

Mike had blood running down his forehead and his cheek showed signs of swelling. Mike rubbed small fragments of glass against his wrist as he stammered, "Shitshow. Really bad shitshow."

"What happened?"

"Let's get the hell out of here!" Mike beckoned as he crawled toward the minivan.

Father Coady, confused by events and feeling a surge of adrenaline, drove Mike to a nearby empty church parking lot to determine the next actions. Father Coady waited several minutes for Mike to calm himself.

For the entire ride, Mike curled into a fetal position in the front seat, whimpering incessantly about his wife, the penis, and the biting. When

Mike had gathered his composure, he turned his red swollen eyes to Father Coady, who had figured out that Mike's wife had been unfaithful.

"The bitch named her dog Faith. How ironic," Mike spat.

"Try to remain calm and tell me what happened."

Father Coady had been wrong. For some reason, he had concluded paranoia had overtaken Mike. He now realized Mike had justification for his suspicion. In was an odd emotion, but Father Coady could not shake his great annoyance at Mike, feeling that his pathetic personality might have driven the wife to such an act. Coady slapped himself, upset that he let such a disturbing thought into his mind at such a time. He took a towel from the car and wiped blood from Mike's face.

"Why?" Mike cried. "Why must God make me suffer?"

"We do not know why God lets things like this happen."

Mike shook his head as though there was a fly on his nose. He did not want to hear excuses for God at this moment. God had seemed to have forsaken him. "Not only is he better looking, he's better fighter," Mike whimpered.

"Who's a better fighter?"

"James, that fucking bastard," Mike coughed through tears.

Father Coady, not fully aligned with Mike's thought process, uttered, "Jesus's brother James?"

"No, not Jesus. I'm talking about *my* brother James. He's fucking my wife!" screamed Mike.

"Your brother is sleeping with your wife?" Father Coady staggered out of the minivan and around to the back-passenger door. Father Coady pulled the bottle of rum from the back floor, filled up the sippy cup, and then drank for a moment. "That's not what I expected."

Jesus's Brother James

"Oh, my good God, my brother is balling my wife!" Mike screamed, devolving into a desperate ball on the ground. Mike's words transformed into primitive sounds as he curled and rolled back and forth.

Father Coady, shocked at this information, could only mutter, "Your brother James is sleeping with your wife?"

"Not sleeping, fucking!" Mike screamed, able to regain his vocabulary.

"My God," Father Coady uttered, looking up to the stars. They sparkled back at him, silent passive observers, unable to help him deal with this man's pain. Coady marveled at their tranquility, wishing the current event did not demand him to say any more.

He peered silently into the darkness. He wanted to assure Mike everything would be okay, confirming God would fix everything, but he lacked the conviction. He knew Mike's road would be difficult and that this episode would haunt Mike until his last moment on Earth.

Crawling to Father Coady, Mike asked, "You said everything happens according to God's plan."

Father Coady nodded "yes."

"Then why would God make a plan for my wife to fuck my brother?"

"We can't understand God's plan," Father Coady admitted.

"Why would God do this to me?" Mike pleaded with Coady.

Father Coady remembered miserable scenes in Iraq, when people beseeched God from their knees. Mike's less dramatic pleads irritated Father Coady. "God did not do this to you," he snapped.

The tone shocked Mike, who slumped over his knees. "If everything happens according to God's plan, he knew that my wife would be unfaithful, didn't he?"

"So God is to blame for everything?" Father Coady asked. "Can you think of anything you did that could have led you to this place?"

Mike stopped crying, glared up at Coady and moved onto his knees. "Are you saying I deserve this?"

"No, I'm not saying that," Father Coady stated, softening his tone as he grasped the callousness of his words.

Mike, still kneeling in front of Father Coady, said, "No, I don't mind. I admit I'm a fuckup. Maybe I deserve this. Put me out of my misery?"

"Kill you?" Father Coady stammered.

Father Coady couldn't look directly at Mike, but instead gazed at the scratched face of Thomas on the sippy cup. Coady recalled an Iraqi man begging for death after his children had been killed by an IED. The man wailed as he held their broken, lifeless bodies in his arms. Then the father smiled at Father Coady and shot himself.

The dreadful image still woke him up in the middle of the night. Father Coady staggered in a tight circle like angry drunk man looking for something, trying to shake the idea of execution, but the more he pondered, the more merciful being dead seemed. Mike, a weak pathetic suffering fool, might be better off dead. Father Coady glanced at the car seats, trying to grasp at something to get the horrible notions to vacate his mind.

"What about your kids? They would lose a father."

"I'm not even sure they're mine. I have a low sperm count. It shocked me when Alyssa got pregnant. Life is too tough."

"That's pathetic," Father Coady snarled, angry that Mike would so easily disavow his children. The image of the man holding his dead children returned to him. "You're going to just throw it all away 'because life is tough.'"

"Life is too hard."

"Sure, life is hard, but you've got it. You don't appreciate the gift that God gave you. Do you know what I've seen? How people have struggled for life? How many people would give anything for one more day with their child? And you're just going to give it all away?"

Mike, not listening to Father Coady, continued to beg, "I'm ready to speak to Jesus face to face. Send me to him."

Father Coady tried to walk away from Mike, but the desperate man clung to Coady's pant legs. Father Coady turned back to face Mike, pointing the gun at his forehead, which caused Mike to smile, broad and pleasant. The enthusiastic grin surprised Father Coady.

Mike saw the gun as the termination of his pain. Mike looked like a child on the floor in front of the Christmas tree, eagerly waiting to open a present. Father Coady cringed. He did not have an answer. He knew he could not shoot Mike, but had no clue as to his next action. He gripped the gun with frustration as he recalled the awful smile of the unfortunate Iraqi father.

"You want to meet Jesus?" Father Coady said and Mike enthusiastically nodded. "You really think you want to meet Jesus?"

Father Coady fell into old memories, recalling the army major who had indifferently pushed aside the bodies of the tragic family from the road. He again saw the father falling into a ditch, covered with the bodies of his two children. Father Coady hated that major. Father Coady had reprimanded him for his insensitivity, asking, "Do you think Jesus would approve of your actions?"

The major dryly replied, "I'll find out when I meet Jesus."

Becoming frantic, Mike screamed, "I want to meet Jesus. I want to meet Jesus!" partially bringing Coady back from his wartime flashback

"You want to meet Jesus?" Coady asked again.

Mike nodded "yes."

"You want to meet Jesus?" Coady asked a fourth time.

Mike nodded again.

Father Coady looked at the quiet stars for several moments as he tried to quell the rush of emotions surging through his body.

"You know there's no answer coming from there. It's up to you now," Mike cried. "End my pain."

Father Coady, his body shaking from his eyes to his toes, looked back down at Mike's pleading face. Then without realizing what was happening, Father Coady's index finger moved and the trigger was pulled. A loud piercing sound erupted, Father Coady's arm jerked backward, and Mike's body slumped lifelessly to the ground.

Chapter 7
Hangover

A vibrating cell phone popping up and down on the slick surface of the end table woke Amber from her slumber. Her snooze had been so deep, she did not know what day it was. She wiped the crusty sleepers from her eyes and started reading the numerous unread messages in her inbox. A sharp, intense pain shot through her head.

"Fuck, my head," Amber cried.

Amber dropped her phone, crawled off the bed, stumbled across the carpeted floor and into the bathroom. She grabbed a large bottle of Advil and the Pepto-Bismol from the medicine cabinet and then plopped on the floor. Without even glancing at the patient instructions, Amber swallowed several pills followed by two chugs of the pink liquid. She tucked her head under the tap and gulped water for several long minutes, trying to moisten her dry mouth. Amber placed her hand under the faucet and splashed cold water down on top of her head.

Why did I drink so much? she asked herself rhetorically.

Leaning over and resting her cheek on the cool tub, Amber replayed the previous night's events. Being a person addicted to numbers, she started counting each glass of alcohol she consumed. She had two glasses of champagne at a bar to start the evening, a glass of chardonnay with crab cakes, and three glasses of cabernet with her petite filet mignon.

That's not too bad, Amber said to herself. Then she remembered she had tried a cucumber martini, a fig Manhattan, and two glasses of Tokaji dessert wine with her cherries jubilee. After dinner, Amber and Jennifer went to the bar for more wine.

As Amber counted those drinks, the image of the handsome priest came back to her. Had she really flirted with him? She felt more than a twinge of embarrassment, which motivated her to pop two additional Advils. Then she lay down on the freezing tiled floor.

With her cheek on the floor next to the toilet, Amber tried to gather the motivation to get back to her emails. She always worked on Sunday.

"Come on, Amber. You can do this."

Amber built the reputation in her division as a workaholic and hated the thought that someone at work anxiously waited for a response. She had maintained this frenetic pace for more than a decade, diligently spending more hours at work than anywhere else. This dedication allowed her to climb the career ladder and now, on her thirty-fifth birthday, she eagerly anticipated a promotion to lead the sales force for her region, earning the title of director, three years ahead of her predicted schedule.

Come on, Amber. What's a little headache? Amber said as she tried to push her face from the tile, but her body remained on the cold surface.

This job ascent pleased her not only for a sense of accomplishment, but she treasured the idea she would soon leapfrog professionally over several older men—sexist male colleagues who had snickered at her when she entered the department. These soft wrinkled men, obsessed with pontificating their views while working as few hours as possible, annoyed her. A former boss, who forced her to listen to Rush Limbaugh drone on and on about evil entitlements, had the worst work ethic in the company. While she spent endless hours on the road, going from doctor to doctor, he snuck off to Home Depot to plan house projects. Then, after her record-setting figures, the hypocrite had the audacity to lecture her on the proper way to get sales. She grew to despise these men.

When the sales group met, these old men often isolated themselves into a huddle in the corner of the room. At lunch, they refused to eat with her, but she overheard their conversations. They whined about the changes in the organization, mainly the large percentage of women who were hired in the department. They mocked forced diversity, but did it in a passive aggressive way to avoid action from human resources. Amber found them weak and fake. She now relished the clear fact that since her first year she had consistently outperformed them and hoped to hear these pathetic men whining about her promotion in the near future.

Come on, Amber, just a little longer, she told herself.

Amber did not want any of her clients to grumble discontent, which could be used by these pathetic corporate male sloths as an excuse to block her promotion. She crawled to her phone, started an email request for product samples, and then, still holding the phone, retreated to the bathroom when a wave of nausea overwhelmed her.

Keeping her head above the toilet in case she needed to vomit, she processed the order to ensure delivery to the doctor's office by Wednesday. Many physicians did not have any patience, so she wanted to make sure all the orders to the fulfillment houses were completed today.

In the past, pharmaceutical sales representatives carried samples in their cars so they could hand out their products like the Jehovah's Witnesses handing out their *Awake!* and *The Watchtower* magazines on a corner. Now, due to new federal laws, the Prescription Drug Marketing Act (PDMA) had sales reps reconcile the sample handouts and make health care professionals submit requests for samples that were shipped to the suppliers' offices. Amber did not want to take any chances. After completing her orders, she rolled onto her back, looking up to the ceiling.

Now I can stop thinking about work for a little while, she gasped. As she looked at a shadow on the ceiling, she pictured the priest's striking face. *What the hell was I thinking?*

She laughed at her bold flirtatious interaction with the priest until she saw a vivid fantasy scenario of the fine-looking man getting into her Uber car. Although it partially disturbed her, she let the scenario play out for a moment as she pondered how good a kisser the priest was. A groundswell of guilt stopped the fantasy.

Amber, the man took a celibacy vow, she exclaimed. *But I didn't take the vow*. Amber thrived on doing things people told her not to. *It's no different than skydiving, river rafting, and bungee jumping. Kissing a priest can now be taken off my bucket list.*

Not only did her culpability dissipate, but a feeling of pride emerged. After all, not every woman had enough feminine charm to tempt a holy man into considering breaking such sacred vows. The pride mixed with the forbidden nature of a relationship produced a special kind of excitement within Amber.

Would he have broken his vow? Amber tempted herself with the tantalizing question. *Is it a vow not to kiss a woman or only not to sleep with a woman? I assume it is sex or some form of sex that would push it across the line.*

Amber fantasized about being in the back seat of the Uber in the clutches of the powerful man, passionately kissing him as they rode through the city. The driver catching glimpses of them through his rear-view mirror, chuckling at their high level of passion. The car slowing as it approached Amber's townhome, causing them to stop fondling each other and to ensure their clothes were straight enough for public display. Amber opening the door and stepping out into the cold air, allowing her cravings to calm.

She would look at her townhome and then back at the handsome priest, considering whether or not to ask him in. Amber's daydream suddenly stopped at this serious thought, unsure of whether she had the nerve to seduce a priest all the way to copulation.

It's just a silly fantasy, Amber huffed as she brushed off the thought. *Plus, it would be his vows, not mine.*

As she sat up on the tiled floor, with her head swimming from the effects of alcohol, she heard a series of loud knocks. She waited for a moment, hoping the knocker would leave. The series of knocks happened a second time. Gingerly getting up, Amber huffed out her frustration and looked in the mirror.

Shit, I didn't wash my makeup off, Amber snarled. She held the firm belief that women accelerated the aging of their skin when they slept with cosmetics hardening their faces. Amber believed that her face would age one day for every full night spent with makeup on it. The knocks interrupted her again. Disappointed with herself she barked, "Who the hell is bothering me on a Sunday morning?"

Cursing, she managed to descend the stairs without falling. Her feet stomped heavily across the hardwood floor. Amber yanked the door open, expecting to see a religious person pushing their propaganda. Instead, the familiar face of her boyfriend Paul stood with flowers, a package tucked under his arm, and a piece of luggage at his feet.

Smiling, Paul, who had come directly from the airport, held the flowers high up in front of Amber as he grinned with pleasure. His smile met Amber's stern grimace. Her displeasure heightened as the aroma of the flowers triggered nausea. She frantically motioned for Paul to move the flowers as she stepped back into the townhome.

"You're back early. I thought you were busy in New York," Amber commented. She retreated to the kitchen to pour herself a large glass of water.

Paul entered the townhome, amused at Amber. "Early? It's nearly twelve o'clock."

Amber glanced at the clock. "Shit, I didn't realize."

"It must have been a great birthday party." Paul smiled, hoping Amber no longer possessed lingering annoyance over his absence during her celebration. Moving to the kitchen, Paul retrieved a vase and filled it with water to ensure the flowers didn't wilt. Like a peacock displaying its bright feathers, he arranged his gifts and placed them in the center of the table in full display for Amber.

The hundred and fifty-dollar gift, even in a vase and prominently displayed, did not impress Amber. She simply huffed. "What's the damn reason for the early morning visit?"

Paul, sensing her agitation, moved back to his luggage and picked up the package. Recreating his vivid grin, Paul announced, "I'm sorry I missed your party, but I was thinking about you."

Amber showed no excitement at the gift, but indifferently strolled to the recliner and plopped into it. "Can we do this some other time?" Amber wanted to crawl back into bed and sleep for a few more hours.

"I think you're going to enjoy this," Paul persisted.

"This can't wait?"

Paul, like a child waiting for parental approval before charging to the Christmas tree to open presents, vibrated with anticipation. "I just think you're going to love it."

"All right, all right," she said, motioning for the gift.

Paul took out his phone and played Matchbox Twenty's song, "Unwell," as he handed her the package. Matchbox Twenty was Amber's favorite group. In her senior year, she had driven her faulty Honda Accord all the way from Raleigh to Madison Square Garden to see the band. In a rare emotional moment, she spent hours outside lead singer Rob Thomas's hotel in hopes of getting his autograph.

Paul loved this story because it showed how spontaneous Amber could be. She normally planned, with incredible detail, every aspect of any activity she undertook. She not only organized her tasks, she even organized other peoples. Whether it was Christmas, Valentine's Day, or birthdays, she sent cards to family and friends and provided them with links of where to purchase presents for her. Amber simply did not leave her gifts in the hands of others.

Irritated at this unapproved gift, Amber pleaded, "Please turn that off, my head is going to explode."

Paul, wanting to appease her, obliged and turned the music off. He nudged Amber to open the package. She placed the glass on the table and reached for the gift, wrapped in cartoon records, Elvis Presley silhouettes, and jukeboxes. Roughly two feet long and a foot wide, she turned the heavy package back and forth, wondering what was inside. Paul, impatient, tugged at the top of the wrapping to start Amber in on opening the gift.

Amber, not wanting Paul to steal her task of opening her own present, gently slapped his fingers. "I can do it."

Methodically and deliberately pulling the paper along the crease to save its integrity so she could neatly fold the used material and carefully place it in the recycling bin, Amber was taking too long for Paul, who lurched forward to help her with the unveiling.

Pulling a large picture out, Paul displayed it in front of her. It was a personally autographed picture of Rob Thomas. "To Amber, sorry I missed you in 2003 in NYC, but I would like to wish you a Happy 35th Birthday. All the best, Rob." Paul gleefully looked at his cell phone and played a message.

"This is Rob Thomas and I want to say 'happy birthday' to Amber." Rob Thomas proceeded to serenade Amber with a two-chorus rendition of birthday wishes.

Paul clapped his hands and announced, "I'll send you the file so you have it."

Although excited about the incredibly creative gift, Amber's reaction was to sprint to the bathroom to unload last night's dinner in the ceramic basin. Paul, confused, carried the framed Rob Thomas photo into the bathroom and held it above Amber as though it had medicinal power. He wanted to be compassionate, but Paul could not hide his dissatisfaction over her lukewarm reaction. Feeling guilty, he tried to help.

Like a doting father, he brought her paper towels, wiped her mouth, and retrieved several soft terrycloth towels, which he positioned around her head in the living room's arm chair. After propping her up into a comfortable position, he dampened a washcloth with cold water and dabbed her forehead. Amber, not wanting to be helpless, retrieved her phone and checked her inbox.

"Please put that phone away, would you?" Paul chided her in a soft voice.

"Just one more email," Amber stated. "Not everyone can to go through life without checking their phone the way you do."

"Are you mocking my philosophy on emails?"

"No, if I only checked my messages once per week, I'd have more free time, too."

"Yes, only checking emails once per week leaves me more time to do other things."

"Like attend your girlfriend's birthday," Amber snapped.

Paul sighed with a mixture of pleasure and frustration, happy Amber's strong spirit had returned, while annoyed at her attempt at making him feel guilty. He retrieved the autographed photo and played Rob Thomas singing "happy birthday" again. He smiled wide, hoping it would brighten Amber's mood. It didn't. Avoiding eye contact, she felt mixed emotions in a similar way as Paul.

She liked this attention from Paul, but felt annoyed that she let his indifference ruin her birthday. She hated that. Her promotion, weeks from final fruition, did not allow her time to be distracted. For these Sunday emails, she copied her boss on each one, sending a clear signal she exceled in dedication. She imagined a see-saw, with Paul on one side and her promotion on the other, and her promotion weighed much more.

"I'm sorry. I will make it up to you," Paul suggested as he muted Rob Thomas. "We could go to La Mella's for dinner?"

The idea of consuming food did not appeal to Amber. "Maybe next weekend," Amber said, letting out long sigh, like a bicycle tire that had run over a nail. Changing her tone, she decided to stop complaining. "It was an awesome gift; I'm just feeling under the weather."

"I understand," Paul replied, happy with her compliment.

Moving over to Amber, he slipped her phone from her tight grip. He placed the washcloth on her forehead and closed the blinds, darkening the room. Amber relaxed for a moment, before he slipped the phone back into her hand.

From the shadows, Paul gazed at Amber and digested her new neediness, while at the same time considering his possible international move in a few months. Immediately he worried that this relationship with her might be an emotional obstacle for his new Russian adventure. Paul focused all his attention on the new trip, so he did not hear the soft buzz of his phone vibrating. Amber did. Even though it was not her phone, she could not stand to have a message go unattended.

"Are you going to answer that?'

"No, my call service, Google Voice, will convert the message for me."

"What if it's important?"

"I will read them as soon as I get the chance. It saves me time because most things aren't urgent."

"You're so rigid sometimes."

"Hey, that gives me time to plan life-altering things like..." Paul stopped before he uttered the word "move."

"Sure. You always have an answer," Amber coughed not wanting to discuss Paul's philosophies on life.

Amber, never one to take no for an answer, crawled over to Paul and pulled his phone out. He gave a half-hearted attempt to stop her, but she clutched the phone as though she were checking it for some secret.

"Oh, my God," Amber exclaimed.

"What is it?" Paul asked.

"A friend of yours has been shot," Amber informed him.

Chapter 8
James

Opening his eyes, Mike could only see a large white intense blur emanating from a round bright center, surrounded by a dark background. He closed his eyes, pressed his eyelids together, and reopened them once again, hoping his vision would improve. It didn't. He could only see the same fuzzy whiteness.

After another attempt to clear his vision, he could still see a bright haze in front of him as though he were at the bottom of a pool looking up at sunlight bouncing off the surface of the water. As he stared at the clearest part of the gray, a dark silhouette of a long-haired olive-skinned man came into view and blocked part of the light as he moved in front of Mike. The figure hovered over Mike, staring silently down at him.

"*Rahkama*," Mike heard floating down from the figure in a soothing manner.

"Jesus?" Mike tried to yell, but his dry mouth muted his voice. The olive-skinned man uttered something, but Mike couldn't understand the man's words. "My God. My God. Jesus, is that you?" Mike questioned, his voice fracturing from emotion. He tried to raise himself up toward the figure, but the man pulled back away from him. "Jesus, please talk to me, for the love of God. Are we in heaven?"

"*Rahkama*," the looming figure stated as he leaned back toward Mike, again hovering near him. Staring deeply at the man's features, Mike noticed his strong Middle Eastern chin, dark brown eyes, long black hair, thick unkempt beard, and deep, dark olive complexion.

The man epitomized Mike's ideal image of Jesus Christ. Tears flooded from Mike's eyes, like waterworks from St. Peter after his third denial, at the thought of meeting his Lord and Savior and the anticipation that his suffering was at an end.

The moment of judgment brought memories of his life, both good and bad. The charitable acts dueled with selfish ones, like volunteering at a "brown bag" event to feed the poor versus sleeping with his administrative assistant. The pleasant thoughts of his wedding against the signing of divorce papers. His first date with Alyssa versus the horrible scene of his naked brother on top of his wife overshadowed every other moment of his being. Mike's tears flowed faster.

"My God, I am sorry," Mike apologized, feeling as though he had ruined the gift of life that Jesus had offered him.

"*Rahkama*," the man repeated in a language foreign to Mike, but at the same time in a tone that Mike understood. Mike's tears stopped.

The man, who Mike hoped was Jesus, put his elongated rough palm on Mike's cheek to wipe a stream of tears. Jesus's fingers felt strong and hard. Mike shook in fear, waiting for something dramatic to happen, but nothing did.

Mike, feeling pressured, attempted to pack every good deed into his thoughts and project them to Jesus. Feeling as though he was being judged, Mike hoped he could persuade Jesus to let him into heaven. Mike waited, wondering if Jesus performed some form of new patient evaluation. Mike wanted to be patient, but now he shook with anxiety, rocking back and forth to soothe himself.

"Will it take long to get to heaven?" Mike inquired.

The figure did not say anything. Jesus simply sat and stared at Mike with a steady stoic stare.

"Is this some kind of test?" Mike asked, hoping it would cause some reaction.

Jesus stayed silent.

Feeling unnerved, Mike started to babble. "I know it might have been a sin to want to kill myself, but I didn't go through with it. The priest shot me." Mike waited for a reaction from Jesus, but the figure did not say anything. Mike tried to change his tone, concerned that it was negative. "But I forgive him for shooting me. I forgive everyone."

"*Rahkama*," the man repeated.

The figure stood and hovered around Mike as though he were an alien examining a new fascinating life form. With a stern look and unblinking glare, Jesus tilted his head, first to the right and back to the left.

His eyes were soft, but at the same time intense, and they made Mike's insides squirm. Jesus's mouth started to form a word. He stopped and moved closer to Mike's nose to examine him a little further. Jesus placed his hand on Mike's head, heavily wrapped with gauze, running his finger along a seam.

Jesus said firmly, "*Rahkama*." Mike put his face closer to Jesus so he could better understand what Jesus was saying. "*Rahkama*."

Mike, although he did not know what the word meant, burst into deep sobs at the thought of hearing Jesus's voice. So loud were his cries that it made him gag. Jesus put his hands on Mike's chest to prevent Mike from falling forward. Mike cocked his head in confusion. "Rock-ah-ma?" Mike repeated.

"*Rahkama*," Jesus repeated.

Mike touched his bandaged head and looked around him, discovering, as his vision started to improve, that he was lying in a hospital room. The priest's bullet had not killed him. For a nanosecond disappointment stunned Mike as he realized he was still far from heaven. Jesus touched Mike's face once more, cupping Mike's cheeks in his large warm hands. Mike, trying to stay optimistic, wondered if Jesus had come to Earth to show him the way to heaven.

"Jesus, are you here to take me from Earth?"

"*Rahkama, rahkama.*"

At that moment, Father Coady briskly barged into Mike's room, started toward a chair in the corner, and then realized Mike was awake. Putting his one hand on Jesus's shoulder and his other hand on Mike's leg, Father Coady's eyes were wet with joy.

"Thank God, you're awake," Father Coady exclaimed. "The doctors told me you would be fine, but I was so worried."

"Fine? I'm going to be fine?"

"Yes, you're going to be fine."

Mike turned to Jesus to see his reaction, but he wordlessly stared back at him. After a lengthy moment of watching Jesus, the image of being shot flashed into his mind. He turned to Father Coady, "You shot me."

"It was an accident," Father Coady explained. "I explained that the gun misfired to the police during the lockdown here."

"Lockdown?"

"Yes, they lock down the hospital whenever there is a shooting. They lifted it when they determined you were suicidal."

"Suicidal? But you shot me."

"Yes, but you kept telling the nurses you wanted to die. Do you remember?"

"You shot me," Mike repeated in a louder, more accusatory tone. Jesus made a humming noise, causing Mike to flinch with guilt. Mike, while never taking his eyes from Jesus, reached out his hand and lightly patted Father Coady's forearm. "But I forgive him for that. I do."

"I'm so glad you said that. And I hope you now realize how sacred life is."

Mike, still looking at Jesus, assured Father Coady. "You're right. Life is a precious gift from God."

"That's right. You've seen the light."

"Almost. I'm waiting for Jesus to tell me what to do next." Mike said, nodding his head toward Jesus.

"Jesus?" Father Coady asked.

"Yeah, I don't know how you did it, but I wanted a face time with Jesus and you made it happen."

"Face time?"

"Yes, face time. Me and Jesus."

Father Coady stood erect, shooting quick glances back and forth between Mike and Jesus. He put his hand to his chin, feverishly rubbing it as though he had an itch. He paced as though he was thinking about a complex mathematical equation. "No. This is not Jesus."

"Not Jesus?" Mike snapped, yelling in surprise. "What do you mean this isn't Jesus?"

"Getting Jesus to make a house call is tough—he's quite busy these days. It's a big world filled with so many million desperate prayers," explained Father Coady.

"If this isn't Jesus, then who the hell is this?"

"This is Jesus's brother James."

"Jesus's brother James?" Mike replied as he inspected James. He wanted to spit the bitter taste from his mouth, but the smiling James transformed his foul mood. He turned back to Father Coady, asking in a more pleasant tone, "You called James and he came all the way down here from heaven?"

"Don't focus on the specifics," Father Coady assured Mike. "You wanted face time with God."

Mike glanced at James with apprehension. "You are James?"

James answered, "*Ana. Yaakov.*" James said something in a foreign language as he moved his hands in a circular fashion. "*Rahkama. Rahkama.*"

Father Coady shook his head as though James has uttered something profound. "Yes, yes, James."

"Can he answer in English?" Mike questioned.

"James speaks Aramaic," Father Coady answered.

"In his two thousand years of visiting Earth to speak with people, he hasn't picked up any English?"

"He only speaks Aramaic."

"Aramaic," Mike stated with a huff as Father Coady nodded his head. "He found his way all the way from heaven to speak with me, but he doesn't understand a word of English." Mike gasped in frustration.

"I don't think that speaking English is critical."

"Not critical? You don't think it's critical for James to give me spiritual guidance in words that I understand?"

"Not critical."

"You're going to translate for me, right?"

Father Coady shook his head no. "There are two reasons why I really shouldn't." Father Coady moved to James and scrutinized several tassels hanging from his robe.

"And they are?"

Father Coady turned his attention from James back to Mike. "For one thing, you should hear his answers for yourself. It is critical that you have a direct and personal relationship with God."

"This is not God." Mike grimaced as though he had just bit into something extremely unpleasant. "And the second reason is?"

"I don't really speak Aramaic."

Mike looked back and forth from James to Father Coady in disbelief. "You brought me a divine man to give me advice so I would no longer want to blow my brains out." Father Coady nodded his head yes. "And he doesn't speak English? And I've not been granted the ability to speak Aramaic?"

"Exactly."

Frustration swelled throughout his torso as though he was allergic to bees and he had just absorbed thousands of stings. Following the frustration, depression overwhelmed Mike's mind. Then the awful idea, the possibility that James, as a direct agent of God, sat silently mocking him, surfaced.

Turning to Father Coady, Mike considered the concept that Father Coady was a sadistic priest and Coady's only interest in this situation was for sick pleasure. Mike started to undo his bandages in a desperate attempt to inflict damage on himself, with the thought he could rip all the negative memories out of his brain.

Father Coady rushed to Mike's side, clasping at Mike's hands to stop any destruction. "What are you doing?"

"If I can't blow my brains out, maybe I can pull them out," Mike screamed, trying to break out of Father Coady's clutches.

"Trust me," Father Coady pleaded. "Spend a few weeks with James. If he doesn't change your life in thirty days…"

"Thirty days?" Mike barked. "You sound like some cheesy infomercial with a lame money-back guarantee."

"Please, please." Father Coady subconsciously nodded to James, who sat smiling indiscriminately.

James sat next to Mike, never breaking his continuous smile. Although James appeared deranged, he had a pleasant effect on Mike, causing Mike to start to chuckle. A large round nurse waddled into the room. She leaned over and checked his bandages.

"Things are looking much better," she said as she inspected the wound.

"Looking better," Mike repeated with disbelief. He started laughing, like a preschooler chuckling over a burp or fart joke, until tears started streaming over his cheeks again. "It's looking better."

"What is all this about?" the nurse asked.

"Nothing in my life is looking better."

"Don't worry," the nurse assured him as she finished adjusting the bandages that Mike had loosened. "Everything happens for a reason. It's all according to God's plan."

"Did God plan for my brother to screw my wife?"

"It's not our place to question. You've got to have faith." The nurse said as she exited, clearly not listening to Mike.

"That's what the captain of the *Titanic* told the passengers before they hit the icy water." Mike called after her, leaving him alone with James and Father Coady. "I'm sure God had a good reason to turn all those people into popsicles," Mike stated to James.

James leaned over and put his large hands on Mike's face again. As though James were practicing Reiki on Mike, warmth emanated from the large man's hands. The feeling seemed to absorb all Mike's negative thoughts, and he fell back to the pillow. With a large admiring smile on his face, Mike gazed at James.

"You wouldn't fuck my wife, would you?" Mike asked.

James smiled and replied, "*Rahkama.*"

Jesus's Brother James

Chapter 9
Modern Man and Old-World Beliefs

Paul, who had rushed immediately to the hospital from Amber's place, jogged into Mike's room, thick with perspiration. Mike greeted his friend with a stream of loud clacking snores as he lay soundly sleeping in his bed. Paul staggered to Mike's bedside, absorbing Mike's current state—head bandaged, skin pasty, and stubble dark on his cheeks—and contemplated the dramatic erosive changes in his friend's appearance.

The word "friend" seemed to ring hollow. After all, they had grown apart since Mike had dropped out of college. "Dropped out" might have been inaccurate, because Mike never attended a class. Their friendship now consisted of getting together for dinner a few times a year when Paul was not gallivanting to a new exotic location. The dinners had grown even more infrequent after Paul decided not to spend time with people he deemed negative.

The message from Mike's wife Alyssa shocked Paul—both in the incident, as well as Alyssa's comment that Paul was "such a good friend" for Mike. Paul had grown uncomfortable around Mike. The more confident Paul became in his life choices, the more awkward encounters with old friends became. The melancholy concept of the shrinking pool of Mike's friends saddened him.

Mike had always been the most popular person in Paul's universe. Mike, who used to possess a positive outlook and energy, constantly packed people into his Porsche and drove to Wrightsville Beach for pizza near the boardwalk and a bonfire on the beach. Paul often silently sat in the shadows, admiring the parade of tan pretty girls that clamored for Mike's attention.

Paul approached the bed and contemplated the change in Mike's features. *He's losing that thick, wavy hair the girls loved so much.*

Paul recalled the road trip to Manhattan with Mike the summer before they started at Wake Tech Community College. Paul's old Ford Escort GT blew a fuse in the middle of the night outside of Baltimore. Unable to pay for a hotel room, they slept in the parking lot of a Days Inn. Mike volunteered to sleep on the hood, which provided a buffet for the mosquitoes, while Paul crawled in the back on top of their luggage.

You were always such a nice guy, Paul admitted.

When they arrived near Manhattan, they parked their car in Hoboken, New Jersey, and took a ferry across the Hudson River to the city. They had planned to take the PATH train, but a cute, curly-haired blonde waitress named Elaine convinced them to take the ferry. Mike had struck up a conversation with her when he helped her disembark from a train and navigate the crowds while carrying several large pillows. Impressed with Mike's gentlemanly gesture, as much as his good looks, she agreed to lead a tour for them through the city.

After dropping off the pillows, she showed them Battery Park and Wall Street. She took them on the A train to Times Square, and they finished the day watching the sunset from the observation deck of the Empire State Building. When she stepped inside off the observation deck, Mike coyly commented, "Today's been so perfect, I could die right here and right now." Mike looked down at Manhattan and sighed. "If I ever get sad, remind me of this place."

Paul, with emotion and guilt overwhelming him, reminded Mike, "Remember the Empire State Building. Remember that day."

Paul violently shook his head, hoping to stop his tears. Examining Mike's condition, he contrasted the bald, overweight, pasty man with the image of the fit, thick-haired guy waving in the wind on the observation deck. Elaine had snapped several photos of Mike and Paul all over New York: at Ellis Island, in front of the Statue of Liberty, on the backs of the large cement lions in front of the New York Public Library, and in the middle of the street in Times Square.

The Times Square picture topped them all. As angered cabbies beeped at them, Elaine barked out calls for them to pose with the lights in the background. Now Paul wondered where his best friend had gone. Even if Mike recovered from this wound, he would not be his same friend from high school.

"Fuck, life can be depressing," Paul said.

"*Rahkama*," James stated from the floor on the far side of the bed.

Paul, stunned, spun to see a tall, bearded Middle Eastern man sitting on the floor in the corner of the room, holding his hands in front of his chest with his eyes closed. The man was dressed in a long robe and wore sandals. The man hummed in small spurts at very specific intervals, which sounded like an old air conditioning unit churning on a hot humid summer evening. Paul, after rubbing the tears from his eyes, leaned forward to scrutinize the man. In a slow deliberate motion, the man opened his right eye to display a large brown iris looking back at Paul.

"What kind of hospital is this?"

"*Rahkama*," James said in a happy tone.

Although a pleasant introduction, the sound made the Paul leap away from James, knocking over a bedpan as he moved. The clanging sound resonated through the room, causing Mike to moan and roll over toward the noise.

"What the fuck?" Mike uttered.

Paul scurried over to Mike's bedside and reached for Mike's forearm, "Mike, it's me, Paul."

"Paul?" Mike questioned as the name did not register at first. He tried to stir himself from his sound sleep, wiping his hands on his pants, and finally recognizing his old friend. "Paul."

"Yeah, it's me."

Mike pushed himself to a sitting position. "It's been a while. How did you know I was even here?"

"Alyssa called me." The name of his wife caused Mike to flinch with pain as though someone had jabbed him in the side with a sharp spear.

"Oh, her," Mike hissed from the corner of his mouth as the awful images danced across his thoughts.

"She said you shot yourself?" Paul mumbled in an awkward way.

Anxious to find fault in his wife, Mike corrected. "Actually, it was a priest that shot me."

"A priest shot you?"

"It was kind of a team effort, but technically he pulled the trigger," Mike clarified. Paul, unable to hide his disbelief, grimaced from confusion. "It's a long story. I'll tell you some other time."

Paul, happy to change the subject, asked, "How are you feeling?"

"The wound is not serious and they should be discharging me soon."

"That's great to hear," Paul stated in an excited tone, which trailed off before he finished the sentence, realizing he did not know what to say at this point.

On the way to the hospital, Alyssa had called, telling Paul various details about their dysfunctional marriage. Alyssa's openness about their dysfunction amazed Paul. Still reeling from the dramatic event, Paul did not want to hear about domestic issues.

But Paul's silence did deter not her from launching into Mike's lost job, the underwater mortgage, and her lack of affection and recent affair with Mike's brother. Concluding she was a callous bitch, Paul hung up without saying anything to her.

"That's really great to hear," Paul stumbled to say something comforting. The conversation halted. Paul surveyed the room, scanning objects, hoping something would trigger a topic. He saw James on the floor. "Did the hospital provide this medicine man praying on the floor?" Paul joked.

"Praying?" Mike leaned over and saw James. "Oh, that is Jesus's brother James."

"Jesus's brother James?" Paul asked.

"Yes, the real Jesus. This guy's brother is the one who died on the cross as a human sacrifice for our sins."

"Jesus," Paul mumbled in astonishment. Paul strolled over to James. "He looks pretty good for being two thousand years old."

"The priest couldn't get Jesus. I guess I'm not important enough," Mike huffed.

Paul, baffled not only with James's presence but also with Mike's answer, concluded that the head shot wound had affected Mike's brain. Not wanting to upset Mike, he did not ask for clarification; instead, he looked at James for a possible distraction. "He looks Kurdish."

"Kurdish?"

"Yes, you know, from the northern part of Iraq."

"Stop," Mike bellowed, putting his hand up to his bandaged head. "I'm in no condition to hear about one of your mini-retirements you spent helping homeless kids in the Middle East."

"I'm sorry. I didn't mean to upset you," Paul commented, surprised with Mike's snarky reaction. "I was just trying to find out a little about him."

"I don't know him well. Go ahead and ask him anything you want," Mike said with a sneer.

Paul moved over to James, squatting down in front of him in order to get a better look. "Are you from Iraq?"

James said nothing, only answering with a long smile.

"Are you Kurdish?" Paul asked him.

James responded in a foreign language.

"What did you say?"

"*Yakov.*"

"Yahk off," Paul repeated with a chuckle. "I can't quite understand him, but it sounds like something nasty," Paul chuckled at Mike.

Mike, like a stoic heckler, stared at Paul's attempt at humor. "You mean to tell me you know hundreds of languages, but not this one?" Mike responded in a sharp tone. Mike's eyes rolled up to the top of his head as though he were playing the role of serial killer in a murder mystery.

Mike's cutting tone informed Paul that not only Mike's appearance had eroded. Paul, realizing the gulf that existed between himself and Mike, decided to change the topic. Paul moved over and sat in the chair next to James, glancing out the window.

"Do you remember that trip to New York?" Paul asked.

Mike gazed blankly ahead, exerting a tremendous effort to retrieve the images of that day. At first Paul's mention of the event pleased him, until Mike realized that the memories had worn down until they were vague and indistinct. "It seems like that was someone else."

Wiping away the unpleasant thoughts, Paul tried to make small talk. "When will you be discharged?"

"I don't know, but I'm in no rush." Mike stated as his tone changed from sharp to pitiful. "It's not like I can go home anyway."

Paul stiffened as though he stood on the tail of a poisonous snake, realizing how each potential conversation could be challenging. *A good friend would graciously offer to take him in*, Paul mumbled to himself. Images of Mike planted on his couch caused Paul to shudder with fear. Emptying his apartment, not filling it, was the next step in Paul's preparation for his sojourn.

Combined with this, Paul had to start the painful process of dismantling his relationship with Amber, which probably represented endless hours of explaining to her why he wanted to end it. Paul had once spent an entire weekend, with only bathroom breaks, escaping from a previous relationship. How would this be possible with Mike sitting in his living room?

Paul felt trapped and guilty for not being willing to help his old friend. Paul, blocking all thoughts of inconvenience, turned to Mike and assured him, "If you need a place to stay you can crash at my place for a while."

"Are you sure?" Mike asked, trying to hide his desperate enthusiasm.

Mike, picking his eyes up from staring at the floor, felt a rush of warmth in his chest. Since he discovered he had not died, the disagreeable thought of his wife arriving in the hospital room had plagued his mind.

Knowing the encounter represented dreadfully reliving the humiliating events, Mike had prayed for deliverance. Mike now hoped to escape from the hospital and hide from the awful reality of his life until he could formulate some course of action or kill himself.

"Sure? Hell, yes, I'm sure. I have plenty of space. I am supposed to move in a month, but you can stay as long as you like."

Mike glanced at James and blurted, "Thirty days would be perfect."

"Great."

Mike shook Paul's hand and clarified, "Can James come too?"

Chapter 10
Sensing the End

Amber seethed as she watched arrogant Paul, with meticulous care, gently open a bottle of Argentinian Antigal Uno Malbec and pour it into a decanter. The fact that Paul pointed to the large golden laurel on the label, signifying he was serving a fine wine, annoyed Amber more. Taking out his phone, he set the timer to five minutes to allow the wine to sufficiently breathe.

While the timer moved and the wine readied, Paul took a pork loin from the oven and delicately placed it on the cutting board. In precise measurements, he sliced the pork and placed it on fine china, along with baked Brussels sprouts and ginger rice. While he worked, Amber fantasized about the wound she could inflict on him with the various utensils and items in close proximity.

He doesn't know I found out, Amber thought.

The sharp cleaver, an obvious choice, represented the bluntest method of pain. She had recently purchased it for Paul so she knew it remained sharp, which would easily permit her to open a large wound on his neck. But an easily-opened wound was not her preference.

Other objects offered a slower form of torture to Paul's anatomy. The corkscrew seemed ideal. As she twisted the device, deeper into Paul's ear, it would not only release her anger, but inflict tremendous pain.

A small Dremel drill in the kitchen would allow her to put a small hole into his forehead.

What am I doing? Amber wondered. *Why am I spending all this energy?*

Amber picked up her phone, checked her inbox, and replayed in her head the meeting she had earlier with her friend Jennifer at a small coffee shop.

"So how are things going with you?" asked Jennifer as she added sugar to her raspberry mocha coffee.

"Things are so crazy with work," Amber replied without ever taking her eyes off her cell phone as she checked the orders forecasted for the week.

"Sometimes I envy you," Jennifer continued as she watched a woman in a dark business suit stroll by them. "Being stuck at home day after day, taking care of the kids, can wear on you mentally."

Amber made a noise that sounded something like "uh ha," but Jennifer concluded Amber wasn't listening.

Growing annoyed, she changed the subject to a topic that might grab Amber's attention. "You're thirty-five. Are you ever going to have kids?"

Amber stopped typing immediately. Jennifer's passive-aggressive way of expressing displeasure could not go unchallenged. "After your constant complaining about marriage and motherhood, I'm not sure I want to."

"I'm just curious," Jennifer said with a sneaky smile on the corner of her mouth. She had gotten Amber's attention. "I know it's quite a bit of pressure. If you don't have kids now, you're going to lose your window of opportunity."

"So be it," Amber huffed. "I'm swamped with everything at work and I don't have time to worry about all those things."

"Does Paul want kids?"

"Paul?" Amber coughed, surprised Jennifer would pose such a question. Amber, who never seriously considered children, never contemplated Paul's opinion on the matter. Amber didn't see why it mattered what Paul wanted and tried to deflect the conversation with a meaningless utterance. "Paul is Paul."

"Not sure what that means."

"It means, who cares what Paul wants?"

"Problems with Mr. Perfect?"

Amber released her phone from her hand, letting it slide onto the table—a sign she was giving Jennifer's question serious thought. Amber, suddenly somber, look steamed, not from the need to answer the question about Paul, but instead from a doubt of whether this topic was worthy of serious thought. "We don't talk about that topic."

"You guys have been dating for almost two years now."

"Does that mean we have to have kids?"

"No, but he's taking the best years of your life."

"Best years of my life," Amber sighed. She wondered if the past two years had been the best years of her life. "That's kind of a strange expression."

"You know what I mean."

"Actually, I don't," snapped Amber, dissatisfied with the direction of the conversation.

"I'm not trying to piss you off. I'm just looking out for you."

"If he wanted to get married he would tell me, right?"

"You sound kind of passive, which is not like you. Why don't you just ask him?" Amber, using a defense mechanism to avoid the question, picked up her phone and started typing. "Amber, could you put your phone down for just a minute?"

"You sound like Paul. He's always saying I'm addicted to my work." Amber stopped in midsentence and started typing a work-related email on her phone.

"He might have a point about your addiction," Jennifer said with a small chortle. "Speaking of Mr. Perfect, is he moving?"

Amber stopped typing. "Moving?"

"Yeah, I saw someone selling Argentinian wine on Craigslist and figured it was him."

Amber immediately switched from her email to Craigslist. Amber noticed the wine, which sounded like Paul. There was a note that the seller needed to move the items quickly before an impending move. As Amber browsed the items, her pride took a severe blow as she contemplated the possibility that he would move without alerting her. Amber gripped the phone with anger. "He wouldn't move without telling me, would he?"

Jennifer simply shrugged her shoulders.

"No," Amber answered sheepishly.

Since that discovery earlier in the day, Amber had stewed with annoyance as she waited for her planned belated birthday dinner. She did not worry about their relationship ending. She did not fret over being alone. She fumed over the disrespect shown by Paul's complete indifference to her. After all, she wasn't some high school girl with a crush. Her fury had only grown as she sat on his Craigslisted furniture, waiting for Paul to make some mention of his intentions while he cooked. But he said nothing.

"You're going to love this Malbec," Paul assured her. "It's from a vineyard in the Mendoza region of Argentina."

Amber tried to seem aloof, but her voice fractured with aggravation. "You know I prefer California cabs."

Paul, focused on the final preparation of the food, did not detect Amber's sour tone. "I worked on this vineyard for more than a year. Have you ever been to Argentina?"

Amber clenched her teeth as she processed this question. He only asked it to display the breadth of his worldly travels. Paul had been to more than fifty countries, while Amber had been to four. Well, four, if you counted Puerto Rico; Amber wasn't sure if a trip to Puerto Rico was considered a trip out of the U.S. She attempted to avoid answering Paul's condescending question.

"Have you ever been to Argentina?" Paul asked a second time.

Amber scowled at Paul, positive he was mocking her. "You've seen my passport. What do you think?"

Paul poured a small amount of wine into Amber's glass for her to taste. She motioned for him to fill the whole glass. He complied. "This is the last bottle I have from that vineyard. I wanted to share it with you on your special day."

"Special day? You have something to tell me?" Amber took the wine glass, absorbing Paul's soft appeasing tone, without expressing any gratitude. Swirling the red liquid, tilting the glass to the side and moving it upright, she did not want to sound needy. She did not want to sound whiny. She wanted Paul to crack without her saying anything.

"I just wanted to share something special with you on your birthday."

"Oh, yeah, birthday," Amber said in a slightly mocking tone. "I thought you had big news."

Paul tilted his head, aware finally that something was bothering Amber, but hoping she was not still spiteful about him missing her birthday. He continued as though he had not detected anything. "Yes, it was on my last quest." In a reflex motion, Paul poured more wine into Amber's glass even though she had only sipped the Malbec.

"And you brought back this treasure."

"You're the only person in the U.S. that has tasted this, I bet."

"I feel privileged," Amber answered with a sarcastic tone.

"Yes."

"Wasn't there a girl with you before your last quest? I mean, didn't you conquer her too?"

Paul sipped the wine. "It's not like that."

"That's right, you're fairly self-centered. Did you dump your girlfriend before or after she took you to the airport for your flight to Buenos Aires?" Amber commented as she sipped her wine.

As obtuse as Paul had been, he now realized Amber had uncovered his impending trip. He remained calm, acting as though her comment did not faze him. "I don't see what that has to do with anything. Yes, I ended it before I moved to South America. It's too hard to maintain contact from a distance."

"Whatever," Amber stated, now drinking the wine more freely. She realized the conversation had taken a wrong turn.

Paul reached over, taking her phone and placing it on the table near him. "Some studies have shown that cell phones are habitual and people have a hard time breaking many of their habits."

Amber's phone started vibrating. Amber reached for it, only stopping after she noticed a knowing smile overtaking Paul's face. Letting out a huff, she leaned back and drank a bit more. "So what did you make me as your *belated* gift?" emphasizing the word "belated."

"I was addicted to my phone too. I know it's a very hard thing to give up. But once you give up material things, you will feel free."

"You seem like the type that's really good at giving up things without a thought," Amber snapped.

Her phone vibrated with a fresh new batch of emails, causing the cell to hip hop on the top of the table. Although she wanted to prove Paul wrong, she knew her promotion would be announced soon. Amber wrung her hands like an upset janitor wringing a mop. She emptied her glass and motioned for Paul to fill it up once more.

"It's good, isn't it?"

Paul passed the plate of pork, hoping the aroma of rosemary and sage would distract Amber for a moment. She froze, determined not to express pleasure to a man who had been lying to her. She huffed, annoyed with herself for putting so much energy into playing this sad game with Paul. She pushed the meal away from her.

"You don't like it?" Paul questioned.

"I'm not hungry," Amber answered.

Paul, obviously disappointed, went to the kitchen to show her the dessert. In Paul's absence, Amber snatched her phone and opened her inbox. She had wasted enough time with this dinner; she had work to do. As Amber read she heard footsteps coming from behind her.

"I told you," Paul said with a childish smile. "You couldn't even make it through dinner without working."

Amber, at first embarrassed to be caught, quickly reversed her opinion and resurrected her anger with Paul. "I wasn't checking work. I was looking at all this great stuff you're selling on Craigslist!"

"Listen, Amber," Paul started, but Amber gave him the hand.

"Save it. You had plenty of time tonight to tell me about your move and you did not say one fucking word."

"Amber."

"No, I want to get past this. I need your help. I'm thinking about selling something on eBay." She stopped for a moment, "What's a good price for an autographed photo of Rob Thomas?"

"You're going to sell my gift?"

"Sure, you said I would feel free if I let stuff go."

Paul froze. "Yeah, but that was a special gift."

"Oh, it was a special gift. You mean a special gift like this," Amber looked at her phone at the list of Paul's items on Craigslist. "A handmade chess set."

Paul did not say anything; he couldn't. Amber purchased that set on their first trip together to Mexico. "That's different," he uttered. "I forgot you purchased it for me. I didn't do it deliberately."

"Oh, I didn't realize you forgot. That makes it all better." Amber typed a price for the special gift. "I think five hundred dollars for the photo should work nicely."

"That's heartless," Paul quipped.

"Heartless?" Amber replied with a cool stare. "Being a man without a heart, I would think it's something you would admire." Amber finished her post on eBay and picked up her purse to march out of the house.

Chapter 11
Mother's Baby, Father's Maybe

Mike, sitting at the end of a large, long, empty conference table, fidgeted with the height of his chair, not wanting to be too low during the proceedings. He shot a quick glance at the legal documents piled next to him. He had not read the papers and had no desire to read them. He knew they could only be bad. When his unfaithful wife's lawyer sent him a package of official forms (he no longer used her name), he knew it meant divorce.

She had not gone to the hospital to see him; instead, she said the children should not see their father in "such a state." Her exact words were, "a weirdo with his head wrapped like a deranged New York City taxi driver." Luckily, James, who had become Mike's most loyal companion, had agreed to come along with him to the lawyer's office. Mike closed his eyes and listened to James's soothing chants.

Finally, after a twenty-minute delay, a well-dressed Alyssa and her lawyer strolled into the room, chatting strategy as they moved. The large-framed lawyer set an expensive leather briefcase on the table in front of him, retrieved several stacks of paper, and organized them into three neat stacks. Mike, in a reflex motion, reached for his papers, which were stuffed into a plastic grocery bag. Mike plucked out a store circular mixed in with the other documents and handed it to a grateful James.

"Rahkama," James stated as he proceeded to glance through the coupons with excitement.

"Good morning. Thank you for coming to the office," the lawyer stated in an artificially practiced, cheerful car-salesman tone.

"Not sure I had a choice. I was served these papers," Mike responded with a sad twinge. He glanced at Alyssa, who did not take her eyes off her phone. He could only see her forehead, which reminded Mike of the image of his brother mounting her from behind and the sound of her moans filling his ears.

"Is this your legal representation?" the lawyer asked in a hesitant voice, motioning to James.

"Rahkama," James said again.

The words brought a smile to Alyssa's face, which caused Mike to grimace because he loved her smile. Mike had a vivid memory of the first time he saw it.

As an MBA student, Alyssa had entered his former office as a consultant on an efficiency project. From the moment she entered the building with the regional VP, flirting as she walked, all of Mike's male coworkers were in love. Mike, who had been divorced before twenty-five, avoided eye contact, while every other male and even two females in the office started flirting with her. Alyssa had instantly charmed everyone.

The office, normally painfully dull, became chaotic with spontaneous energy. Mike's colleagues busied themselves drafting schemes to impress the beautiful new consultant. Mike attempted to stay clear of the wild scrum, but his friend and office mate, Tim, recruited him into a plan to lure her to a happy hour. Tim, a former college linebacker and fine physical specimen, did not seem to need the help, but admitted that he intimidated women and needed a guy like Mike to make her feel at ease.

"Hey, Mike, I'm guessing with your recent divorce so fresh you're not going to make a move," Tim asked him his blunt manner.

"You're right, for a change. I'm not interested," Mike responded.

"Well, I'm going invite her out this Friday at Harry C's saying it's a company get-together," Tim explained.

"There's a company thing at Harry C's this Friday?"

"There is now. I'm going to tell her a bunch of us are going there. You can vouch for the story and then you can cancel on Friday around lunchtime."

"Why the deception?" Mike asked.

"I think it will be easier to get her to go."

"Fine," Mike agreed reluctantly.

Mike did his part, first stating he was going to the happy hour and then later informing Alyssa that something prevented him from attending. Tim circled the office all day Friday, beaming with happiness over his ability to get a manufactured date. Every other male was jealous.

Mike, unable to endure the endless chatter among his colleagues about Tim's success, hid in an empty conference room on Friday afternoon. Then, at 3:50 p.m., ten minutes before Tim and Alyssa were scheduled to leave for drinks, Alyssa barged in breathlessly into the conference room.

Wearing her classic grin, she hovered around Mike, obviously in an agitated state. Mike tried to act aloof, but her every movement bedazzled him. Her long legs popping out of her short business suit and her bright, deep-blue eyes made it impossible for him not to ogle. Alyssa, with her short hair and preppy style, seemed like a co-ed with a cool confident air about her.

"Busy with work?" Alyssa asked as she slid up next to him.

"Yeah," he said.

"Too busy to make it to the happy hour?"

"Yes, I'm way too busy."

Alyssa peered over Mike's shoulder and let him smell the perfume she just applied, causing Mike to roll his eyes as he struggled to remain placid. "Too busy," she stated as she looked at a crossword puzzle sitting in front of Mike. "Are you sure?"

"Yeah," Mike stammered.

She batted her eyes and put out a girlish pouty lip. "It seems that the happy hour group has shrunk down to just me and Tim."

"If you were to ask some of the other guys I'm sure they would tag along."

"I'm asking you."

Mike said nothing, staring at her as though she were Count Dracula, hypnotizing him into obedience. Even though he normally would have leapt at the chance to go with her, the freshness of his recent divorce made him hesitant. "I'm not sure that's a good idea."

Alyssa pranced around the table, displaying to Mike all of her wonderful anatomical attributes, but Mike kept his gaze at the papers in front of him. In a sweet voice Alyssa said, "I was talking to Kim and she was saying what a nice guy you are."

"Kim?" Mike replied, surprised that Kim, the disillusioned, bitter receptionist, had said anything nice. "She said I was a nice guy?"

"She said you're the only one who always volunteers for charity events she organizes."

"Oh," Mike said, happy that his philanthropy did not go unnoticed, but wondering if he was vulnerable to manipulation.

Alyssa moved to Mike and put her hand on his. "As a consultant I don't want to ruffle feathers. Come with us and I won't forget it."

Mike tolerated a long bumpy ride in the covered bed of Tim's old pickup. Tim and Alyssa sat alone in the cab. Tim had taken a long circular route to the bar, allowing him more time to be alone with Alyssa. Then Mike spent three hours standing near Tim and Alyssa as Tim unleashed a flurry of macho stories about bloodying opponents during his football days. To Mike the stories, jokes, and embellishments appeared to be working as Alyssa laughed, smiled, and patted Tim on his broad shoulders after each tale. Mike's endurance ended, and he asked the hostess for the number of a taxi service.

Tim danced with excitement when Mike returned. "I am so going to get laid tonight,"

"Where did Alyssa go?"

"She's in the bathroom," Tim bellowed as he rubbed his hands together.

"Okay, I'm heading back to the office," Mike stated, slipping out of the bar and waiting for the taxi to take him back to the office. Once there, he packed up his belongings to drive home and was surprised to see Alyssa walking down the hallway. She plopped her firm butt cheeks on his desk. She looked down at Mike with a cheerful pout and a playful stare.

"I thought you were a nice guy," Alyssa asked in a tone normally reversed for young girls asking a father for a toy.

"I am a nice guy."

"I begged you to stay with me," Alyssa asked in a silky tenor.

"I stayed."

"Not long enough," Alyssa whispered his Mike's ear. "Maybe you're a nice guy, but you aren't the swiftest."

"What?"

"You don't read women very well." Alyssa reached down and ran her fingers through Mike's thick wavy hair. Leaning forward, she kissed him in a hard, but at the same time, soft way. It had been the best kiss, stunning Mike as he leaned back after it had ended as though a powerful shock wave had barreled into him.

"That was the best kiss ever," Mike uttered in a sincere and honest way.

"I should have held back, I'm not sure you deserve such a good kiss."

"I'm not sure anyone deserved such a great kiss."

Mike's comment caused Alyssa to lunge for him and the kissing went from hard to animalistic. Alyssa ripped at Mike's clothes, like a person ripping Christmas presents open, popping the buttons off his shirt and tugging at his zipper. She did not stop until Mike sat in his chair with his chest bare and his boxers on his knees.

Alyssa turned her attention to her own clothes, tugging open her blouse and then, like a magician, pulling off her bra without taking off her shirt. She reached under her skirt and pulled off her red panties and tossed them on Mike's chest before mounting him.

After their passionate lovemaking, Alyssa collapsed on Mike and then hit him again with her wonderful lips. As she collected her breath, she whispered complimentary things in his ear and kissed his cheeks, while Mike wondered if the whole thing had been a dream.

"Tim thought he was going to get lucky," Mike chuckled.

"I always had my eyes on you," Alyssa said as she tried to button her blouse, but realized she was missing several buttons.

Alyssa, with her outright rejection of the muscular Tim, had filled Mike with such overflowing pride. Much later, now with her affair with his brother, Alyssa had delivered the lowest, most humiliating moment of his life. She was responsible for his biggest pride and lowest point, which baffled Mike. Unfortunately for Mike, painful memories were ten times more powerful than pleasant ones, so she would forever be the wickedest person he had ever met.

"Do you remember that first day in my office?" Mike mumbled to Alyssa. "You know, that first date?"

Alyssa froze as an annoyed look drenched her face. Putting her cell phone to the side, she coldly replied, "That's the problem with men. They can't separate sex from love." Alyssa motioned for her lawyer to speak and returned her attention to her phone.

"You're saying you didn't love me then?"

"No, I'm not saying that. I loved bottles when I was an infant. Now I'm different. You know what I mean?"

"No, I don't know what you mean."

"I think we should get to the point of the meeting. I've drafted the divorce papers," the lawyer stated and pointed to the center stack of papers.

"I see that," Mike replied in a defeated voice. "You know I always pick the slutty girls. She fucked me the first time in a public place. Before we even started dating."

"That's right, and you begged me to marry you. Not the other way around," Alyssa snapped.

The lawyer loudly cleared his throat, trying to derail the pending argument. "There's one more thing we would like to request as we proceed."

"Request? You make it sound like you are asking me to volunteer for something," Mike's bitterness filled his mouth.

"Mike doesn't volunteer for anything anymore."

"In the paperwork you will see the request for samples in order to perform DNA testing for the two children."

"Is that necessary? Do you really think I won't support my kids?"

"So says the man who was fired months ago," Alyssa exclaimed.

"I will support them," Mike tried to say in a stern voice, but his tone fractured after the word "will."

"This is not about *you* supporting them," Alyssa stated, emphasizing the word "you."

"What?"

"I'm requesting your brother James submit for testing too," Alyssa stated in a lawyerly way. "If I can find him. Where did he disappear to?"

"I'm not my brother's keeper," Mike answered. "Do you think I'll ever speak to that scumbag again?"

Alyssa casually shrugged her shoulders. "Knowing him, he's already starting seeing someone else. Men are pigs."

Mike leaned forward to Alyssa, changing his tone in hopes she might show some pity. "Do you really think the kids are James's?" Mike asked.

Alyssa's face turned serious. "Mike, you saw what happened. You know that's been going on for some time." The lawyer, not wanting Alyssa to say something inappropriate, attempted to stop her, but she waved him off. Alyssa knew that even U.S. presidents ignore legal counsel when they want to. "You must have known."

Mike muttered, "Some time?"

"Mike, let's not create an alternate set of facts. You know things have not been good with us. I mean, your libido has been subpar for some time now." Alyssa's tone had changed. She sounded like a guidance counselor helping a student select the best career choice. "Your brother can better provide for the kids. You should be grateful I'm offering you a way out. This would give you time to get your life together."

"My life together?"

"You're not the man I married. You've become this pathetic shell of a person. I'm not sure what happened."

Although Alyssa spoke in a smooth, charming voice, it repulsed Mike. Mike stood up and walked to a shelf full of books. He started to methodically bang his head against the books until James came over and put his hands on Mike's shoulders.

"*Rahkama*," James stated.

Mike hugged James. "Thank you for standing by me." Turning back to Alyssa, Mike barked, "Thanks for small favors." Mike grabbed his jacket and started to leave.

The lawyer waved for Mike's attention. "We still need your sample before you go."

The lawyer retrieved a small package and pushed it across the desk to Mike. Inside was a paternity test kit. James picked up a cotton swab from the kit, sniffed it, and then rubbed the swab along the inside of his cheek. He ran it along his bushy eyebrows, giggling as it moved along the hairs.

"You don't want to contaminate that," Alyssa cautioned.

"You really need to prove the kids aren't mine?" Mike asked in a pathetic tone. "You actually want me to take a test to see if the kids are mine or my brother's?" he asked rhetorically, peering at Alyssa. She had returned to her phone and acted as though Mike had said nothing.

"Yes, otherwise the state will assume you're the father because they were born during the marriage," the lawyer explained.

"What a fucking novel concept! Assuming that the children belong to the husband," Mike snapped.

"Can you spare us all this drama? When you left the house and did not return, I did not see any concern for your kids." Alyssa made air quotes around the word "your." "You know it's kind of hard to support your children when you commit suicide."

Mike hated Alyssa, but she was right. He hadn't even thought about the kids in the past few weeks. Whatever sins she had committed, Alyssa did not feel she needed to beg for Mike's forgiveness, which became evident to Mike. A cringe-worthy silence filled the room as Alyssa glared, Mike stared, and the lawyer froze. James broke the silence with a series of giggles as he rubbed a second cotton swab on the edge of his nose.

Mike took out his own swab and angrily swabbed the inside of his cheek. He handed it over to the lawyer.

"If we're both lucky you're not the father of my children," Alyssa barked, standing and moving toward the door. "You can get your freedom."

"Freedom?" Mike questioned.

The lawyer nodded, bagged the swab Mike had handed him, and said nothing, and the two left the room.

Chapter 12
Passed Over

Amber sat at the end of long table in a conference room, which looked as if it had been dully decorated for the opening scene of a Kafka novel. She diligently checked summary tables of sales data while waiting for her sales director, who was perpetually late, to enter. The numbers were good. The numbers were excellent.

Amber had memorized the numbers, but she relished recounting them. There had been a ten percent increase in the last two quarters—a much higher ramp up than corporate had expected. Her sales were higher than any other person on the entire East Coast. She could taste her promotion. Like a straight-A student waiting for her test to come back from the teacher, she was giddy with anticipation.

Although ecstatic about the promotion, she hated the promotion giver, the director of sales. His being fifteen minutes late on this day did not represent an anomaly. The man, never on time for a meeting, had been the head of the corporate "Manager of the Future Program," which amazed Amber.

For fun, she had taken the company's manager's handbook and listed the number of rules this leader had routinely violated. Late to meetings, incomplete annual reviews, and inappropriate language were common themes. Amber hated this incompetence. She despised the company for allowing a man with such dramatic flaws to climb the corporate ladder.

Amber organized the data supporting her performance into simple visual displays, knowing her ill-informed director wouldn't understand any of it. Not only did he consistently arrive at meetings late, but he never came prepared. He knew nothing. Even though she sent him notes, PowerPoint presentations, and spreadsheets, her director never read of her emails.

Amber did not think this; she knew it. She had coded her emails to know when her director opened them, but he never did. She felt this was disrespectful. She hated his rudeness. She hated his ignorance. She hated everything about him. She did not even think of him by his name, Steve. Instead, she thought of him by her invented nickname, Skitters, due to his nervous anxiety and poor communication skills.

Sixty-year-old Skitters had been trained at a different time for this industry. He referred to his administrative assistant as a secretary, asked for people to send him memos, and still asked for free drug samples even though the Prescription Drug Marketing Act (PDMA) forbade sales reps from carrying them on doctor calls. He refused to change.

Skitters spent more time on the golf course than he did in meetings, excusing the laziness as a relationship-building exercise. Biting her tongue proved to be a major piece of her job. Skitters, as well as others in management, did not allow for any type of criticism.

Amber, who viewed Steve as being a recipient of corporate welfare, could not always contain herself. Once she accidentally complained aloud to a colleague that Steve was stealing from the company when Steve spent an entire business trip golfing with college buddies. Steve happened to approach her near the end of the rant, but could not quite understand the full extent of the monologue, yet he caught the gist of her complaint. Steve made a point to comment on her "judgmental" personality.

"You're a high performer," Steve stated in every review, "but you have to tone down your personality. You rub people the wrong way."

"Can you give me an example?" Amber always asked.

"No, nothing specific, you just have to be more of a team player," Steve would answer, which meant he wanted an employee who did everything he said and never complained.

After each review, Amber did the same thing: she dropped the completed forms in the shredder bin on the way back to her office, called friends, and mocked Steve's feedback. She found the idea absurd that a lazy, ill-informed, technically-illiterate individual gave her reviews.

She did grudgingly try to endure the human resource's evaluation requirement until the buffoon retired. Amber looked at her competition, concluding no one had the results she compiled. She also knew that this promotion to regional manager was critical to her ultimate plan to replace Steve as sales director when he did leave the company.

Amber's director—his brash, irritating voice dozens of steps in front of his pace—finally entered the room with an overstuffed binder and an old leather briefcase. Steve, a tense balding man with an unkempt mustache, mumbled something to Amber. She rolled her eyes at the sight of the aged briefcase, which she had concluded was unprofessional.

From the binder, Steve fumbled for some paperwork, which fell across the table to Amber. As Amber gathered his papers, she noticed Steve had printed out the salaries of all her colleagues. Amber rolled her eyes again at his lack of sense.

"Sorry for being late, Amber, things are a bit hectic."

Amber nodded again. She refused to say it was okay. She felt that Steve disrespected her every time he was late, which she refused to accept. He always waited for her to accept his apology, so both of them sat in silence at the start of each meeting.

"There's quite a bit going on," Amber finally stated, anxious to get to the news about her promotion.

"Yes," Steve said as he continued to fish through his binder. "I have your review here somewhere."

He took the paper out, pressed out the wrinkles with his sweaty palm, flicked a hardened piece of food from its edge, and slid it in front of Amber. Steve had handed Amber her self-assessment, but had not completed his section of the form. "Do you have your comments on my self-assessment?" Amber asked with an acidic tone.

"Hmmm, I'm sorry, I thought I completed them."

Amber exerted all her strength not to scream at this fool, knowing such an outburst would kill her promotion. "Well, can you give me your verbal feedback?"

"Very good numbers, Amber. You are very strong," Steve said as he still attempted to organize his mess.

"Any numbers in particular?" Amber stated with glee, knowing Steve had not reviewed her numbers in detail; she wanted to embarrass him.

Steve did not flinch, but used his trademark vagueness to answer, "Across the board, nice job, and that is reflected in your merit increase."

Amber flinched at his lie, because she had just seen the salaries of two colleagues who had a higher merit increase, but had lower numbers last year. She bit her lower lip and stayed silent.

Steve, when he finally corralled his papers, turned and asked, "Any questions?"

Amber hesitated, not wanting to appear too forward, but she wanted to know her start date for the new position. An awkward silence returned. Amber tried to stay quiet as she pretended to examine the review. She finally grew impatient and blurted, "What is the status of the regional manager position?"

"Oh, I am glad you asked." Steve stood, went to the door and called in a middle-aged, plump, well-dressed woman. "Amber, I want you to meet Tina. She is going to be our new Regional Manager of Mid-Atlantic Sales."

Amber, stunned with shock and awe, dropped her large smartphone loudly on the table and her mouth hung far under her chin as she surveyed her director in the hope he was joking. She turned her attention to the woman in front of her who politely said, "Well, it is nice to meet you, Amber. I look forward to getting to know you better." When Amber didn't stand or shake Tina's extended hand, the new regional manager had the common sense to smile, nod, and quickly exit the room, gently holding the door as it closed.

"Mid-Atlantic? You're filling John's open position with someone from the outside?"

"Yes," Steve replied with a strange smile.

Amber, still shaken from the announcement, stammered, "Can I ask the reason why no internal candidate was considered?" The question only pertained to one internal candidate.

"No particular reason. I wanted to go in a new direction."

"New direction? Was there something wrong with the successful old direction?" Amber asked barely containing her anger.

Steve shot Amber an unpleasant glance, returned to his corporate robotic response mechanisms, and confidently replied, "The sales have not been what we expected."

"The sales have exceeded target by almost thirty percent."

"Are you sure about those numbers?" Steve asked, with an intentional obtuseness rising in his demeanor. Steve, a company propagandist, had the endurance to continue an emotionless, irrational conversation intended to wear down the most passionate employee. He possessed the uncanny ability to release illogical vague statements in an indifferent manner; it always deterred his reports from attaining any satisfactory answer.

"Yes, I'm more than positive," gasped Amber, forgetting Steve had transformed into his "intentional obtuseness" mode. "I've been sending you sales updates every Monday, and I just sent you the quarterly," Amber continued as her voice elevated to a level that suddenly unnerved her director.

Steve, realizing his normal techniques were not achieving the desired result, firmly scratched his chin as though it would loosen a clever retort. It did not.

"Amber, this is not about performance," Steve commented in a stern calm voice.

"Not about performance? Then what the fuck was it based on?"

"Amber, that is not appropriate."

"Is this what you think of your current staff?"

"I am not sure why you are translating this as a negative to the current staff."

"Because none of your current staff got the promotion," Amber interrupted in a tone that bordered on a yell.

"I'm not following your logic. This passion is something you need to work on."

"You don't want me to have passion for my job? You want me to not care, like you?" she screamed.

Steve, a veteran of annual two-week management trainings for twenty consecutive years, used his favorite management tool and left the room without saying a word. Amber stood in disbelief, waiting for someone to come into the room and explain that this was a prank, but no one did.

Amber stood there for several minutes, frozen with anger, disappointment, and incredulity all mixing together. Finally, after ten minutes, her cell phone buzzed with a new message from Steve. Amber read it to herself.

Can you prepare some thorough orientation material for Tina? She is new to this type of sales and could use a basic introduction.

Amber screamed with a passion not normally witnessed in a corporate setting and smashed her phone against the wall.

Jesus's Brother James

Chapter 13
Friendless

Mike sat on the floor of Paul's apartment, afraid to spill something on the sofa or chair. Paul had made it clear that everything needed to be sold on Craigslist. Mike had spilled a little blood on the futon when he changed his head bandages and Paul had had a conniption. As Mike sat on the finely buffed hardwood floors, he thought about the DNA test.

Mike turned to James sitting on the floor next to him. "Can you believe her?" Mike asked.

James smiled and giggled.

"I'm glad you think it's funny." Mike's statement caused James to break into a laugh, but it unleashed tears down Mike's cheeks. James leaned forward and wiped Mike's tears with a napkin while he patted Mike on the shoulder.

"*Lev*," James said, which, although Mike did not understand the spoken word, caused him to nod his head in agreement. James tapped his chest over his heart and repeated the word several times: "*Lev.*"

"*Lev*," Mike repeated as he touched his own chest. "Does *lev* mean heart?"

"*Lev*," James responded.

"I should have known all along," Mike commented, still thinking about the DNA test.

"*Lev*," James said.

"Yeah, it hurts," Mike said.

James continued to clear the tears from Mike's face, meticulously dabbing each small stream until every speck of moisture was removed. The front door flung open and Amber stomped into the living room. Stopping for a moment to examine the strange scene of Mike and James on the floor together, she shook her head and dropped pictures of Paul on the floor in a thud, causing a glass frame to crack. She rushed into the bedroom with a small bag.

From the bedroom, Mike could hear dresser drawers being thrust open and slammed shut, while Amber served a series of curses directed at Paul. After a five-minute, unintelligible one-woman show, she reappeared in the living room.

"This is the dickhead's key," she announced in a loud voice that bounced off the walls. She threw it down on the coffee table and started for the door, but stopped after three steps. Pivoting hard on her sneakered heel, she changed directions and headed back to the coffee table and glared at the key.

For a moment, she stood in silence staring at the key as though she were watching an exciting movie. Every few seconds she let out a short huff as though her mouth was a vent releasing excessive pressure that had built up within her.

"*Lev*," James said as he tapped his chest and then tapped Mike's chest as he motioned to Amber's chest.

Amber squinted her eyes in confusion, "Are you two insane?"

"I think he's saying that we both have pain in our heart."

"Is his name Captain Obvious?"

Amber growled, picked up the key, and scratched several squiggly lines into the top of the glass coffee table. When she was finished, she stepped back to critique her work. Although the lines were drawn randomly on the surface, it was a clear "Fuck You" written on the surface. It made her smile. She dropped the key on the table again, turned for the door, and was greeted by James, who had risen to his feet.

"*Lev*," James said in a soft voice.

James reached out to her and took her hand. Amber, at first, recoiled from his touch, but then relaxed into his warm hands. A warm sensation ran from her hand through an imaginary meridian from her toes to her ears, melting her anger as the warmth ran through her body. Calmness took hold of her. Stunned, Amber backed slowly away toward the door, unable to process what had happened. She wanted to thank James, but the strangeness of the encounter caused her to be silent.

"I've got to go," she finally managed to say.

"*Lev*," James concluded.

"You said it. Relationships are a beast," Mike said with a sigh, crawling over to inspect Amber's handiwork. Although he had just witnessed the defacement of his friend's coffee table, he could not help but smile as he felt a bond with Amber's pain.

"*Lev*," said James as he started to get into a mediation position on the floor.

"I guess I should have figured out earlier that our marriage was doomed," Mike lamented.

James stopped humming and turned his attention to Mike. Although James said nothing, he peered at Mike as though he were a marriage therapist intently absorbing each word with careful analysis. He made a circular motion with his hand to signal to Mike that he wanted Mike to continue his story.

"I always go for the shiny car," Mike stated. "You know the car that impresses, but that always breaks down and needs a lot of maintenance. For some reason, this whole thing reminds me of when I put all my money into my uncle's old Porsche 911. It was the winter of my freshman year of..."

Mike stopped his sentence before he could finish the word "college," and remained silent as he ran his finger along the newly carved imperfection in the glass. From his wallet he took out his treasured acceptance letter from Cal Poly and gazed at it for a long time. His face started to droop as though the gravity of the earth had increased tenfold. The letter had streaks of blood on it, which must have happened the night that Coady shot him. His eyes started to water once again.

"You know Alyssa said I changed. She said I was a pathetic shell."

James took Mike's hand and took the letter from him and stated, "*Shwoqqan.*"

Mike tried to utter something, but his words could not travel across the dryness of his throat. James leaned forward to hear the next sentence that was yet to cross Mike's lips, but no sound emerged.

"*Shwoqqan,*" James repeated.

As the two men sat there, Paul came through the front door with a robust positive vibe emanating from his face, which eroded when he saw the two sitting almost in each other's laps. Shaking his head like a dog twisting a play rope, Paul attempted to return his focus on his happy thoughts.

Dropping his briefcase on the counter, he bounced over to the sofa and pushed a sheet of paper across the coffee table in Mike's direction. As his fingers moved the paper on the glass, Paul noticed the scratches and jumped up in horror.

"What the fuck?" Paul said as he rushed into the kitchen to grab a wet rag, returning to feverishly wipe the marks without success. "How am I going to sell this now?"

Mike reached over and retrieved the paper, which contained a job description for a Human Resource Director of a local company. "What is this?" Mike asked.

"Huh?" responded Paul, barely able to turn his OCD-attention from the damaged furniture to his friend.

"Did you bring this for me?"

"I'm a little busy. Give me one second," Paul commented. "What the fuck were you guys doing here anyway?"

"Look at the key. It's not the one you gave me." Mike snapped as his eyes brought Paul's attention to the single key sitting on the table.

"Didn't you try to stop her?" Paul snatched the key. "Oh, never mind. She's still pissed. This is not like her." Paul grabbed his phone and browsed to search eBay for the autographed photo of Rob Thomas. It was still posted. "She's really pissed."

"Your girlfriend left that for you too," Mike said, trying to keep a smile from appearing on his face, pointing to the pile of broken pictures on the floor. Paul walked over to look at the mess.

James rose and moved to Paul, placing his large hand on Paul's chest. "*Lev*," James stated in a soothing voice.

The gesture did not soothe Paul, but instead he recoiled away from James's touch as though his hands were toxic. "No offense, but I don't want strange guys feeling me up."

"He's trying to comfort you," Mike commented.

"Why would I need comforting?" Paul said as he placed Amber's key in his pocket.

"Doesn't everyone?" Mike replied.

Paul sat down and looked again on eBay. From a second account that Amber would not recognize, he made an offer to purchase the photo. Although re-purchasing a gift from an ex-girlfriend seemed illogical, he felt compelled to buy it. After making a bid, fifty dollars less than what Amber had asked, he put his phone away.

"Is there something you wanted to tell me?" Mike asked, waving the paper around.

Moving briskly across the room, Paul grabbed the paper and sat back down on the couch, trying to avoid looking at the scratches in the coffee table. "I have some good news for you."

Mike shuddered as though he were naked in the middle of an ice storm, fearing what Paul was about to say. He turned to James for comfort, but James had turned his attention elsewhere and was giggling to himself.

Noting Mike's distress, Paul suddenly asked, "Hey, how did the meeting with your wife and the lawyer go today?"

"Not well. They made me take a DNA test."

"Your wife made you take a DNA test?" Paul asked.

"She wants to prove the kids belong to my rich brother," Mike spit out.

"You're fucking kidding," Paul said, not able to hold back a chuckle.

"I guess for you this is funny."

"I'm sorry," Paul apologized, embarrassed with his reaction. "You know what I do when I'm thinking about the future?"

"What?"

"I think of the worst-case scenario."

"I've already done that and I ended up being shot by a priest in a park," Mike coughed.

"Tell me, what's the worst-case scenario?" Paul insisted.

Mike took a long moment to ponder the question. "I guess if the test proves that the kids I've been loving and raising aren't mine."

"Right. So you find out those two lovely kids are your niece and nephew. Isn't it better that you find out now? Better for them, while they are still so young?" Paul stated in a pleasant tone that irritated Mike.

"You say that like it's a good thing."

"Is that the worst thing that you can think of?" Paul asked in a more serious voice. "You caught your wife cheating on you with your brother. There's so much hate now between you. Don't you think that is going to poison any relationship with those kids?" Mike rubbed his bandaged head as he pondered the idea. "Don't let your pride get in the way. Why hold onto a bad situation?"

"That's easy for you to say."

Mike started to cry again, not because he disagreed with Paul's questions, but from the harsh idea that he found logic in Paul's conclusion. The nothingness, the not caring, frightened him. If Mike accepted Paul's thesis, he would be free, but he would be alone, negating the past several years of his life. He had no career. He had no wife. He soon could have no kids. He would be completely alone.

Paul sat motionless, not wanting to get too close to Mike while he cried. Paul distrusted any male tears. James, on the other hand, moved over to Mike and tapped his chest again. "*Lev,*" James stated. The words soothed Mike, who stopped crying. James returned to amusing himself.

"Did you ever think what your life would be like if you had made different choices?" Mike asked Paul.

"I try not to. It's water under the bridge," Paul answered with confidence. He felt a twinge when he thought of how badly he had handled the past few weeks with Amber. He peered at his phone and saw a message that Amber had rejected his initial offer.

"So you never look back?"

"No point to it. You can't change a past decision. You can only change the future," Paul replied and sent a new message to Amber's eBay account offering fifty dollars more than her asking price.

"Why did you bring me this paper?" Mike asked, wishing to change the subject.

"Oh, yes, I have a friend who is the director of human resources at a local medical device company. I convinced her to give you an interview for some open positions."

Mike looked at the information, desperately wanting to argue about the idiocy of going to an interview in his condition, but feared Paul would think him weak. "A job interview should be interesting."

Chapter 14
Interview with Buffy

Father Coady pushed his face in the dirt, taking cover from the sound and fury of the IED exploding on the side of the convoy. Wiping the dark earth and dust mixed in with his perspiration from his eyes, he tried to gauge the danger. With his chin barely in the air, Father Coady saw a father holding two small bodies. He tried to crawl through the sand to help them, but his body started to sink. From the sky a bomb fell down toward them, but Father Coady couldn't move. He screamed, which woke him from sleep.

Clutching a glass of water from his nightstand, Father Coady gulped several mouthfuls. The coolness of the liquid dampened the vividness of the nightmare. Father Coady stood up and walked to the bathroom. He would now be up for hours. After washing his face, he strolled to his computer.

On nights like this, Father Coady tended to surf eBay and Craigslist looking for bargain items for his poor parishioners. Once on eBay, his eyes were directed to the "items you may be interested in" list. A framed autographed photo of Rob Thomas. Father Coady's favorite band was Matchbox Twenty.

Five hundred dollars represented a large sum to any priest, but Father Coady really wanted that signed photo of Rob Thomas. He had always loved Matchbox Twenty; Thomas's haunting vocals always gave him chills.

As he stared at the computer screen, the photo seemed to be calling to him. He knew he shouldn't buy it, but he wanted it so badly. He knew there would be financial repercussions, but he was willing to risk it for the prized item. Clicking back between the photos he drooled with desire. Its beautiful, structured frame and alluring design made all the difference. He clicked in his offer.

Why did you spend all that money? Coady asked himself, with a touch of buyer's remorse.

Shaking his head, he tried to forget the negativity. A response came to his inbox. His offer was accepted with a big smiley face. *A feminine gesture*, Coady concluded. When he purchased the photo, he would be interacting with a person of the opposite sex. He smiled and thought of Amber. He gently slapped his cheeks.

Father Coady checked his email to see if he had any messages from Mike. Coady smiled at the soft tone of Mike's response. He hoped James had been making progress on improving Mike's outlook. Father Coady's initial worry that something awful might happen with the two seemed groundless.

He pictured the two men spending time together and Mike turning his life around. A small ping signaled a new email. The eBay seller had sent him directions and signed it "AM." Images of the note Amber left in his pocket filled his mind. She had signed it "AM." *What are the odds the photo's seller is Amber?*

Keep it together, it's just a coincidence. It might not even be a woman, he instructed himself. *The seller wants to meet me at someone named Paul's place. It's probably her boyfriend.* Father Coady took a long swig of water to cool the heat of his thoughts. *Relax, there's no possible way it could be Amber.*

With James next to him, Mike sat in an office conference room painted in a light green, reminding him of the administrative office in high school. He had often been sent to the principal's office for his comedic antics. Every memory he had from high school held laughter. He longed for those days.

While Mike waited for his interview with human resources to start, James chuckled as he tried to untangle a pen from his long beard. James had no trouble amusing himself. Mike intently watched James braid his long beard, pondering the details of this mysterious person. Was he even real? Mike now considered that James was a real-life guardian angel.

James noticed Mike's stare. *"Rahkama,"* he stated with another chuckle.

"Rahkama," Mike replied and started to smile, but was interrupted when the conference room door sprang open.

A young HR coordinator named Buffy flew into the room, stopping for a moment as she surveyed Mike's bandaged head, then regained her composure and slid into her seat. Mike timidly offered his hand to her, which she briefly shook, barely touching his hand.

In a deliberate manner, she took out items and placed them in specific locations on the conference table. Mike reached for his portfolio, but realized he had come to the interview with nothing other than James, so he leaned back in his chair and waited for the awkward session to begin. The HR person looked at James.

"Is this gentleman with you?"

"Yes. Don't worry. He won't interrupt. He doesn't speak English."

For a moment, Buffy digested this information. Not wanting to extend this process, she decided to proceed without delay. "This is just a preliminary screening for two open positions," the young woman said in automatic manner.

The rehearsed delivery reminded Mike of his wedding day, when Alyssa practiced her lines over and over before the wedding. Ironically enough, when they were standing in the church in front of the priest, Alyssa stumbled on the word "poorer." In a loud voice, which echoed through the cathedral and over the assembly, Alyssa said, "For richer or po... po...po... or...poorer," never able to fully deliver the whole phrase. At the time if seemed like an innocent slip of the tongue. For years, people teased him about the slip, which he now found painful and deliberate.

"Now it all makes sense. It was all planned," Mike said in a voice loud enough for the HR person to hear.

James reached over and placed his hand on Mike's heart, "*Lev,*" which calmed Mike.

The young woman, whose default was a robotic tone, tilted her head as she absorbed this unique scene. She analyzed various possible reasons for the interaction and when she could not find a palatable explanation, decided to continue the interview as though she had not witnessed it.

"As I mentioned, this is the preliminary interview. The next step in the process would be an interview with the hiring manager and a panel of impacted employees," she stated, never making eye contact with Mike. "We carefully screened your resumé and feel that you have the talent and experience we are looking for. We would like to initiate a discussion to see if you could become a valued member of our team."

Mike chuckled at the false statement, "carefully screened the resumé." He did not have a resumé. He felt amused and annoyed at the same time. "Screened my resumé," Mike repeated in a stale tone, which caused the young woman to look up from her notes.

"Yes, resumé," she assured, for the first time allowing a twinge of uncertainty to enter her voice. For a moment, she pondered whether to ask Mike about his head bandage. Promptly concluding the best course of action was to ignore the topic, she turned her focus back to her notes and restarted her monologue. "Our interview process intends to find the best candidate from a diverse pool of people, which will engage in bringing our company forward. Our system is based on a triangle, the shape that is the strongest shape, consisting of integrity, diversity, and quality."

Integrity, Mike thought. *Who in this world has integrity?*

"Do you have any questions or comments before we get started?" the young woman asked in artificially pleasant voice.

"What on my resumé impressed you the most?" Mike asked with a devilish smile.

The young woman, again focusing on finishing the interview within the allotted thirty minutes, showed some adaptability. "Actually, I didn't read your resumé," she admitted sheepishly, completely converting her robotic tone to a sweet feminine one. "I'm sorry."

"Sorry?" Mike stammered. The word melted his anger. For some reason, he wanted to hear it so badly. His eyes watered.

The young woman, concerned with the reaction, steered the conversation back within the realm of her scripted outline, transforming into her machine-like conveyance. "In order to get this started, can you please let me know which position intrigued you and why you thought you would be a good fit." The young woman stated briskly, placing a large checkmark next to the question.

James made a noise as though the question amused him, which caused Mike to start to laugh. After he finished his chortle, Mike pondered the absurdity of trying to answer the question, because he thought he offered nothing to this company. With no possible honest answer, Mike turned to creatively fabricating responses.

"The idea of managing people is something special," Mike lied. He had hated managing people and dealing with petty disputes and constant whining. He preferred to be on the road, away from the office politics. Mike smiled at the young woman as she feverishly scribbled notes. He started to formulate a reply to the second part of the question, but the young woman was fixated on ending the interview on time.

"Can you describe a time in your life when you directly worked to make a positive change? Please explain your involvement, the challenges you faced, and how you overcame them?" the young woman asked without taking a breath.

Mike laughed again as he considered describing the night he attempted suicide, fought his naked brother for sleeping with his wife, and was shot by a priest, but decided that those incidents had not worked to make a positive change. Mike's laugh deteriorated as he found it difficult to recall a change with a positive outcome.

He remembered Alyssa's statement that he had become a pathetic shell. The heavy thoughts weighed Mike down, causing him to place his forehead on the table for a long pause. Buffy glanced at her list of questions, hoping the encounter would soon end. After gathering himself, Mike sighed and delivered a fabricated answer.

"In my last position, I restructured the department through intensive synergies, resulting in a ten percent increase in the KPI annual output."

The incomplete answer, to Mike's astonishment, caused the young woman to smile, delighted with Mike's meaningless corporate jargon. She commented, "Very good answer."

The young woman, whose name he still did not know because she never introduced herself, clapped her hands with enthusiasm. Suddenly, Mike feared a successful outcome, which would mean more sessions filled with these awful questions. He twitched. He started to pick at the scabs hidden beneath the gauze on his head. At first the young woman did not notice as she reviewed the next question, but she reacted when the bandage loosened and she caught a glimpse of the wound.

Trained not to react, or in layman's terms, indifferent to human emotions, the young woman plodded along with the next question.

Jesus's Brother James

"Can you describe a time when you were presented with a difficult challenge and how you reacted? Please provide specific examples if you can."

Mike grew steadily more tired of this tedious interview and his initial attempts to have fun with the young woman grew stale. Only a short time removed from the traumatic events, he could not perform this artificial dance with such a soulless individual, even if this craziness was normal for corporations. Afraid this interview would crack the remainder of his sanity, he decided to end this session as soon as possible after trying to crack his interviewer.

"A difficult situation," Mike stated as though he were pondering a serious thought. "That's a tough one. I would have to say the time I caught my wife sleeping with my brother in my own bedroom."

The young woman's pen stopped. She played the answer again in her head. The bizarre answer proved successful to Mike. He jolted a reaction out of her. An uncomfortable expression covered her face.

If this man was joking, it meant Mike had a weird sense of humor. If this man was serious, it meant he was mentally ill. Either way, she had a Starbucks gift card in her pocket and office gossip to share with her officemate.

"Now for the second part of your question, how did I react?" Mike continued, pressing forward with hopes to fully crush her spirit to continue. "I tried to kill my brother with a lamp as he beat me senseless."

The young woman pretended to scribble notes and launched into her next question. "Very good, let's move on. In this job, you'll need to ensure your team stays current on industry standards. What do you do in your spare time to stay informed?"

"I surf the internet looking for ways to kill myself."

Unable to contain herself, she blurted, "You're kidding, right?"

His comments had had their desired effect, but he decided to pull back, thinking it wasn't fair to the young woman to scare her. "Of course I'm kidding," Mike stated in a fractured voice that failed to convince the young woman he was not serious.

The young woman sat bewildered, lost without a detailed script to follow. She concluded that her salary and her training were both inadequate for this situation. Her body started to shake. She made breathing sounds like she was practicing for a Lamaze class. The noises startled James, who made his way over to the young woman and held her hand.

"*Rahkama*," James stated in such a pleasant tone it caused the young woman to not only smile, but giggle.

"Oh, my," she commented, instantly releasing all the angst Mike had given her. "You were just joshing me." Now absorbed with James, she dropped her professional expressions and giggled like a girl at prom. Studying his features, firm jaw, and strong cheekbones, she forgot about the interview.

"Is the interview over?" Mike asked.

Ignoring Mike, she kept her focus on James, "You remind me of that handsome star on a soap opera I used to watch in college." James giggled, but she continued, "I used to snuggle up on my couch with my sister on snowy days." The young woman sighed from the deep pleasure of the vivid memory. "My name is Buffy."

Mike coughed with surprise.

"Now you say your name." Buffy ignored him and could not take her eyes off James.

Mike asked, "Is there any way we could just end this?"

Buffy, with her focus still on James, responded, "I can just make a note in here that you have other offers and would like to remove yourself from consideration. It will make you look more desirable." She said all this to James, which caused him to chuckle and she laughed in return.

The young woman stood, straightened her clothes and her hair, smiled one last time and turned for the door. As her hands touched the door, she suddenly turned back to James, but placed the coffee gift card in front of Mike. "This is a little gift for coming down here today."

"Thank you."

"No, thank you," she said to James.

Jesus's Brother James

Chapter 15
Amputated Career

Amber sat squeezed in a booth between two round male colleagues at the welcome lunch for her new boss Tina, wondering why men smell much worse after the age of thirty. Not only did she not want to attend this lunch, but Steve, the oblivious director, refused to pay, so everyone had to chip in on the bill. She was paying for the opportunity to celebrate a stranger getting her promotion.

"Pathetic," Amber spat as she pushed away a plate of hot wings her chubby colleague had ordered.

On Amber's left was Peter, who spent his life endlessly complaining about the difficulty of his job. For the past thirty minutes, he had alternated from complaints about complicated company software to challenging travel situations.

Amber hated working with Peter, who was meticulous, but so slow at everything. Now, Peter informed her, through a mouthful of chewed chicken wings, he had been promoted to her same level, which seemed incredible, so she slid to her right.

Moving away from Peter brought Amber closer to Willy, who was also a stout man, full of high energy with a piercing voice. Willy, always on the lookout for attention that might be brought to himself, spoke as though he were a professor in an auditorium without a microphone. Willy also liked to flirt with all the women and never realized all this flirtation was inappropriate and unwanted. He felt neglected from his wife's lack of affection.

He now took Amber's shift to his left as an opportunity to try his stale pickup lines with the most attractive salesperson at the company. He placed his arm around Amber and announced, "Doesn't everyone love Amber?"

Most of the group retorted, "Oh, yeah."

"I love it how Amber will send me an instant message, I will respond, and then she'll not respond to me for like thirty minutes," Willy stated with a wink to Amber.

Someone in the group called, "I know, right?"

"I also love that she types all through my calls with her. She's not even paying attention. For a girl with such dainty fingers, she can really plow down on those keys." Willy smiled at Amber as though he had just covered her with the most poetic compliment. "No wonder she didn't get the promotion. It would've sucked reporting to her."

Amber had enough. She firmly pushed Willy off the end of the bench so she could exit the booth. She dropped fifty dollars for this awful lunch next to Tina. "I'm sorry, I have to leave," she stated without making an excuse.

Amber sprinted to her car and jumped inside, hoping to block out the awful world. As though she were in a sci-fi movie, with monsters roaming everywhere, she slid down into the seat, hoping to hide. She did not hide from creatures, but from horrible thoughts, such as a failed career and failed relationships.

At thirty-five, she had nothing meaningful. Amber wanted to drive home and hide under the covers, but feared Paul would be lurking about. Instead, she blasted her favorite Matchbox Twenty song, "Unwell," hoping she wasn't crazy, but just having a little trouble.

Jesus's Brother James

The night before, Paul had come her house, along with two dozen red roses, her favorite flowers. Thinking this was an attempt at reconciliation, Amber allowed him to come into her house. The meeting started well, especially when Paul made her a drink of cucumber and mint, which Amber liked to drink when she was stressed. He also placed a box of tea on the counter.

She even smiled as she booted up her computer to catch a few last-minute tasks for the next day. Amber couldn't wait to get her replacement phone tomorrow—hopefully that one would last a bit longer if she held her temper in check.

"I made reservations at La Mella's tonight. My treat," Paul said in a tone so soft it was almost a whisper. The reconciliation started to turn sour when Paul ended his apologetic gestures and tried to steer her evening.

"Sure, I just need to get some things done for work."

"Say, did you find a buyer for the Rob Thomas photo?"

"Not yet," Amber stated, not wanting to discuss the fact that she had indeed found a buyer.

"I was just looking for the photo and didn't see it."

"Can I please just focus on my work for a few more minutes?" Amber whined.

"You must have a lot of work with your promotion," Paul commented in a soft, sympathetic tone.

The comment stung Amber, realizing she had not informed Paul about her disappointing news. "I did not get the promotion."

"I'm sorry. Did they give it to Peter?"

"No, they brought someone in from the outside," Amber seethed. "Someone with no experience whatsoever, a friend of Steve's."

"The corporate world is unbelievable," Paul concluded.

"The whole thing is complete and utter bullshit. Steve's the worst director I've ever had. He's a completely incompetent, balding, little skittering twit," Amber ranted. "He even has me training my new boss!"

"I agree," Paul stated, which caused Amber to smile. "They're screwing you."

Amber nodded her head in agreement.

"They're too stupid to realize the value and the skills that you bring to that place."

Amber clapped with agreement.

Then Paul shocked her. "You should quit."

Amber's smile disappeared. "Quit?"

"Sure. You aren't a slave."

"What the hell? I can't quit."

"Why not?"

"Why not? I haven't got a choice. I have way too much invested in this company."

"Come on, be serious, Amber. After a corporation amputates a person's legs, they're no longer able to climb the corporate ladder."

"That's a bit dramatic."

"Trust me. If they weren't upfront on this promotion and went outside, then they've pegged you to be a worker bee."

"You don't understand."

"I do understand. You act like a slave, so they treat you that way."

All the positives Paul had collected—flowers, gifts, and sweetness—evaporated in two short arrogant sentences. Amber knew she wasn't perfect, but she was right. "You don't get it. You don't have ten years hanging in the balance," Amber yelled with frustration.

"Yes, I do. Remember, I worked in the corporate world. They treated me as badly as they treated you. But I changed. I freed myself." Paul took out his cell phone. He showed her that the phone was not turned on. "Do you see me attached to my phone?"

"You don't understand."

"Do you see me dealing with the humiliation of training my replacement who doesn't deserve the job? I'm not a slave to anybody. No phone, no computer, no chains."

"Arggghhh," Amber groaned, motioning for Paul's phone. He handed it to her. She examined it closely. "It's not turned on?"

"That's right."

Amber stood up, strolled to the sliding glass door, "It's really not turned on?"

"That's right."

"Well, I'm not turned on either." She opened the door and then threw the phone into the parking lot. She threw it so hard that it bounced five times before coming to rest under a large SUV. "Oh, and by the way, I sold your stupid birthday gift."

Paul, not amused, stood and picked up his spare key, sliding it into his pocket. He moved to the front door, then stopped momentarily. "You might not believe this, but I was just trying to help you."

"Oh, my bad. I thought you were just trying to be a condescending, lecturing, emotionless jerk."

"I know change is tough, but you're the one staying in a bad situation."

"Good advice. I think it is time to move on."

Jesus's Brother James

Chapter 16
Crawling Experience

Mike never wanted a minivan. It not only represented domestication, it represented dysfunctional domestication. The family vehicle burst with aching memories and tokens of his futility. From a damaged stereo, the Wiggles's "Big Red Car," ran on a continuous loop. Baby Einstein stickers were on the side windows, and Happy Meal toys kept rolling underneath the gas pedal. With each reminder, Mike huffed or slapped his right hand firmly against the dashboard. He had to keep his left hand on the steering wheel.

"Those kids have so much crap," Mike concluded as he gripped a plastic Happy Meal toy in his palm so hard that it caused pain. Mike smiled because the physical discomfort displaced his emotional agony. Mike rolled down the window and chucked the toy out to the side of the road. Jettisoning the toy brought him great joy.

Needing more pleasure, Mike bent over and ran his fingers over the sticky car floor mats with his fingers, searching for another toy to unload. Finally, all those trips to McDonald's bore fruit, with an endless quantity of worthless plastic objects strewn throughout the minivan.

With each toss, a slight amount of delight warmed Mike's chest. Feverishly, Mike searched for more items to generate more joy. Switching from small cheap toys to his wife's music, everything that Alyssa owned could go. The minivan swerved as Mike found delight in tossing her sunglasses, lipstick, and the expensive dreamcatcher she purchased on an extravagant trip to Sedona, Arizona.

"Fucking stupid. Why do you keep a dreamcatcher in a car? Do you nap while driving?" Mike screamed as he used all his force to throw it out the window. By doing so, Mike turned the steering wheel, swerving the minivan into oncoming traffic.

Tires screeched, horns honked, and motorists screamed. But none of this deterred Mike's enthusiasm for the purge. Mike twisted his body to retrieve his wife's iPad from the back of his seat. She had started to sit in the back seat with the kids instead of, in her terms, "being close to him."

After stretching to a point that would have impressed a yoga master, Mike snatched the electronic device and tossed it on the pavement so hard, he thought he heard it splintering beneath him. Mike raised his hands and hollered, "Good luck at your book club now!" James, not sure of what was happening, joined in the celebration.

"*Rahkama*," James chirped.

The two men cheered as though their team had scored a touchdown in the Super Bowl. The celebration did not last as blue lights flashed in the rearview mirror. Mike imagined the cost of the tickets: two hundred dollars for littering, three hundred dollars for changing lanes without a signal, and four hundred dollars for driving in a manner to endanger.

After a quick glance to James, the presidential demand to crack down on illegal immigrants generated another huge imagined fine. Pulling over to the side of the road, Mike put his head down on the steering wheel and placed his hands out the window for easy access to the handcuffs.

"I'll make it easy on them," he told James, who copied Mike and also put his arms out the passenger side window.

Ignoring Mike's hands, the police officer stated, "License and registration."

"Yes, sir," Mike replied, relieved the officer did not clasp the handcuffs on him immediately. Fumbling through his wallet for his license, his shaking hands could not pull his license from its clear pouch. After three feeble attempts, he simply held the whole wallet up in front of the officer.

"Please remove the license from the wallet, sir," the officer demanded.

"Of course," Mike complied, but the next attempt was also unsuccessful. Apparently, he had left his wallet on the dashboard so the plastic had melted to the license.

Frustrated, the officer barked, "Give it to me." Mike handed the wallet to the officer, who yanked the license out. Like a nocturnal animal gazing into a bright light, Mike stared blankly at the officer. "Is it possible for you get the registration while I look at your license?" the officer commented sarcastically.

"Oh, yeah, I guess I could do that."

Mike frantically shuffled items out of the center console to locate the registration. Unable to find it, he turned his attention to the glove compartment. Stretching over James, he popped open the stuffed compartment, allowing numerous prescription bottles to fall into James's lap. James collected the bottles and proudly displayed them for the officer.

"*Rahkama*," James announced.

"All of these are your prescriptions?" the officer questioned.

"I think my name is on all the labels," Mike coughed, putting his hands out, again anticipating handcuffs.

The officer simply took a prescription bottle, examined the label, and asked, "Pain medication?"

"My head wound," Mike replied, pointing to his bandaged head.

"How did that happen?"

Mike nodded in reply.

"That was not a yes or no question. What happened to your head?"

"Gunshot," Mike stammered, realizing the answer might sound odd. Mike lowered his head once again, returning to his search for the missing car registration.

"Gunshot?" the police officer asked in an interested tone. He looked up and intensely examined Mike's bandaged head. In the meantime, Mike found his registration and eagerly handed it to the officer.

"Gunshot wound?" the officer repeated his question.

"It's not what you think," Mike explained. "I did not shoot myself."

James, perhaps sensing the stress in Mike's voice, proclaimed, "*Rahkama.*"

"Not what I think? Actually, I wasn't thinking you shot yourself," the officer commented.

"I mean, it's not like I was shot in a drug deal gone bad or anything."

"Not a drug deal?" the officer asked.

"No, I was shot by a priest."

"*Rahkama,*" James added as he held up a second prescription bottle.

"Okay, you two are acting a little weird. Could I ask the two of you to get out of the vehicle while we run your information?" Mike fell out of the car and down onto his knees.

"Sir, there is no need to be on your knees."

Mike, thinking the worst, put his hands behind him, "I don't want any trouble."

James climbed over the driver's seat and down to the ground next to Mike. "*Rahkama*," James repeated.

The officer dropped his stoic expression and moved back several steps away from the two. Sensing drugs behind the odd behavior, he motioned for his partner to flank him on the right to scope any potential trouble. The partner, who had started to run a background check, moved to the side, keeping his full attention on James's hands, which were obscured underneath the long flowing robe.

"Are you on drugs at this moment?" the officer asked in a stern voice.

"I'm taking several prescription drugs for my wound, but only at night," Mike replied, his breathing becoming erratic. As motorists drove past them, he felt very much on public display. The novel *The Scarlet Letter* popped into his consciousness. He remembered the large "A," but could not remember the woman's name who was forced to wear it. Suddenly it came to him. "Hester, fuck, I remember."

"What did you say?" the officer asked in a strong tone.

"Hester Prynne wore the A," Mike called out with anger surfacing in his tone. "And where was her lover, that pastor, hiding?"

"We might have a problem here," the officer signaled to his partner through his walkie-talkie mounted on his shoulder.

Mike looked up, realizing that he might have inadvertently startled the officer, put his head down, pondering the possibility of being sodomized by a large tattooed man in order to get toilet paper. James smiled, so Mike tried to be positive.

"Okay, buddy, what drugs have you taken today?"

"Nothing," Mike replied, his voice cracking.

"Please stay away from him," the officer commanded James.

James stood and took a few steps away from Mike, but stepped onto the road in the path of oncoming traffic. Mike, seeing the potential danger, lunged for James's ankle to stop him from moving into a car. "No!"

The officer, realizing Mike's intent, assisted in grabbing James's robe, safely guiding him back to a sidewalk on the far side of the car. "*Rahkama*," James commented.

Mike burst into tears and scolded James as though he was a child. "You have to be more careful. You could've been killed by that car." James embraced Mike, holding him for an extended period. "Promise me that you will never ever do something like that again."

"*Rahkama*."

The officer stood there puzzled. He felt some sympathy for Mike, but was feeling impatient. "I want you to start talking."

"I don't think I have to tell you anything," Mike spoke in an excited voice, still agitated from the recent events. "You're just abusing your powers as an officer. We haven't done anything."

"Oh, you've forgotten about your little drive."

"I don't have to cooperate with you."

"Would you rather have this conversation at the station?" the officer said as reached for handcuffs.

James, still wearing his permanent smile, said, "*Rahkama*," one more time in a tone so soothing that the officer released his handcuffs and stared at James. Normally cynical, the officer felt a strong connection with James and all his anxiety suddenly dissipated. "*Rahkama*," James stated once more, which caused the officer to smile.

Turning to Mike, the officer, in a stern, but sympathetic tone, asked, "Do you really want to do this?"

Mike replied with his chin on his chest, "The reason for my crazy driving is that I'm angry with my wife. I was throwing my wife's shit out the window because I caught her sleeping with my brother a few weeks ago."

The officer nodded as though he had heard this story many times. "And the gunshot wound?"

"I was accidentally shot by a priest who was trying to stop me from committing suicide."

The officer, a twenty-year veteran who had seen it all, did not flinch as the story rang true. The second officer returned to the scene and loudly informed his partner that Mike had a clean record.

"And what's with the story with Jesus here?"

"He is not Jesus, but Jesus's brother James. He doesn't speak English," Mike stated. "He's helping me get through this tough time."

"Well, it must be working because he saved you from being handcuffed."

"Saved me?"

"Yeah. And because of him, I'm going to give you a chance to cool down. There's a Starbucks right over there. I'd like you to go over there and have a cup of coffee. After a few minutes, take a bag and pick up all the shit you tossed onto the road."

Mike enthusiastically nodded. "Sure. Thank you, Officer."

The officer nodded and commented, "I'm going to be looking for you walking on the road cleaning up your litter in about thirty minutes."

For some reason the phrase, "walking on the road," appealed to Mike. He gazed over at James and imagined that James was a good walker. "You know what, Officer, I think I'm going to sell that minivan. Get rid of all those bad memories."

"Whatever you want, but move it off the road and into the parking lot."
He and his partner walked back to their patrol car and drove off.

James bent down to pick up a plastic card that Mike had dropped in his
haste to pull James to safety. It was the Starbucks gift card from Buffy.

"My God, you're so amazing," Mike shouted at James. "It's like you
knew we were going to end up at Starbucks." He hugged James with
such force that James let out a little yelp. "I'm sorry, James. I'm just
really thankful that you are here with me. I don't know what I would
do without you."

James smiled and hugged Mike once more. James had a serious look on
his face and finally uttered, "*Rahkama.*"

"You're right, James, we could spend some time meditating to get these
negative thoughts out of my mind."

"*Rahkama,*" James stated.

"Yes, and I will text Father Coady to let him know everything is fine.
Thanks for reminding me."

"*Rahkama,*" James answered.

Chapter 17
No Action Is an Action

For Paul, college campuses were much more inviting than corporate buildings. After leaving the business world, he spent whole days at Duke University, strolling across campus to mingle with students. He never spoke with them, but only observed.

He envied their smiles and laughter. Paul never experienced those emotions in the corporate world. His first boss, who fancied himself a mentor, informed him that only lazy people smiled and laughed at work. If you were laughing, it meant you weren't busy enough. Paul grew to hate his mentor, but appreciated him for helping him to flee the corporate world.

Once free of the business jail, he wanted to go back to college. Not any college, but a prestigious college. He had always wanted to attend this respected private institution, but he did not possess the grades or money when he graduated from high school. Instead, he went to a local community college and finished his bachelor's degree online while working to pay for it.

Now creating his own world, he purchased Duke golf shirts, attended numerous home basketball games, and pretended to be an alumnus. To cement the illusion, he enrolled in an online certification business class offered by the university.

Today, instead of heading to Duke Gardens, he drove to the archenemy of his fantasy college, the University of North Carolina at Chapel Hill. He had a mission. He had to fix things.

Paul, who prided himself on success, recently witnessed two large failures. His oldest friend had gone suicidal and now for help turned to a stranger who spoke no English, while his girlfriend ignored all his charm, rejecting all of his attempts at reconciliation. Between Mike and Amber, he could not seem to win.

Today, Paul was focused on helping Mike. With a little research on the internet, Paul discovered that there was a world-leading expert on early Christian studies at Chapel Hill. Using his talent and confidence, he convinced the professor to meet, figuring the professor could translate Aramaic and communicate with James.

Arriving early for the meeting allowed him to relax near the Graham Student Union by Raleigh Street. He watched a young couple toss a Frisbee on the lawn. He watched another couple lounging on the grass, reading from their respective textbooks, the girl's head resting on the small of his back.

A third couple sat next to him, trading small random kisses between spoonfuls of frozen yogurt. Each couple was different, but all shared the same broad smiles and energy. As he watched them, the sad thought that he might never again experience such a relationship invaded his mind.

Am I too old for such playful antics? Paul questioned himself as he continued to stare at the second couple on the grass, who now stopped studying to embrace and kiss.

As though he were a video editor, Paul plucked his historical romances deep within his cerebellum and compared them up against the young couples near him. He remembered Kim from NC State, the cute blonde he dated his freshman year at Wake Tech. Always self-conscious, Paul never gave her public affection, which she took as a sign he was not interested.

There was Cathy, a Campbell University tennis player, who often invited Paul for late-night rally sessions. She ended the relationship with a huff, frustrated that Paul never called her. Finally, there was Karen, whose father was a powerful VP at Porsche. She broke up with Paul after he objected to her vacationing with an ex-boyfriend in Asheville.

I've got a talent for getting girls to break up with me, Paul thought as he sipped his sparkling water.

A Frisbee smacked into Paul's temple, ending his review of his former lovers. The co-ed smiled, apologized, and called to her boyfriend to end their Frisbee session. "Let's blow off class and go back to your place." The boy smiled and the two turned and walked in the direction from which they had just come.

Relationships are great at the beginning. Before expectations get in the way, Paul mumbled to himself.

In the first days in his relationship with Amber, they spent whole days lounging in bed, watching reruns of *Star Trek: The Next Generation*. They both loved watching sci-fi movies and TV shows. Although Amber often snuck into the other room to check messages, the rest of the day consisted of lying in bed, cuddled together, watching episode after episode, only breaking for food or lovemaking. Sometimes both. One-time Amber found dessert in the refrigerator, smeared it across her torso and dared Paul to lick it off, which he was happy to do. Those were the best days.

Stop this. Spending time trying to change the past is pointless. Paul shook his head to shake the distracting thoughts. *There is nothing wrong with you. There were good reasons you lost interest in all your relationships.*

Kim, the NC State student, sobbed hysterically after every test or exam, thinking she had failed it miserably. Instead of a movie or dinner, Paul had to massage her fragile self-esteem closer to normal with hours of pep talks. Paul, running low on motivational hints, started reading self-help books to ready himself for such nights. The therapy sessions ate into his own study time. In the four months they dated, Kim never failed a test, and she never received lower than an A minus. Proudly dancing around the room after each A, she lectured Paul on his lower grades. Kim did not react well when Paul concluded, "I'd get better grades if my girlfriend had a little more maturity and could handle stress better." This sent Kim hysterically from the room, saying she never wanted to see Paul again. He left, happy she had ended their relationship. Later he received a surprise call on his way home from Kim, tearfully begging him to return to her apartment.

That's bipolar, isn't it? Paul asked himself.

His next girlfriend, Cathy, possessed the firmest body Paul had ever seen, but had the same soft mentality as Kim. Cathy played hours of tennis, hiked most weekends, and competed in triathlons. Paul assumed the exercise and scenery provided Cathy with serenity. It didn't. Cathy, having spent all this time creating the perfect body, wanted all males and some females to notice it.

She often undressed in public spaces, asked strangers to feel her flat stomach, and often flung her firm chest in front of people. On a trip to Wrightsville Beach, she asked a married man to rub suntan lotion directly on her chest. When the man's wife objected, Cathy snapped, "Haven't you heard of the skin cancer problem?"

That's a sign of more serious mental issues, isn't it? Paul asked himself.

He thought Karen might buck the trend of his dating the emotionally handicapped. She was smart, charming, cute, and above all—wealthy. Paul assumed financial stability stood behind Karen's easy-going confidence. The self-assurance proved false.

Karen, lacking any academic, athletic, or other accomplishments, constantly jabbered about the pedigrees of her ex-boyfriends. The collection included a class president, football captains, and older men. Simon, a college offensive tackle, proved her favorite. Karen not only bragged about him, but she also made several trips to see the former football star, telling Paul they each had the right to see whomever they wanted.

Paul complied, spending time with an actress who believed Paul had the talent to write a screenplay. Ironically Paul's casualness toward the relationship transformed Karen's indifference into jealousy. Appearing at Paul's apartment in tears, confessing her sudden change of heart, she pleaded for a monogamous relationship. After one six-hour marathon discussion, they both agreed to reunite.

While eating breakfast following the all-night negotiations, Karen coolly stated she had one final trip with Simon for a weekend in Asheville. She informed Paul she would break the news to Simon on that trip. Paul scoffed at the idea, telling Karen she was insane. This sent Karen into a frenzy, where she called him "conceited, cold, and harsh." She broke up with Paul immediately.

You sure know how to pick them, Paul reflected. *They were all wacky*.

Paul stood up, walked over to a random piece of trash, and tossed it into the garbage bin, thinking this action symbolized his ability to discard his brooding. Looking to the past created an obstacle for accomplishing his future goals. Seeing no value in spending precious mental effort on his past loves, he returned his focus on the task of getting help for his troubled friend. He grabbed the notes he prepared for the upcoming meeting and headed to Carolina Hall.

Professor Bart, busy with tasks varying from speaking engagements to lecture notes, did not have time for a meeting with Paul. His field of study, early Christian studies, had generated enormous notoriety. Atheists wanted him to speak to legitimize their doubt in Christian teachings, while Christians wanted to meet with him in hope of using God's limitless power to bring him back to the faith. Professor Bart chose this field thinking he would spend his life alone in a library reading ancient texts and still enjoy his limited fame. Hah. Never taking his eyes from a book on his desk, Professor Bart motioned for Paul to sit.

Paul surveyed the room stacked with old books, notepads, and various tattered clippings. Paul felt as though he were still a college student, visiting his professor during office hours. It unnerved him. He suppressed these feelings of intimidation and focused on attaining what he needed. Paul took out the notes he had prepared.

"Thank you for seeing me," Paul stated. "I've read all your books and find your writing interesting."

"Thank you," Professor Bart replied, with a strong tone of doubt in his voice. "Is there any of my writings that stand out in particular?"

"I found your writing examining how the evolution in the early Christian writings of Jesus being a prophet to being a God fascinating."

"Yes, it's an intriguing topic," Professor Bart replied, happy Paul could articulate a clear opinion on his books. Still, he leaned over to his desk to read his planner and determine why he had accepted this appointment. "You wanted to speak to me about Jesus's brother James?" Professor Bart asked.

"That's right," Paul said in a purposely excited tone.

The professor stood, went to his shelf, snatched up a copy of *Just James*, and then returned to his desk. He handed the book to Paul in the hopes of ending their meeting. "I feel this is the best biography of James. This should help answer any questions you might have." The professor returned his attention back to his notes.

Paul, like an intimidated college student, started for the door, but remembered he had not come to Chapel Hill for a book recommendation. Spinning back around, he returned to his seat. "I had a few more questions," Paul explained.

"A few more?" Professor Bart asked as he looked at his watch.

"I've been introduced to someone," Paul hesitated, now flustered, at the idea of bothering a serious professor with questions about a strange man claiming to be the two-thousand-year-old brother of Jesus. When he drafted this plan, determining James's real identity seemed to be a way to help Mike. Paul sensed that the gun-wielding priest represented a danger. Originally, he planned to convince Professor Bart, whom he assumed spoke Aramaic, to interview James, but this now seemed like an odd request.

"James spoke Aramaic, is that correct?"

"Yes, that is correct," Professor Bart huffed, exasperated he had not yet rid himself of this pest.

"I am sure that you have studied Aramaic extensively."

"I can translate some things."

"Can you speak Aramaic?"

"No, I would not be able to speak it."

"How am I going to be able to speak to James if I can't learn Aramaic?" Paul sighed.

Professor Bart's eyebrows rose at Paul's statement. "You need an expert in Aramaic," the professor stated and reached to the bookshelf once again. Without even looking he pulled a book from the shelf and handed it to Paul. "This book was written by a famous linguist."

Paul accepted the book. He glanced at the back cover, which described the journey of a young Kurdish Jewish girl traveling from Northern Iraq to the United States. At the bottom of the page, Paul scanned the photo of a beautiful woman in her late twenties. "Wow, she is absolutely stunning," Paul stated out loud.

The comment, attracting Professor Bart's attention, caused him to lean over to see what Paul was describing. "Oh, I gave you the wrong book.

I meant to give you another." Professor Bart retrieved a second book. "You have the book by the daughter, Mina Sabar, but you really need the book written by her mother, Professor Sabar."

Paul did not pay any attention to the second book, but fixed his eyes on the photo of Mina Sabar. He read her bio aloud. "An award-winning author who now lives in New York City." Paul, a strong believer in destiny, felt a special connection to this person. Immediately, the idea of a road trip to Manhattan popped into his mind. "It would be like our college days, driving to New York," he said out loud.

"No, Professor Sabar is based in California."

"The book says that the daughter speaks Aramaic too."

"The book does not say anything," Professor Bart commented, annoyed at Paul. "Yes, she speaks Aramaic, like other Kurdish Jews do."

"And she lives in the Village. It's going to be so great to have her meet James."

"James?" Professor Bart asked.

"I need something translated," Paul started to explain.

"I'm sure that there is someone closer who could help translate."

At this point, Paul had stopped listening, busy jotting down the author's information. Paul thanked Professor Bart for his help and dashed from the office. As Paul crossed the quad, surveying the young college students, vivid memories of his last trip to New York with Mike filled him with glee. He felt certain that he was meant to do this.

Chapter 18
Lifestyle Dysfunction

Amber could not decide whether her desire to speak with Mike was pathetic or endearing. She pulled into the Starbucks, uncertain as to why she had made a quick U-turn after seeing Mike and James being interrogated by two police officers.

Her first impression of Mike was of a pathetic loser. His slovenly appearance, his strong body odor, and his whiny voice put her off before she knew anything about him. The odd circumstances of Mike's recent injuries perplexed her. The presence of his strange nonspeaking robed companion frightened her. His idleness and lack of accomplishment disgusted her. Perhaps her desire to have her impressions verified drew her in to investigate.

She first observed from a distance while Mike and James picked up trash along the highway. Amber assumed Mike was lazy, which seemed validated from her observation. James, although heavily robed, picked up items, while Mike sat in the grass, constantly playing on his phone.

Mike only stopped looking at his phone to bark orders to James, usually telling him to stay clear of the road. After ten minutes of watching, Mike ordered James to clean the minivan. Again, Mike sat and was on his phone, only going to the minivan to take pictures of it after James had finished.

This guy is unbelievable, Amber concluded.

The two headed into Starbucks. Amber, unable to contain her curiosity, followed them. At first, she did not see them, but then noticed the two were sitting cross-legged on the floor near the restroom. James sat with his eyes closed with his hands on his knees, humming a gentle noise as he sat perfectly still. Mike sat next to him, also with his eyes closed, but he was not calm.

Mike kept fidgeting from side to side as though he were sitting on a bundle of dry hay irritating his legs. Customers, who were picking up their complex coffees at the counter, shot surprised glances at the two as they attempted to move past them. Amber decided to take a direct approach to get answers as quickly as possible.

Amber stomped over to them and demanded, "Why were the police talking to you?"

Mike opened his eyes and looked up, catching a full view of Amber's chest through the opening in her blouse. He did not answer, but instead traced the contour of her black and flowered bra. Noticing his leering, Amber straightened up and huffed a sigh of aggravation. "I'm sorry," Mike stated, embarrassed to be caught.

"Whatever," Amber huffed, not willing to accept his apology.

Mike now became irritated with Amber's reaction. "Look, I'm sorry, but when a man opens his eyes and is confronted with a beautiful woman exposing her wonderfully shaped chest in your face, what do you think he should do?"

The surprising compliment did not soften her, because she still found Mike repulsive. "It's fine," Amber commented.

"Look, all I can do is look," Mike snapped in a sad and melancholy tone that startled Amber.

"It's not a big deal."

"It is a big deal for me," Mike took out a prescription bottle of Viagra. "I need help." Mike held the bottle in front of him.

Amber was flushed and embarrassed with the strange direction of this conversation.

James, opening his eyes, moved over and took one of the blue pills. "*Rahkama*," James said as he swallowed a pill.

"Hey, those are thirty bucks a pill," Mike remarked in a harsh tone. James frowned, so Mike softened his tone. "Don't worry, I've had these for quite some time. I'm not using them much."

Amber, hoping to get the conversation away from this topic, interjected, "The police?"

Mike, started to answer, but turned to his phone when it pinged. "We've got a message from a potential buyer on the minivan." Mike smiled. "You're my good luck charm."

"Did you have a problem with the police?" Amber asked impatiently.

"Yes," Mike started to answer and realized "no" would have been a better response. "Not a problem." Amber stared expressionless at Mike, signifying she was waiting for a different, more informative answer. Mike sheepishly added, "I threw something out the window. But they didn't give me a ticket or anything."

"Threw something out the window? They pulled you over for littering?" Amber asked as James started to hum loudly.

"I threw a bunch of my wife's stuff out the window," Mike admitted in a huff. "The wife who was sleeping with my brother."

Amber flushed a second time, embarrassed for Mike again. The bottle of Viagra rolled and bumped into her foot. Amber bent down and handed the bottle back to Mike. "I think this belongs to you." Amber, without a further question or goodbye, left the two men and exited the shop.

Mike, watching Amber leave, commented, "I have that effect on women." James shook his head as though he were acknowledging Mike's comment. "I shouldn't have snapped, but I'm a little sensitive when it comes to sex."

"*Rahkama.*"

"The past couple years I've had such a low libido. I like to look at women, but my desire to have sex has collapsed." James pulled Mike back to the floor.

"*Lev,*" James said as he pounded his own chest.

"Yeah, you're right. There's something wrong with my heart."

A woman in her late fifties interrupted the conversation. "Is this a prayer group?"

"A prayer group?" Mike looked over to James who had closed his eyes and started humming in a low tone. "I guess it is more like a meditation session."

"Wow, really?"

Mike nodded his head "yes."

"My name is Sarah."

"My name is Mike, and this is James."

"May I join you? It looks like a hoot." Mike nodded agreement and the older lady joined them on the floor. "You know, I used to teach meditation."

"I could use a little guidance."

"Can I ask why you're starting meditation?"

"I guess life is tough."

"You got that. You know that life ends up killing all of us eventually," Sarah said with a long laugh.

"Ain't that the truth."

Sarah smiled and placed her warm hand on Mike's chest. "Just remember to breathe deeply," Sarah instructed in a soothing voice that reminded Mike of a girl he knew in high school.

"Breathe?" Mike asked at such an obvious necessity.

"Yes. It's never a good thing when you forget to breathe," Sarah said with a chuckle.

"Right."

"Close your eyes and breathe in one nostril and out the other. Repeat that again and again."

Mike sighed with discomfort because Sarah's instructions sounded goofy. "In one nostril and out of the other," Sarah repeated in her soothing voice. Persuaded by her appealing tone, Mike decided to give it a try.

While Mike practiced his alternate nostril breathing, Sarah encouraged Mike to control his thoughts, "Think of an enormous white billboard. One that goes on for eternity. Let your essence expand within you like helium in a balloon."

The alluring frequency of her words caused Mike to open his eyes, tracing Sarah's face as though he had just picked her up for the prom. His pulse started to race as he felt his blood throb through the arteries and veins as though Sarah had just turned his heart back on. He felt a strong warming sensation bubbling within him.

Drifting deep away from reality and into his imagination, he strolled naked along a lake, holding Sarah's soft hand. The sensations were so vivid that he could feel soft muddy leaves under his bare feet. As he ambled, Sarah, also naked, laughed with a youthful energy. He found her long brown hair resting on her bare pale shoulders erotic in a subtle and simple way.

She winked as though she could read his thoughts. They arrived at the edge of a blue lake. She dipped her small toes gingerly into the water, but Mike hesitated. She tugged for him to follow. He still hesitated. The tug turned into a yank, forceful enough to pull him completely into the water.

Frigid water shocked all of his skin, except his hand that was warm from Sarah's grip. Mike gravitated toward her. She placed her forehead on his cheek and clutched him so tightly he felt her hot breath on his neck. Mike could feel every aspect of her body, her feet against his feet, her chest against his chest, and her privates against his privates. Mike, aroused, tried to pull away, but she pulled him closer.

The sensations forced Mike awake. He opened his eyes to find Sarah staring at him with a huge smile.

"Wow, you were really in a Zen mode there."

"Really? I didn't think I ever cleared my mind."

"Well, you were in a zone for quite some time."

"How long were my eyes closed?"

"You had them closed for almost twenty minutes."

"Wow." Mike looked at his watch in disbelief. Sarah smiled at him and hugged him. Mike, still thinking about the skinny-dipping in the lake and still aroused, felt embarrassed. "Meditation is powerful. It's not what I thought it was going to be like."

"That's a good thing." Sarah took a napkin and jotted down her phone number. "If you are ever interested in more meditation, let me know." She got up, gathered her things and left the Starbucks.

Mike turned. "That was really bizarre. That's the most turned on I've been in a couple of years."

"*Rahkama*," James replied.

"Is it normal to get turned on during meditating?" Mike asked.

"*Lev*," James answered.

"Maybe it just allows me to clear all the garbage out of my head," Mike's phone beeped. "Hey, that guy who wants to buy the minivan is here." Mike stood and headed for the parking lot.

Mike, energized from the stimulating mediation session, sauntered to his minivan with a positive air. An older, intense man was busy inspecting the minivan as though he worked for the border patrol. Down on all fours, he shone his flashlight along the bottom. The man's wife sat in their car, reading a copy of the tabloid *Weekly World News*. Mike strolled over and extended his hand, which the man ignored. The buyer straightened up, brushed off his knees and moved to the front of the minivan.

"Hey buddy, can you pop the hood?" the man asked in a tone sounding more like a command than a question.

Mike obeyed, pulling the release hatch, which allowed the eager buyer to dive underneath the hood. Grunting and mumbling to himself, the man poked deep into the various dark crevasses of the engine. The man coughed, which caused a scoopful of leaves to float above the man's head. Mike suddenly felt ashamed.

Early in life Mike had been a "car guy," plastering posters of Porsches all over his wall. He had felt comfortable getting grease on his hands, tinkering with cars. As he looked at the engine, he detected various signs of neglect.

The man grumbled, "Young people don't take care of anything anymore."

Mike glanced over at the man's old Lincoln Town Car and thought to himself, *It's not like he takes care of his car.*

The older man plopped himself in the front passenger seat. After examining the owner's manual, he sighed. "There are no notations for oil changes or maintenance," as though he had finished a sad tale.

Mike rubbed his bandage, longing to meditate. "They track that stuff electronically. I'm sure my wife changed the oil."

"I don't know," the older man pointed to an oil change sticker on the windshield. "According to that sticker you haven't changed the oil in close to two years." The older man shook his head in disgust. "They usually replace those stickers."

"Look, I'm not asking much for it," Mike stated, not wanting to fight with the man.

The older man placed the manual back in the glove box and proceeded to crawl under the minivan and fiddle with the housing on the oil filter. He had a small flashlight on his belt and he shone it up at the housing and started to mumble numbers to himself.

"This is fucking unbelievable," Mike huffed at James. "I'm almost giving this piece of shit away." James came over and tried to calm Mike with a few short pats on his shoulder. "This guy doesn't want to buy a minivan; he just wants to bust my balls."

The older man came up from under the minivan, a strange expression on his face. It reminded Mike of the time a doctor diagnosed his father with lung cancer. "I don't think the oil has been changed for a while. There's an old date on the oil filter."

Suddenly, as though he had just endured two years of torture at the Gitmo prison camp, Mike cracked. He did not have the patience to deal with this, and he blamed everything on his wife. She spent thousands of dollars on contractors, expensive trips with her girlfriends, dinners with friends, but she could not spend money to maintain her minivan. Anger swelled within him. Mike snatched a Buzz Lightyear doll from the back seat and slammed it against ground, cracking the clear helmet.

"I'm not sure I want the minivan," the man stammered, afraid of Mike's fury.

Mike, disregarding the man, continued his tirade, grabbing an old Boppy pillow which Mike had been tasked with donating to a shelter, ripping the stuffing out and throwing it into the air. "Fucking bitch is always buying these stupid fucking pillows and I have to pay for them." The stuffing fell to the ground like snow during a storm. James rushed over to Mike and put his hand on his shoulder and called loudly to him.

"*Rahkama.*"

Mike's anger suddenly dissipated, causing him to drop the destroyed pillow on the ground. "I'm sorry, James."

James nodded, moved over to the buyer, and smiled at him. The grumpy old man started to babble nervously. "I'm just trying to find something for my daughter. We don't have a lot of money. I'm not trying to be difficult; just trying to get a good deal."

"I thought the price was a steal," Mike interjected.

"It was. It was. This is your wife's minivan?"

"Not anymore. She took the nice car. She took the kids. She took my brother. And left me with this piece of shit."

"Divorce?" the old man whispered to James.

"*Rahkama.*"

The older man moved over to the side of the minivan and rested his hands on the car seat then lowered his head as though he were deep in contemplation. After a minute, he raised his head and looked at Mike. "The mileage is pretty low and the price is more than fair."

Mike nodded his head. "That's what I thought."

"Would you be willing to throw in the car seats too?" the older man interrupted Mike's melancholy thoughts. "My daughter has two kids."

Mike, stunned by the reversal, stammered, "Sure. I'll even throw an expensive dreamcatcher in with the car."

The older man put his hand out. "When can you part with it?"

"*Rahkama*," James stated.

"As soon as we can transfer the title."

Chapter 19
Holy Covetousness

Father Coady stared at the initials "AM" for hours as though he gazing at the initial of a cute girl in his high school homeroom. He kept imaging it might be the Amber from the bar. Her face haunted him each night when he put his head on his pillow. When he slept, he dreamt of following her into the Uber car and going back to her place.

Although he had only met her one brief time, he had recorded every feature of her face and every nuanced inflection of her voice. The moment of her soliciting him on the sidewalk played on a continuous loop in his mind with meticulous detail. He could see her face, smell her perfume, and feel her breath.

Stop thinking about her, Coady told himself, but failed to heed his own advice. He continued to fantasize about her. *Stop playing this awful game*, he yelled at himself as he pulled into the trendy apartment complex.

Father Coady peered down at AM's address. It looked familiar. Shaking his head, he tried to clear his mind. Reaching for a small bag on the back seat, he snatched his stiff black shirt and white collar, thinking the seller might lower their asking price for a man of the cloth.

Originally, he had chosen more casual dress, wearing jeans and a plain white T-shirt, but now he felt the need to put on the clerical wardrobe. Perhaps this AM would not demand the five hundred dollars, which was a huge sum for him. As he pulled the black shoes from the bag, he saw his war medal. He clutched it while he remembered the grim images of Iraq.

His pulse raced and his throat dried as the stress of those recollections invaded the present. He got in the back seat and closed the door. Frantically he undressed and started to put his priest clothes on. Wearing his clerical garments calmed him like a security blanket.

He plunged his face into the black shirt and thought he could smell the odor of the incense they used at mass, but it was only cheap laundry detergent. Shimmying, wiggling, and twisting in the back seat, Father Coady stripped down to his T-shirt and boxers as he changed. Suddenly he heard a noise outside the car.

"Hey, buddy, there could be kids around here. Can't you do that some place private?"

Father Coady instinctively ducked down as far as his large frame would allow, pulling the black shirt over his head. Through the arm sleeve, he shot a glance to see an attractive woman momentarily standing next to the car and then striding away from him.

Using the shirt as a primitive periscope, he watched her graceful figure sway the sleek business suit from side to side. Father Coady enjoyed a woman in a power suit. Like a scout on a mission, he diligently observed her motions. She dipped her slender fingers into a small bag and retrieved her phone, putting it to her ear as she continued to walk.

"Are you here alone?" she asked.

That voice—oh my God, it's her. It's Amber, Father Coady cried.

Father Coady swung his head, trying to lose his shirt for a better view, but slammed it against the front seat. "Ow," Father Coady yelled, but quickly gathered himself.

Pulling the shirt off his head, he gazed at her. The hair color, the figure, the walk all matched Amber. Clawing at the window handle, he tried to push it open, but the engine was off, so the glass remained up. He shoved open the door, falling out onto the hard blacktop with a thud. The stress of the situation dried his throat, causing Amber's name to be garbled in his throat. He frantically tried to stand tall, thinking he could make a better attempt at yelling from a standing position.

From his worm's eye view, he traced Amber's long legs moving in a small pirouette. His heart raced as he caught a glimpse of her wonderfully sculpted cheeks and dimpled chin. Unfortunately, she moved at a brisk pace, quickly disappearing from his view as she rounded the corner of the nearest building. Father Coady crawled to his feet, feverishly hopping along with only one leg in his pants.

"Come on, come on," he yelled at himself.

Afraid of missing this magical opportunity to reunite with Amber, he hopped faster and faster, like a one-legged intoxicated Easter Bunny. Unable to keep up the frantic pace, he lost his balance and collapsed down on the wet grass of the pocket park.

When he pushed himself up from the moist turf, a woman pushing a double stroller greeted him with a deeply annoyed huff. "Weirdo." Father Coady grabbed for his plastic white collar and wrapped it around his neck, hoping to soften the woman's disgust, but she only repeated her original comment in loud sustained groan, "I'm calling the police."

Forget her, Father Coady scolded himself, rolling forward and pulling up his trousers, allowing him to charge faster.

By the time Father Coady zipped his trousers, stood up, and dashed over to the corner of the building, Amber had vanished. Zig-zagging across the courtyard, he checked every path to no avail. Finally, out of breath, he bent over to refill his lungs, while bemoaning the sad idea that God had sadistically tempted him.

If that was a test, he had failed with flying colors. He did not understand this fierce attraction to a stranger, but he enjoyed the adrenaline she created within him. Into his soulless existence, she imbued him with strong emotions he had not felt since he had returned home from Iraq.

While he tried to comprehend all these feelings, a penetrating humming echoed through the courtyard. Looking up, he noticed long thick hair draped over a balcony. He stepped closer. To his amazement, James sat squatting around a small table where several long incense sticks burned. He rubbed his eyes in disbelief.

"James, is that you?" Father Coady asked, but when he looked up, the balcony was empty. "I've got to get a grip. Let's focus on this Rob Thomas photo."

Pulling out his phone, he checked the address and adjusted his priest outfit for the upcoming negotiations. Strolling up the steps to apartment 66, he heard a low humming drifting down at him. James came to mind. Father Coady checked the address one more time. He had the correct place. All of a sudden, the door swung open and Mike stood in front of him.

"Hey, Father Coady, are you coming to check up on James?"

"Mike?"

"Yeah, you forgot my name already?"

"No, I mean. I thought I saw James on the balcony," Father Coady stammered.

"Have a seat," Mike pointed to the lawn chairs that had replaced the living room furniture.

Father Coady slumped down in the chair, trying to gather his thoughts like a man trying to sweep confetti on a windy day. "I'm here to buy an autographed photo."

"Oh, you're the one. Wow, what a coincidence. Why is she meeting you here?" Mike said with a chuckle. "Paul's ex-girlfriend is selling it." Mike returned to the floor surrounded by prescription bottles. He counted cash with a blood-stained piece of paper on his lap.

Father Coady surveyed the room, which resembled a scene where a drug deal might take place. "Paul's ex-girlfriend?"

"Yeah, well, I think so, it's kind of hard to tell with them."

Just then, James dashed into the room, immediately hugging Father Coady. He exclaimed, "*Rahkama.*"

"It's great to see you," Father Coady coughed as James squeezed him tight.

Mike stopped counting the bills on the floor to view the reunion. "Looks like he's glad to see you too."

"What have you two been up to?"

"James helped me sell my car," Mike commented, holding up cash.

"That's good. Anything else that is new?"

"My wife made me take a paternity test to prove my kids aren't mine," Mike said. "And Paul is moving to some exotic locale, which will leave me homeless."

Father Coady cocked his head to the side, unable to determine Mike's mood, unsure whether the statements were a complaint. He glanced over to James. "Has it been helpful to have James with you?"

"James has been wonderful."

Father Coady nodded. "Yes, you said something about Paul. This is the boyfriend of the woman I am going to meet?"

"Yes, the same. He's an old friend from high school. He's going to live in Russia for a year or so."

"Wow, that's dramatic. It seems a bit dangerous," Father Coady replied.

"Paul is a very exciting kind of guy."

"Do you have a place to stay?"

Mike coughed as though the question irritated his throat. "Paul's working on that. He said he has some big plan regarding me and James."

"You and James?"

"Yeah. He said he's researching how to find someone to translate Aramaic."

"Researching?" Father Coady questioned in a tone that clearly expressed concern over Paul's meddling.

"Paul thinks he has all the answers. He's become some kind of genius. I guess it'll take a genius to put my life back together." Just then, James let out a large chuckle. "I wish I could laugh as easily as you can," Mike commented to James in a manner that pet lovers speak to their animals.

Father Coady moved around the room, inspecting the empty apartment. After a moment, he turned back to Mike. "Are you expecting Paul's girlfriend?"

"She's in the other room on a call."

"Other room?" Father Coady asked as he tilted his head to peer into the other room.

"Is my time up with James?" Mike asked in a frightened voice. "I thought I had thirty days with him."

"No, I didn't say that," Father Coady assured Mike. "Paul's girlfriend is here right now?"

"Yeah, she's taking a conference call or something," Mike responded. "You know the business type, always on the phone."

The phrase "business type" conjured up an image of a business suit, which conjured up an image of Amber's figure in a business suit. Father Coady's breathing became heavy, he started to perspire, and he shook himself before finishing his sentence. "Business suit," Father Coady muttered. Just then, Coady heard a noise from the other room. "Business suit," he repeated louder.

"Let's not talk about our time ending in front of James; he's has really grown attached to me."

"Sure."

"Thanks," Mike with a slam on Father Coady's shoulder. "Firm. You are one built priest."

Just then, a flood of noises filled the apartment. A key opening the front door met the noise of the office door opening, with Paul entering the apartment and Paul's ex-girlfriend walking down the hallway. Father Coady did not know where to look. From one eye, he saw Paul holding an armful of books, while with the other, he saw trim legs underneath a bright red business skirt.

"Oh, there's Paul and his girlfriend now," Mike announced to Father Coady.

Jesus's Brother James

Chapter 20
Wine and Whine

Amber's entrance astonished not only Father Coady, but Paul as well. The two men both stood, gawking at her nonchalance strutting around the room. Flabbergasted, Father Coady hung his mouth wide open like a hungry fish ready to swallow a large hook.

Paul carried a more annoyed expression. As a man obsessed with controlling his life, the roller coaster ride with Amber had been making him fatigued. She strutted confidently across the room and gave Coady a firm handshake with her tender slim hand.

"My name is Amber," she stated. "Are you here for the photo?"

"Yes," Father Coady stammered, waiting for Amber to recognize him, but she showed no sign that she did.

"It's in the other room. Let me get it," she twisted on her Vince Camuto shoes to retreat to the other room.

"Amber," Paul called after her, but she did not respond. Paul looked at Father Coady. "You're here for the Rob Thomas photo?"

"Yes," Father Coady replied, still overwhelmed.

"What would it take for you to lose interest in that photo?" Paul asked Coady.

"This is a friend of yours?" Father Coady questioned, turning to Mike.

"Like I said, we knew each other in high school," Mike replied.

"Wait a second, you guys know other?" Paul asked Mike.

"He was the priest who was there that night I was shot," Mike stammered in a clumsy way.

"Wait a second, this is the priest that shot you?"

Just then Amber reentered the room with the picture. "Here is the photo, signed personally by Rob Thomas."

"You're really selling your birthday gift to this guy?" Paul snapped as he rushed over to the photo, blocking Coady's path so he could not inspect it.

"Sure." Amber put the picture up on a box, sitting near the kitchen, to allow Father Coady to have a nice view. She noticed the box contained a dozen bottles of red wine. She took one out. "Nice wine," Amber announced in a brash voice. "Would you like a glass as we close this deal?"

"Sure," Father Coady responded.

"You can't serve a priest wine," Paul protested.

"Why not, they drink every Sunday, don't they?" Amber uncorked the bottle, filled several water glasses, passing one to Father Coady. "Would you like one?" she asked James, who shook his head yes.

James smiled, said something in Aramaic, and sipped the wine with joy, emptying it quickly, motioning for more. "I guess he likes it," Mike commented.

Amber pushed past Paul to click glasses in a toast with Father Coady, "Cheers."

"Thanks," Father Coady replied as he sipped the wine.

"Amber, I would prefer that you not sell this."

Amber sipped her wine, not acknowledging Paul's request. "This wine is scrumptious. I have to hand it to you. You have good taste."

Father Coady, playing the spectator, watched this dance between the two, impressed with Amber's self-assurance. Agreeing with Amber about the quality of the wine, he downed the whole glass.

"Amber, you can't sell this," Paul declared.

Amber's mouth rolled wide open, shocked that he uttered such a statement. "Can't sell this?"

"Amber, I am pleading with you. If you want to sell it, let me buy it from you."

"If this is going to cause friction between the two of you, I will rescind my offer," Father Coady interjected.

Amber chuckled, "Silly, you can't have friction between things that have been separated." Amber strode to Father Coady, filled his glass, and patted him on his shoulder.

Either the wine or Amber's touch caused his body temperature to skyrocket. In a reflex motion, he unbuttoned the sleeves of his shirt, pushing back the fabric to expose his broad forearms and military tattoos.

"Tattoos?" Amber bellowed, recalling those arms from her thirty-fifth birthday celebration. Hiding her face from Father Coady, she searched the medial temporal lobe of her brain for the exact memories of that encounter. She wanted to doubt the validity of the recollection, but how many priests sport tattoos? Luckily, Mike interrupted.

"Are priests allowed to have tattoos?"

"Normally, they are not. I got them when I served in Iraq."

Tattoos, Iraq, Amber mumbled to herself. *This has to be the priest I made a pass at.* Embarrassed, she now focused on two questions: how salacious was their conversation, and did the priest recognize her?

"A priest serving in Iraq. That's unusual." Mike continued.

"I guess," Father Coady responded.

"Excuse me," Amber stated and slipped down the hall to the bathroom for a momentary reprieve.

Paul shook his head and turned his attention to Mike. "I've got good news for you."

"Good news? Let's hear this," Mike sighed.

"When I first met James, I thought he was Kurdish."

"Who am I to question your opinion?" Mike answered dryly.

Paul turned to Father Coady for affirmation, but Coady avoided any eye contact. "Anyway, I did a little research to see who speaks Aramaic. Come to find out, there's a professor at Chapel Hill in early Christian studies."

"You want me to meet with this professor?"

"No, he doesn't speak Aramaic, but he told me about a professor at UCLA who migrated from Northern Iraq and is an expert on Aramaic."

"LA is kind of far from here."

"Let me finish. The professor from UCLA has a daughter who is also an expert on Aramaic. And get this: she lives in New York."

"New York City?"

"Yup, right in downtown Manhattan. She's an award-winning author. She wrote a best-selling book about her family's struggles to get to the

U.S." Paul handed the book to Mike, showing him the picture of the author. Mike stared at the photo of the author with admiration.

"She's pretty too. Middle Eastern women are always so striking," Mike commented, handing the book to Father Coady. "Don't you think she's beautiful?"

"Yes, she is very lovely," Father Coady replied.

"This author would be perfect to translate for you," Paul lectured Mike.

"You want me to call up a complete stranger and tell her to translate therapy sessions in Aramaic for me?" Mike questioned.

"Call? No. Let's make a road trip there."

"Why would she meet us?"

"I contacted her publicist. She agreed to meet with us if we get to New York in the next couple of weeks."

"I sold my car."

"Fuck, Mike, why aren't you excited?"

"I can't just go off to New York City. I've got to wait for the paternity test results for Alyssa's lawyer."

"I would think they could call you. I think it would be great to get away from here."

"Why are you so amped up about this? Aren't you getting ready to move out of the country?"

"It'll be like old times," Paul commented.

Mike, irritated from the conversation, rubbed his wound. "No, it won't be like old times. Maybe that Mike is gone forever."

James, who had been listening to the pattern of the conversation moved to Mike, "*Rahkama.*"

"I think James wants you to go," Paul concluded.

"I don't know." Mike moved to the bottle of wine, took two long chugs from it and turned to Father Coady. "Would you take us?"

"You want him to take you?" Paul asked, not trying to disguise the hurt in his voice.

"I would like to help, but I don't have a car."

Amber, who been hovering in the hallway, blurted, "If you need a ride, I'll take you."

"Why would you drive us all the way to New York?" Mike asked.

Mike's question proved difficult to answer. She hated driving. She did not like missing work. Worst of all, she would be trapped in a car with a priest she had propositioned. She ran her finger along the glass of the Rob Thomas framed photo.

She thrust the photo into Father Coady's hands. "You can have this. Consider it a donation to the church." Amber had concluded that this type of impulsive action did not fit her personality, so that's why she should do it. "That's it," Amber exclaimed.

"What's it?" Paul interjected.

"I need to do something out of the norm. I need a change; so what the hell."

"I wouldn't want you to miss work," Mike commented meekly, still uncertain about a long trip.

"Well, I want to miss work." Amber stood up, took out her phone and left a voicemail for Skitters. "Steve, I'm taking a personal day off to take care of family matters. If you need to reach me, send me an email." Amber hung up the phone and turned to Mike, "I'm all set."

"You're going to drive to New York with three guys you don't know?" Paul questioned. "Is this all because you're pissed at me?"

"Not everything is about you."

"Amber?" Paul questioned.

"What?"

"I'm just concerned," Paul pleaded.

"Concerned about what?" Amber snapped. Paul, as clever as he was, did not possess an articulate answer, and his hesitation annoyed Amber. She turned away from him in disgust.

"Mike, are you sure you couldn't use my help?" Paul pleaded in a pathetic voice.

"You've done so much already. And you've got so much to do for your move."

The apartment filled with an awful silence, as for the first time in a long time, a room filled with people all pitied Paul.

Jesus's Brother James

Chapter 21
Road Trip or Pilgrimage

Having spent a year serving in Iraq, Father Coady experienced stressful rides, like being shuttled from one base to another, always anxious about the possibility of encountering an IED. Those times did not diminish the tension he felt sitting in the passenger seat as Amber throttled her Porsche Cheyenne north on Interstate 95.

Amber, considering the job of driving too mundane for her full attention, juggled various other tasks at the same time. Her fellow I-95 travelers did not appreciate Amber's creative driving and periodically laid into their horns to keep her from wandering into their lanes. In response, Amber would jerk the wheel, causing the car to tilt dramatically.

Amber's driving made Father Coady nauseous. He rolled down the window, stuck his head out, and absorbed the air high above the Raritan River in New Jersey. He could taste and smell the ocean breeze. It soothed him.

"Do you get carsick easily?" Amber asked.

"Easily, no," Father Coady replied.

"That's a dig on my driving," Amber laughed. "I've gotten so used to multitasking." She hated her boss, she bemoaned missing the promotion, and she dreaded continuing her job, but she could not break the habitual cycle of work. Her new phone stood propped up in its holder to the left of the steering wheel, while her iPad remained at her side on the console so she could navigate the various databases she needed to access.

"How is your company going to survive with you being away for a couple of days?" Father Coady asked.

"Another joke, huh?" Amber chuckled. "You're kind of a unique priest."

"Would you like me to drive so you can focus on your work?" Father Coady asked as he wiped perspiration from his forehead.

"I'm okay," answered Amber. "I'm really good at multitasking. I used to write term papers while driving back from home."

"Really good at multitasking?" Father Coady questioned.

Mike, oblivious to the constant erratic motion of the car, looked up from a biography on James to announce. "Do you know that James was called 'the Just'?"

Father Coady took his finger and gently nudged Amber's chin upward away from her iPad and toward the road, allowing her a better view. "It's believed that he was an extremely righteous man."

"It kind of sucks no one remembers him. I mean, Apostle Paul, who never even met Jesus face-to-face, gets all the credit."

"You're right. No one remembers James," Father Coady replied. "But he did help found the early church."

"Why is the Catholic Church so against James?"

"The Church is not anti-James. The official stance of the church is that James might have been a step-brother or cousin, but he was not Mary's son."

"Why are they so adamant about such a minor point?"

"For the Church, it's critical that Mary was a virgin when Jesus was born and that she remained a virgin her entire life. Her perpetual virginity has to be preserved," said Father Coady.

"Going your whole life without any sex?" Amber chuckled as she glanced at Father Coady's handsome face. "That poor woman."

Father Coady reddened with embarrassment. "Well, that's the official doctrine of the Church."

"Do you really believe that a married woman went her whole life without having sex with her husband?" Amber pried.

"I guess some people might think that," Father Coady answered without looking in Amber's direction.

"Some people might think that? It sounds like you are avoiding my question," Amber pressed.

"I do not think the virginity of Mary is a critical element of the faith," Father Coady replied in a voice so low Amber could barely hear.

"Hmmm, interesting," Amber noted.

"Life without women might not be a bad thing," Mike interrupted, giving Father Coady a coded look.

Amber's phone violently vibrated on its stand, signaling an urgent message. Reading the email, she sighed. "How hard is it to send a package? The goddamn fulfillment center is going to kill me." Shooting a quick glance at Father Coady, she sheepishly said, "Sorry for taking the Lord's name in vain."

Amber, with one hand on her phone and one hand on her iPad, attempted to review the status of the shipment while simultaneously sending a message to the nurse inquiring about the samples. Because Amber did not possess three hands, she attempted to drive the car with her elbows. The expensive car drifted right into the path of a large F-150 pickup.

"Put the phone down, you crazy bitch," a large man in a construction hat screamed at Amber.

Amber, who had spent one year living in Hoboken, did not flinch from this typical New Jerseyan greeting. Father Coady, on the other hand, needed to get out of the car. Approaching the New Jersey Turnpike Newark Bay Extension, he could see the Holland Tunnel, which held the promise of slow moving traffic, car horns, and suffocating exhaust. He absolutely knew he wanted some head-collecting time before entering the stressfulness of America's largest city.

"Any chance we could take a break before heading into the city?" Father Coady asked.

"Have you ever seen the Statue of Liberty or Ellis Island?" Amber asked.

"You mean take a boat?"

"No, you can see both from Liberty State Park."

"Really?"

"Sure, I mean, you can only see the ass of the Statue of Liberty from New Jersey, but, hey, it's something." Amber coughed. "Sorry, I keep forgetting that you're a priest."

"You forget that I spent a year in the military. I've heard a lot worse than 'ass.'"

"I guess I see the collar and assume," Amber confessed. "It's a nice park; great spot for taking photos."

"Sounds good. We could cross the Hudson when the traffic is better," Father Coady stated.

By the time they parked, Lady Liberty was sending a long shadow out into New York Harbor. A stiff breeze blew, but it was nice after being crammed in the car for hours. James rushed to the waterfront, pointing excitedly from one skyscraper to the next.

Mike, although trying to stay calm, gushed with excitement over the pleasure James experienced. He felt like a father watching an exuberant child ride his new bike. Mike asked Father Coady to capture the moment with a picture.

The only member of the group not enjoying the scenic view was Amber. She lagged behind, diligently answering emails from Skitters, who for some odd reason urgently needed revised reports. Amber, like an angry mother scolding a disobedient child, barked numerous commands through her phone as she walked.

Her voice increased with intensity, scaring pedestrians who were at the park for a stroll. Then, as if she were directing a large orchestra, she waved in various directions. Finally fatigued, she leaned against the railing, staring at the water and wanting to throw her phone in the bay.

"Pretty busy with work?" Mike commented.

"Yeah, the fulfillment center messed up. If the doctor doesn't get them, I could lose a new client," Amber huffed with frustration. Then, as though she were talking to Paul, she blurted, "I know what you're going to say. I'm addicted to my job."

"Actually, when you talk business, you sound so professional," Mike commented.

"Sorry, I'm projecting Paul's thoughts onto you."

"Interesting. Is that a good thing or a bad thing?" Mike asked with a sly smile.

Amber, suddenly struck with an unexpected groundswell of unhappiness, gazed at downtown Manhattan. She imagined herself trapped on the inside of a pinball machine, responding to metal balls charging at her from different directions. She went on this trip for a change, but here she stood, irritated by her director and still hurting from her ex-boyfriend.

"It's a bad thing to compare you to Paul," Amber meekly uttered.

As the sadness spread from Amber to Mike, his expression shifted too. "I hate to say I kind of envy Paul. He's got his shit together."

Amber did not like the comment and huffed out a long breath. "He's got his shit together?" she repeated.

"I mean, he's so free. I, on the other hand, always feel like I'm trapped in some awful existence, being pummeled all the time."

Mike's description of his life shocked Amber, not because it did not suit him, but instead because it could have been used to describe her life. "I know what you mean."

Mike took his acceptance letter out of his wallet, gripped it tightly, and asked, "Do you ever think back on life and imagine that some choices led you down the wrong path, trapping you?"

Amber pondered her choice to go into the corporate world and started to agree with Mike, but resisted the urge to admit defeat. "I've made some bad choices that have impacted my life, but I have to believe we are never trapped. We still have choices."

"Hmmm," Mike responded, digesting Amber's conclusion. "You know what's funny? My wife is kind of like Paul. She does what she wants, not what she feels obligated to do. Doing things you don't want to do makes you bitter."

"Bitter?" Amber repeated, gazing at her phone, thinking about the large slices of her life she spent on company business, only to be left feeling bitter. Her hatred for her director returned with a deep, vivid clarity. He did not feel obligated to be on time for their meetings. He did not feel obligated to read her reports. He did not feel obligated to appreciate her hard work. He did what he wanted, not caring about her.

"I put up with a lot. I just take all that disrespect and keep plugging away for the bastard because I feel obligated to do it."

"Are you talking about Paul?"

Amber cringed, realizing she not only endured disrespect at work, but she also endured it from Paul. "No, I was speaking about my director," she admitted. "Can I ask you a question?" Mike nodded. "If a director, in two years, was never on time for a meeting, what would you think?"

"I would think he didn't care about it."

"If your wife didn't show up for your birthday party, what would you think?"

"That she didn't care," Mike answered. "Can I ask you a question?"

"Sure."

"If your best friend from high school never called and ignored you, what would you think?"

Amber hesitated, but felt the need to be truthful. "He doesn't care."

Mike nodded in agreement. "Can I ask you one last question?"

"Sure."

"Why do you think we hang around with people who don't care?"

"I don't know, but maybe we can help each other find out."

They shook hands, and Mike went over to stand next to James. Amber eyed Father Coady, who stood chatting with a few dog owners. Within a second, Father Coady detected Amber watching him, making him anxious, which Amber noticed. For some reason, she relished the power she had over him. Then, like a moth moving out of the dark cool night toward the light on the porch, she slid up next to him.

"Hello, Father," Amber said.

"Please call me Coady."

"Were you blessing those dogs?"

"Are you mocking me?"

"Should I stop with such jokes?"

"No, I must admit that you're a refreshing change."

"Refreshing change—that doesn't sound bad."

"Oh, it's not."

"My life could use a refreshing change."

"Yes, change can be good sometimes," Father Coady remarked. "But I sense that you're a person with so many talents to offer life that life will offer you fine things in return."

"Did anyone ever tell you that you have a very soothing effect on people?" Amber asked, staring closely at his facial features.

"I do try," Father Coady stated. Just then Mike and James laughed loudly. Although the two were enjoying themselves, Coady grimaced.

"Has this been a tough case for you?" Amber asked him. Father Coady, with the intensity of a detective, stared at her for a long moment. "I mean with the suicide and everything."

"You get used to tough cases. I was a chaplain in Iraq. You see some crazy things."

"Iraq? I didn't know that priests went to war."

"It is not all that common. But I come from a military family and always wanted to serve, so I volunteered. The Church hesitated, but I openly campaigned to join."

"I can't imagine how tough being in a war might be."

"It's kind of funny," Father Coady stopped midsentence and stared out a boat approaching the dock at Ellis Island.

"Funny?"

"In some ways, things are tougher here in the U.S. than they were there."

"I find that hard to believe."

"In a warzone, there is no illusion that life is easy. And in that type of environment, people work harder to help each other. I guess that's why soldiers call each other brothers—because they will do amazing things for each other."

"The stress of danger at every moment."

"Hmmm." Father Coady started to say something.

"What were you going to say?"

"I seemed to handle the stress better there. I made so many deep and real connections with those soldiers. I felt that I was making a difference."

"And you don't here?"

Father Coady had let the conversation wander to an awkward location. Again, with a detective's stare, he peered at Amber, trying to determine her motives for questioning him. He needed to share this with someone, but he could not open up to her. "I don't know. Maybe we should get back to Mike."

Amber placed her small hand in the center of his chest. "I know you're a priest, but life is hard for everyone, right?"

Father Coady shook his head in agreement. "Elie Wiesel wrote, 'the opposite of love is not hate, it's indifference.' I often feel that there are so many indifferent people in the world."

"Indifferent," Amber winced, thinking of the pain indifference had brought her. "You find people indifferent?" She said with a chuckle.

"Maybe I shouldn't complain, but I just grow frustrated with people back here. You have hundreds of people who come together each week, but they seem so indifferent to each other."

"You have every right to complain. You're free to bitch," Amber stated and then blushed, realizing she had cursed again in front of Father Coady. "Maybe I should get a curse jar."

Father Coady, feeling some anxiety lifted from sharing his human side to her, laughed in a deep steady laugh. "That's funny."

"What? That I curse?"

"No, I like the fact that you're so real. You're open and...and..."

"And what?"

"I don't know, you don't treat me like a priest. It's a nice change."

"Okay, then, why don't you speak to me openly? Here's your chance."

Father Coady, like a poker player ready to go all in with his chips, gazed at Amber. Finally willing to gamble he stated, "I wonder how all my parishioners can sit so often in God's presence and be so filled with anger. I see no noticeable impact on them at all. It makes me question my faith."

Amber, not one to freeze up, had not anticipated a holy man expressing a crisis in his faith. Sounding like a youth seeing something new, she uttered, "Wow."

"Perhaps I've said too much."

"No!" Amber grabbed his hand, sticking her nails into his palm to prevent his retreat. "You were honest. I just don't know if I can handle such a weighty topic. You just have such strong conviction."

"I appreciate you listening," Father Coady commented.

A strong sudden breeze blew Father Coady's thick hair into an upright standing position. Amber reached over and patted his hair back into place. After brushing his hair into an orderly appearance, she slid her fingers down his cheek across the thick coarse stubble. Amber found the roughness of his cheeks appealing. He looked more like a soldier than he did a priest. She glanced at his white collar to remind herself of his real occupation.

"Thank you," Father Coady stated.

Amber reached over and tenderly squeezed his hand. "Everyone needs other people. It's only natural."

"Maybe someday I will confess all my dark hidden desires to you."

Amber squeezed his hand more firmly this time. "Listen, not everyone in this world is indifferent."

Father Coady, in an unconvincing way, nodded his head in acknowledgment.

"I mean it," Amber insisted. "I'm here for you. Whatever you need, I'm here for you."

With his hand, Father Coady traced her face from her cute dimpled chin, to her full lips, onto her small rounded nose and up to her often-furrowed forehead. In a slow and deliberate motion, he leaned forward and pressed his lips against hers.

Chapter 22
Perceiving Change

Paul, a sci-fi fan, had often wondered how it might feel to float in the emptiness of space. Now he suddenly felt he was experiencing it. *I should be celebrating*, he muttered to himself.

Just that morning Garry Kasparov called him personally to confirm the details of his sojourn to Stavropol. But now he sat moping on the floor in his bare apartment, feeling like a teenager on prom night without a date. *This is pathetic*, he snapped. *Never whine about the past. You've got to focus on the future.*

Paul bent down to examine a large cardboard box labeled "Goodwill Donations." Filled with various mementos, which had dwindled over the years, the box held clothes, books, and picture frames. Donating the books and clothes seemed logical, but donating the picture frames with photos still inside them suddenly seemed callous.

In the center of the box stood a thick photo album. Paul brushed off the dust and thumbed through photos of himself in high school. He noticed that in all of the pictures, Mike flanked him with a huge smile.

I feel that life as inverted, Paul concluded. *Mike rarely smiles now.*

As Paul progressed through the photos, he noticed a small handwritten note from Mike next to a graduation picture, "Paul-ers, whatever happens, it doesn't matter. We'll have each other to get through anything. Your friend forever."

Paul tasted bitterness. Mike did not have him as a friend to get through a tough marriage. Paul, angry with himself for feeling guilty, flung the photo album on the floor. *Why am I killing myself over this? It's not my fault. I didn't tell him who to marry!*

Paul stood and stomped in a circle until the guilty feelings subsided. Calmer, he returned to the large donation box to see if there was anything else he wanted to retain. He pulled out a framed picture, taken with Amber at the entrance of exotic resort in the town of Loreto in Mexico. It had been their first vacation together, not long after they had started dating. The large picture had been wrapped in a coarse blanket that Paul had purchased on the beach from a vendor named Pedro.

Huh. I used to keep this in my office all the time, Paul mused.

Paul again plunged into a memory of that vacation. While Amber swam, parasailed, and lay on the beach, Paul occupied a quiet spot in the shade of a cabana to read. With a tin bucket filled with Dos Equis dark lager and ice, he relaxed, browsing several books.

From his secluded chair, he watched various vendors schlepping Mexican trinkets, such as ceramic banks and sombreros, up and down the hot sand, under the impression that American tourists would spend dollars on almost anything. Paul, a person who prided himself on living a minimalist lifestyle, did not purchase any of these frivolous items. No matter how much they pleaded with him, either in Spanish or English, he simply uttered, "*No quiero, gracias*," to each of them.

Most of the vendors, when a sale did not happen, resigned themselves to pestering the next tourist, but one round, dark-skinned man in his fifties selling blankets on his shoulder asked if he could sit in the shade with Paul. The man, who Paul learned was Pedro, was covered with a thick layer of perspiration. He did not say anything, but sat quietly to enjoy a brief escape from the hot sun.

As he sat perched on the arm of a wooden chair, Pedro watched a small speedboat trying to hoist a large, pale German tourist off the dock and into the air. It took three tries to successfully get the man airborne, but it appeared he might drop back into the water at any second.

"*Guero gordo,*" Pedro said to Paul, who knew enough Spanish to know "*gordo*" meant fat, but did not recognize "*guero.*"

"*Guero?*" Paul asked.

Rubbing his chin, Pedro contemplated an answer, then stated, with a point of his finger at Paul, "*Guero. Usted.*"

"Me?"

"*Sabe,* white people," Pedro repeated.

"Oh," Paul said, finally understanding Pedro had been commenting on the tourist's size and whiteness. Laughing, Paul not only found humor in the sight of the round tourist, but took pleasure in knowing the word Mexicans used to describe Caucasians.

"Blankets, good price," Pedro stated, switching back to his salesman delivery. For effect, Pedro took out a stiff blue and red handkerchief and wiped the perspiration from his thick black eyebrows.

Paul, who had was sipping his cold beer, offered Pedro a bottle of water. "*¿Agua? ¿Fria?*"

"*¿Agua?*" Pedro laughed, shaking his head "no."

"Beer?" he asked, pointing to a Dos Equis in the middle of the small bucket of ice.

"Sure," Paul smiled, lifting a chilled bottle from the ice.

"*Gracias,*" Pedro replied. He gulped the whole beer without stopping. He wiped his mouth with his sleeve and handed the empty bottle back to Paul.

"*Otra mas,*" said Paul, but Pedro declined the second one. "*Me llamo Paul.*"

"I am Pedro."

That introduction initiated a late afternoon ritual, where Pedro ended his day sharing beers with Paul. Between Pedro's limited English and Paul's pitiful Spanish, Paul learned quite a bit about Pedro. First, he learned Pedro drank quickly so resort staff did not see him drink. Next Paul discovered Pedro lived twenty miles inland, with five children and a demanding wife.

Pedro taught Paul three Spanish words: *latosa*, *mandona*, and *patrona*, which meant that Pedro's wife was very demanding. Pedro did not mind selling blankets on the beach. Paul also learned that his only daughter wanted to study art in France.

There were two common threads in everything Pedro said. He always smiled when he spoke of his family, and he ended each paragraph with the phrase, "Thanks, God." Paul liked that. Reared in a traditional German family, where giving people compliments was frowned upon, Paul found the warmth endearing.

It also amazed Paul that a man lugging blankets across the sweltering beach, begging tourists for a few dollars, could thank God about anything. No matter how large were Pedro's piles of blankets, he greeted Paul with a smile and, "Thanks God for another good day."

On the last full day of his vacation, Paul purchased Pedro's pile of blankets, without negotiating. The sale caused Pedro to dance in the sand in excitement. Pedro asked Paul to order two shots of tequila, along with two beers, squeezing a few bills into Paul's palm. Pedro, a blanket vendor, could not order at the resort. When the drinks arrived and the waiter left, Pedro picked up the shot glass, handing one to Paul and holding the other above his head.

Pedro exclaimed, "Thanks God for Señor Paul," and then downed the tequila.

For Paul, a man who never liked to look back upon life, this moment always made him smile. He kept the blanket on a chair in his office. Whenever he wanted to complain about his life, he glanced at the blanket, cursed himself for being spoiled and worked harder to accomplish a goal. Now, he felt guilty for wanting to donate Pedro's blanket.

I bet you Pedro would invite me to drive with him to New York, Paul mused.

He returned his gaze onto the picture of Amber, who was smiling, clutching his arm with her left hand and holding up Pedro's blanket with her right. Pedro, interrupting his sales, took the picture on their last day at the resort.

"We had some good times," Paul said to the photo. The doorbell rang, interrupting Paul's nostalgia. Putting Pedro's blanket and the photo down next to the box, he went to the door.

"Package for Mr. Anderson," said a UPS driver holding a large envelope.

"That's not me."

"Can you sign for him?" Paul nodded yes, reaching over to sign for the package. Paul closed the door, holding the delivery tightly in his hands. "It must be the results of the paternity testing," he concluded. "I guess Mike's going to find out if he's a father or not."

On his way back from the door, Paul kicked the photo album, causing the high school graduation note from Mike fall on the floor. He read the note again: "Whatever happens, it doesn't matter. We'll have each other to get through anything. Your friend forever."

For a long moment, he looked at the items associated with three different people: the blanket, the photo, and the envelope. He pondered on Pedro's outlook. *How the fuck did that guy say 'thanks God' after every day?* Paul huffed. *I bet he wouldn't say that if he were here.* Paul knew immediately that was a lie.

He slapped the envelope. Should he bring it to New York, he wondered? If the news was bad, bringing it to New York would be a disaster. He could call, but again, if the news was bad, that would be awkward. Holding on to it without telling Mike did not seem like a good idea either.

Shit, if he would have just let me drive him to New York, I wouldn't be dealing with this, Paul bemoaned. *And Amber didn't help. She stepped in, offered to drive, and then gave Rob Thomas to the priest.* Paul's face lit up, *Yeah, the priest is the problem. He's turned my friend and girlfriend against me.*

Paul paced his empty apartment, like the Grinch on Christmas Eve, plotting for a way to get even with the priest. Amber might be annoyed at his behavior, but Paul believed he wasn't a bad guy. He never cheated on her. He never lied to her. He omitted some information, but he didn't lie.

Sure, their relationship would not end in marriage, but it could have ended in a more dignified manner. A manner where Paul was seen in a better light. But it was the priest who had done something. What, Paul didn't know, but it had to be something.

Yes, that guy's the problem. I'm the one who bought her that great gift. I'm the one who found that author. I'm the one who called the publicist. I did all the work. Paul seethed. *Then he swoops in and gets to go on a joy ride to New York.*

Paul dashed into the bedroom where James had been sleeping. Rummaging through robes and underwear, Paul searched for some clue to where Father Coady lived. There, stapled on the inside of a robe, he found an address.

That's where he lives, Paul concluded, typing the address into his phone before sprinting back to the living room for his car keys.

As he opened the front door, Paul froze, realizing he had no purpose in charging into a priest's home. He needed a plan. He shut the door and returned to his pacing.

What did he intend to find there? He imagined finding some lucid information about the priest. A guy who hung around with a robed guy must have something to hide.

That's it. I'm going to find out who this James guy really is. Paul clapped his hands with excitement. *And while I'm there, I'm taking back Amber's gift*.

Assuming Father Coady lived in some form of rectory, Paul crafted a tale about being a lawyer needing access, but concluded such an encounter proved too complicated. He decided breaking into the place was simpler. To his surprise, the address proved to be an apartment on the southern side of Raleigh, not a rectory.

Paul's suspicion immediately intensified. It further emboldened Paul to aggressively pursue his plan to break into Father Coady's home. Paul, ever the strategic planner, worried about an alarm system, but decided a person living in a dilapidated apartment in south Raleigh wouldn't spend money on an alarm.

Walking up to the sliding glass door, Paul hesitated for a moment, struck by the thought that this might not be Father Coady's ground floor apartment. Pushing his face against the glass, he surveyed the interior hoping to see some object associated with the priest.

Paul started to panic, worrying about someone calling the police or a neighbor coming after him with a gun. At the verge of abandoning his mission, Paul noticed the Rob Thomas photo.

There it is. It's his place.

Paul wiggled the handled of the patio door and noticed a bedroom window had been left slightly open. Crawling through a prickly bush, he pushed through the thorns and up to the window.

Although not locked, the aged window did not open easily. Grunting as he pushed hard, he lost his balance and he fell face-first into a sharp branch with very long thorns.

Jesus, that hurts, Paul exclaimed. He immediately swallowed his pain so no one would hear him.

After squeezing through the window, Paul dashed to the picture and back to the bedroom window. For a moment he considered leaving with only Amber's gift, but decided he needed to do a little investigating. He wanted to find something sinister. Going to a desk, he pilfered it for contacts, but only ran into several pieces of paper with Sacred Heart Church logos on them.

Is this his church? He dialed the number listed on the paper, waiting for someone to pick up, but no one did. *It must be too late.*

Paul laid the paper back down on the desk and noticed a photo of Father Coady in Iraq, surrounded by several soldiers and someone who looked to be James. Paul picked up the photo for closer examination. Father Coady, standing in the center, smiled widely. Determining the photo held no damaging evidence, Paul ruffled though more papers. Finding an official-looking document, Paul stopped, read it, letting a smirk cover his face. He found something.

Very interesting, Paul exclaimed. *Let's see what Amber thinks about this guy after she reads this.*

Chapter 23
Gotham

Central Park on any given day offered street performers, people calling attention by picketing for some cause, and those parading in their outlandish outfits. Some people designed their wardrobe for shock value.

Speaking of shocking, Mike banged his head against an ancient oak tree for shock value, gathering a small crowd. James pleaded in Aramaic for him to stop. The harder Mike hit his head, the louder James screamed. Some in the crowd thought the whole episode was staged by local actors.

While Mike started his breakdown, Father Coady strode next to Amber, trying to decide whether or not he should grab her hand. He wanted to. He thought she wanted to hold his hand. He made the best of walking next to her with the warm sun shining down on him.

The sweet moment was abruptly interrupted when he recognized James's voice. He looked back and saw Mike, and then he sprinted over the bridge and up to Mike.

"Mike, what happened?" Father Coady asked, slightly out of breath.

"I don't know. I'm freaking out. Maybe this wasn't a good idea."

"What going on, Mike?"

"I don't know—all these people, the cars, the honking, and the smells. It's too much for me."

Mike had been on edge all night. An hour car ride to get through the Lincoln Tunnel wore on everyone's nerves. New Yorkers relieve their stress by blasting their horns, which only stressed Mike out more. When the group emerged from the tunnel, everyone had needed a good night's sleep, but Mike woke up still anxious.

Amber stepped forward to brush pieces of bark from Mike's hair. "There must have been something to set you off."

Mike held up his phone. "I just got this message from Alyssa's lawyer. He has updates for me."

"The results from the DNA test?" Amber panted after running over here.

"Yep." Mike slammed his head into the tree once more before Amber and Father Coady pulled him away from it.

"The results were bad?" Amber asked.

"You could say that," Mike replied.

Father Coady and Amber remained silent, not wanting to force an answer from Mike. Instead of speaking, Amber simply rubbed his shoulders while avoiding eye contact with him.

While Father Coady and Amber hesitated, James broke the silence. "*Rahkama*," he exclaimed loudly. "*Rahkama*," he repeated.

Mike collapsed into James's chest and tears flowed. "I don't want to know, James. I don't want to know the results."

"*Rahkama*," James assured.

"You don't know the results?" Amber asked.

"I haven't looked at the email, but I know."

Amber took the cell phone from Mike. "Let's worry about all this when we get back. Let's enjoy the morning and meet with this woman," she suggested.

Mike left the phone with Amber and turned to Father Coady. "What do you think?"

Father Coady cleared his throat, "You've only been around James for a couple weeks now and he's had a great impact on you."

"You're right. He has this ability," Mike interjected. "I almost don't believe it at times. But when he intervenes, everything just seems to work out. James helped with Alyssa's lawyer. He sold my car and he introduced me to Sarah."

"Sarah?" Amber asked.

"She's my meditation partner."

"Remember, we're here for you," Father Coady assured.

"Thank you, Father. That's just what I needed to hear."

Father Coady, James, and Mike hugged, which seem to drain the tension from Mike. A group of elderly tourists wanted to take James's picture. Mike temporarily forgot his troubles while he helped arrange the group photo.

With a large smile beaming from his face, James stood surrounded by these women as the impromptu session started. After several photos, James motioned for Mike to join him, communicating through sign language and the word "*rahkama*."

Mike whispered in Amber's ear, "Is there any chance of finding a quiet place to relax until my appointment with Ms. Sabar?"

"Sure. The Museum of Natural History is on 79th Street on the west side of the park. We could tour through the exhibits."

"Exhibits? That sounds like it might be crowded with screaming kids."

"They have various movie theaters. You could see some nature documentary on stars colliding or something."

"That sounds better. You and Coady can wander around while James and I mediate in a dark theater."

Chapter 25
Unholy Romance

Father Coady sat, glued to Amber's side in the pitch-black Hayden Planetarium at the Museum of Natural History, watching stars explode and planets dissolve. The exhibit, "Dark Universe," did not interest him, so he focused his gaze on Amber.

With each brilliant flash of light, Amber's alluring feminine features were illuminated. The dense darkness hid his admiration of her. Amber, in her own stealthy way, detected each action of her devoted priest. She observed his losing struggle not to gawk; she just enjoyed the game.

Men gazing at her was nothing new. For her job, she routinely endured waiting rooms packed with attention-starved elderly men, who drooled at her as they waited for their colonoscopy, EKG, or other medical procedure. But that was not unique. Those men ogle all women, pretty or ugly, young or old, thin or wide. A priest unable to control himself was different. It was taboo. It was off-limits. For a woman battling the effects of indifference, a dose of obsession was welcome.

"Isn't this great? I get goosebumps thinking about the vastness of the universe," Father Coady whispered.

"I'm getting goosebumps all over too," Amber agreed, fumbling for Coady's hand in the darkness. Missing his hand, her fingers hit his hip, and she redirected her touch to gloss over his firm abdomen. "Doesn't it make you want to explore?"

"When I was in Iraq, I use to sit in the desert and dream that I could travel through space," Coady whispered in a low, sincere voice.

"Shush!" came a voice from the darkness.

Amber turned her chest into Father Coady's as she slid her other hand to the back of his neck to pull him closer to her. She started to undo his priest collar and then stopped, deciding it was sexier if he left the collar on while they smooched. She moved her lips to his and kissed him deeply several times.

Coady leaned back, feebly trying to resist his urge to kiss her back. "You've a boyfriend and I am..."

Amber kissed him, stopping him midsentence. She didn't stop until she had kissed all resistance from him. By the time the necking ceased, they were both a little breathless. Amber leaned over to whisper, "I get the impression that we're both the neglected ones in our respective relationships."

"Amber."

"Shush, we can talk later. Can't we have just a moment of distraction?" Amber kissed his mouth again, preventing him from speaking.

Then, as though afraid Coady might pull away at any moment, she latched onto him with a gentle ferocity, never once allowing his lips to be free of either her lips or her skin. As though a master puppeteer, who possessed the ability to move various parts of her body, she guided not only his lips, but his hands as well. Finally, when her passion had heated her to an uncomfortable temperature, she paused as flashing lights from the show exploded all over the room.

"You're so beautiful," Coady whispered as he rested his forehead against her cheek.

"What?" Amber asked, even though she heard him.

"You're the most beautiful woman I've ever seen."

Relishing the compliment, Amber lurched forward, pressing her lips hard against Father Coady's. They engaged in a second round of necking. Like excited teenagers they thrashed at each other, while never letting their lips separate. They never noticed the people around them were aware of what was going on.

As their passion reached a volcanic pitch, the show abruptly ended, the lights went on, and everyone saw them. A slow steady groan rose and increased when people realized a priest was at the center of this disturbing public display. Father Coady turned to a lady near him, scrambling to adjust his priest collar back into its place.

"Excuse me," he apologized.

"What kind of a priest does that sort of thing?" a young woman snapped at Coady as she covered her toddler's eyes with her hand. "I mean, really. There are kids here."

"I'm sorry," Father Coady stammered.

"I mean, what kind of a priest?" another woman said as she pushed past Father Coady.

"Not a very good one," he commented to the woman's back, because she was already in a full-stomp move away from him.

"Oh, my God," Amber said, trying to hold in her laughter. "Are you not embarrassed at all?"

"It's not like I know them," Amber burst from her laughter. "And as you told me, you wanted to be able to be more open."

"I'm not sure that's what I meant."

"You told me you were sick of indifference. I'm being anything but indifferent," Amber chuckled.

Father Coady wanted to kiss her again. This time Coady initiated the kiss, pulling her onto his lap and firmly embracing her. Father Coady kissed her again and again. The two, forgetting that they were still in a crowded place, reignited their passion. Nothing could have come between them, except a young usher trying to clear the room for the next showing.

"You guys are going to have to get a room or something. We've got another show starting soon."

"I'm sorry," Father Coady said.

"Don't apologize," Amber informed him.

"Really, you guys are freaking me out," the usher commented.

Back in the hallway outside the theater, Father Coady adjusted all his clothing. "We should probably go and meet Mike and James."

"There's a different show in another theater," Amber stated as she tilted her head pointing toward it. "I don't know about you, but I haven't thought about work in a while."

"I know you're only playing, but I don't think it's funny."

Amber put her hand on his cheek. "I'm sorry, I was only being playful. Why don't we go see if Mike and James's show is over?"

Father Coady nodded in agreement.

Mike and James, after sitting through a dinosaur documentary, wandered through the African Peoples section on the second floor of the museum. Mike, forgetting James did not understand English, read each synopsis to him. They stopped at the Yoruba People in Nigeria display, long enough for a small group of students to gather around James. The children assumed James worked at the museum and was a living exhibit. Diligently taking notes regarding his dress, a teacher peppered them with questions.

"Can anyone name the culture this man represents?" asked the teacher.

"He looks like Jesus," one student called.

"Very good," the teacher answered. "You notice here the tassels he's wearing."

"*Rahkama*," James announced.

"What did he say?" a student asked.

"I'm not sure," the teacher replied.

The students, clueless of James's identity, were being instructed by an equally clueless educator. Mike turned his attention to the exhibit about Egungun, which was a masquerade performance used by the Yoruba people as comic relief. The performances recounted the history of their people.

As he looked at the mask of Egungun, Mike imagined the performer coming to life, dancing in front of the museum goers, telling the gloomy history of his lifetime. As Mike imagined the plastic figure coming to life, he also fantasized about his wife Alyssa dancing in the hall in an elaborate mask to recount the history of their marriage.

The performer's spirit possessed Alyssa, causing her to twitch and spasm. The half-dressed Alyssa was forced to dance with an image of her lover, Mike's brother James. Here in the hall, in front of the group of young students, the two would be forced to perform their carnal dance, while the Egungun provided comic relief with their wild gyrations and loud heckling. The Egungun would cheer, howl, and scream as the lovers danced and the performer chanted.

Through sign language, the performer would make Mike's flaws come to life: Mike drunk on weekends at a local strip club; Mike neglecting his kids; Mike's pathetic salary; Mike's soft body and bald head; Mike's weak libido.

Mike collapsed on the floor, twisting, and foaming as though he were experiencing a heart attack. James pushed through his group of admirers and rushed to Mike's side.

"*Rahkama*," James said loudly.

"I think I'm ready to hear what you have to say. Let's go see this translator."

Chapter 26
Translation

Amber, Father Coady, James, and Mike navigated south on the crowded sidewalk of 6th Avenue just below West 13th Street. No one here stopped to gape or even acknowledge James's appearance; they were too busy getting to where they needed to be. People moved quickly to their destinations without distraction, only displaying annoyance at the four people slowing the flow of rapid movement down the street.

Although no one noticed James, he observed everything. Often, he stopped to peek into the windows of the various shops, seemingly amazed at objects as well as customers. He also stared at the New Yorkers dressed in various outfits, standing in small areas catching a quick smoke. At one group, he stopped to look at a woman with tattooed arms and several piercings on her face.

"*Rahkama*," James commented to her.

"Listen, buddy, I ain't got time for stupidity today," she snapped as her smoking partner sneered at James.

Father Coady tugged James into a tranquil, tree-lined, pedestrian-free street when they reached 11th Street. They felt as though they had entered a completely different city. Mike followed and huffed, "This is much better. I don't know how people deal with so many crowds every day!"

"Oh, that was nothing," Father Coady commented. "You should see the chaos on the streets of Baghdad."

"I guess I'm a little nervous," Mike commented.

"We don't have to meet with her." Father Coady's anxiety had elevated ever since they left the museum and headed to see the author.

Amber, who kept pace at Father Coady side, put her small hand on Coady's trembling back. "Are you okay?"

"Yeah, I'm okay."

"Don't worry, Father. I need to do this," Mike said.

"Okay, we just need to be relaxed. This might be hard for James."

Amber, noticing the change in Coady's mood, leaned over to give him a gentle kiss on the cheek. "It'll be fine."

As Amber's lips approached his cheek for a second kiss, Father Coady turned his head so her lips landed on his. The small peck transformed into a long lip lock, lasting for several minutes. As Amber tried pull away, Father Coady pulled her toward him to extend the kiss.

"What the hell is that?" Mike exclaimed.

Father Coady reddened, realizing his lack of discretion. "Sorry, I just got carried away."

"I forgive you," Amber chuckled.

"I know it's been a long time since I went to a Catholic mass, but I don't remember the priest kissing parishioners."

"It's not what you think," Father Coady started to explain.

"Hey, I've got too much on my mind as it is. I don't the energy to process this. Let's just get to Ms. Sabar's office."

Mike pressed ahead at a rapid pace until he stood in front of a brownstone building. "I think she's on the second floor," Mike commented to James. "She's going to translate for me. I finally get to hear what you want to tell me," Mike commented in a frightened voice.

"Remember, you're the most important one in that conversation," Father Coady stated in a serious tone. Mike nodded.

"Will I be able to see James after this?" Mike asked.

"Sure," Father Coady replied, but his tone was not convincing.

"You're just saying that. You only gave me thirty days."

"No, you will be able to see him."

"Then why did you tell me it was only thirty days?"

"I'm sure you're going to be able to see James whenever you want," Amber interjected in a voice much more convincing that Father Coady's.

"I'm going to be alone," Mike stated firmly.

Amber and Father Coady looked at each other, saddened Mike was losing his family. Amber started to answer, "Mike, you won't be . . ."

Mike cut her off, "I know the results of the paternity tests. The kids aren't mine."

"Mike, I ..."

Mike cut her off once more. "You've got to have sex to be the father. And we weren't really having sex. I really don't want to go back to Raleigh."

Mike's yelling triggered stress for Father Coady, filling him with bad war memories. Backing away from Mike, he hoped he could subdue them. Not fully coherent, Coady stepped into the street, causing Amber and James to leave Mike for the priest's side.

"Coady, are you all right?"

"Yeah, I'm fine."

Mike, standing alone, screamed, "You are all going to leave me!" He sprinted west toward 6th Avenue.

Father Coady, Amber, and James ran after him. Mike, confused and distraught, ran in a staggered path.

"He's heading into traffic," Amber called to Coady.

"Oh, shit," Father Coady exclaimed, accelerating as fast as he could.

Mike, seeing the flow of cars, thinking the others were abandoning him, concluded getting run over by a car would be better than a world without his newfound friend James. Mike, using the rush of adrenaline to overcome his lack of fitness, maintained his distance in front of Father Coady. Like a tailback moving on the football field, Mike danced between people and darted toward the avenue. His midsection hurt, but he was close to his destination, so he pressed forward through the pain.

Cramping from dehydration, sweating from the heat, and panting from fatigue, Mike struggled to remain steady on wobbly legs. Trying to see his path through a river of sweat running into his eyes, he plowed forward blindly, using the sounds of speeding cars as his guide.

With the traffic noise intensifying, Mike made a final dash toward the street and leapt. Instead of his second opportunity to come in direct contact with the divine, Mike ran smack into the bicycle of a food delivery person riding south. Falling into the gutter, egg foo young, pork chow mein, and General Tso's chicken rained down on top of him.

The delivery person, who remained on his bike, screamed Chinese obscenities at Mike, who remained exhausted and dazed. Pulling an egg foo young patty off his neck and chow mein noodles from his hair, Mike surveyed the feet of people gathered around him. He did not try to get up. He liked looking at these body parts.

Unlike peoples' faces, toes did not cast judgment; they simply followed the commands of the brain. From perfectly manicured toes sitting in designer shoes to work boots, all of them remained silent. When Father Coady arrived, the delivery person still ranted as though Mike had committed the severest crime possible. Seeing Coady, his Chinese switched to labored English.

"Stupid, idiot moron!" the delivery person screamed.

Amber stepped in front of the biker, while Father Coady checked on Mike's condition. "Mike, are you okay?"

"Stupid, idiotic moron!" the delivery person yelled at Amber.

"Hey, enough," Amber snapped, causing the delivery person to lower his complaints to a mumble.

Father Coady, thinking the man was raising his hand to strike Amber, snatched the man's wrist.

"I don't want trouble," the delivery person changed his tune, either from respect from the priest collar or the size of Coady.

"Let's calm down here. It was an accident," Father Coady said in a calm but firm voice. "We can just thank the good Lord that no one was hurt."

"Thank God? Look at all my food! And my bike!" the delivery person yelled.

Father Coady surveyed the old bike, wondering if the delivery person was about to make a pitch to get money out of him. "I don't think that bike could be damaged."

"Look at my bike," the delivery person started to yell, but let his voice taper off when Father Coady leaned toward him. "My food," he said in a much meeker voice at Father Coady.

"Here you go," Amber snapped, handing the man fifty dollars, with a scowl on her face.

"I lose customer," the delivery person pleaded. Amber handed him another fifty dollars. "I lose customer," he continued.

"There are millions of people in New York, let's not be dramatic here," Amber screamed at the man.

Father Coady, playing the peacemaker, stepped between the delivery person and Amber. "I think we should all be thankful that no one was hurt," Father Coady stated in a slow, steady, and firm voice as he clutched the handlebars with his large hands.

"Yes, yes. Thankful," the delivery person replied as he tucked the hundred dollars into his jeans. He pedaled away from Coady.

Amber took tissues from her purse and feebly attempted to wipe the sauce from Mike's face. Instead, she only moved the sauce from one place to another. She noticed tears welling up in his eyes. "It's going to be all right."

"You're not going to take James away from me, are you?" Mike responded.

"Of course not," Amber assured.

James bent down to Mike, "*Rahkama*." Mike took his hand and stood up.

Back at the brownstone, Father Coady, Mike, James, and Amber squeezed into the small odd-shaped office of the author Ms. Sabar, where she greeted them warmly. Mike, worried about his appearance, hid behind the others. She said hello to everyone, but focused her attention on James.

Motioning for James to sit, she looked at his robe and played with the tassels in his hair. She said something to James, but a sudden clang rang through the room as Father Coady knocked a large world globe off its stand. He fumbled to get it off the floor and back into its holder.

"Please let me help you with that," Ms. Sabar commented, steadying the stand for the globe. "I'm in the middle of moving."

"Moving?" Amber asked.

"I'm going to be living in Iraq for more than a year," Ms. Sabar replied.

"Coady was stationed in Iraq," Amber informed her. "It was near Baghdad, right?"

Father Coady did not speak, but nodded his head slightly.

"I will be going through Baghdad into Northern Iraq to work with the Kurds." Ms. Sabar attempted to squeeze between Father Coady and Amber, but the space would not permit that. "This meeting might work better if we have fewer people in the room."

"Are you sure?" Father Coady questioned.

"We should let them be alone," Amber commented.

As Ms. Sabar opened the door for the two, she informed them, "There are a few nice little restaurants not far from here."

"Will it take that long?" Father Coady questioned.

"I would like to take my time, plus I would like to get a little practice before my trip."

"Sure," Amber stated.

"It'll be okay. It's a great day, you can even sit outside," Ms. Sabar instructed. "I'm very intrigued by James and it will take a good hour."

"Are you sure?" Father Coady questioned a second time.

"We should go," Amber replied, tugging Father Coady toward the door.

While being pulled from the room, Father Coady turned back to hear, "Now, let's get to know each other, shall we?"

Jesus's Brother James

Chapter 27
Divine Revelations

Ms. Sabar, dressed in a checkered purple blouse with a black designer jacket, was not what Mike had expected. Imagining a bookish author with disheveled hair, out-of-style clothing, huge glasses, and questionable hygiene, Mike could not have been more wrong. Ms. Sabar looked more like an editor of a high-end fashion magazine. Although her office showed the obvious signs of an impending move, signs of order were prevalent everywhere.

Boxes had computer-generated identification labels, stacks were segregated into areas of research, and her desk remained immaculate. Typed instructions for the move sat in the center of the desk, in front a large framed photograph of her with an older woman. The picture was taken at the Gateway Arch in St. Louis.

"Is that your father?" Mike asked as he leaned over the desk to examine it more closely.

"Yes, it is," Ms. Sabar replied, letting a hint of nerves creep into her voice. "You know my father?"

"Yes, he is a professor at UCLA."

"That's right. Are you familiar with his work?"

"No, I'm not. My friend Paul set this whole thing up." Mike looked at another picture of the father in front of a large shelf of books. "The love of words runs in the family," Mike commented.

"Yes, it sure does," she replied, happy with the way Mike had phrased his sentence. Although curious to hear the two men's stories, the combination of James's robes with Mike's appearance, compliments of his run-in with the delivery person, caused her to fret.

"Have you always wanted to be a writer?" Mike asked as he pondered his life's dreams.

"Yes, I guess I've always wanted to write."

From her early years, when she drafted stories in crayon with drawings, Ms. Sabar had always thought of herself as a writer. She used to sit on her father's lap as he rapidly typed on an old typewriter. When he took breaks, she would pretend she was helping by gently touching the typewriter keys. She did not possess the dexterity to push those old keys.

At first, she simply followed her father's occupation, loving the attention her father drew as he became a leading expert on Aramaic. Unlike unworthy fame, her father drew the admiration of educated people who provided an endless stream of compliments for both his work and his journey.

After graduating from college, it was only natural to write a story about her father's amazing migration from Iraq to the United States. As the story became a bestseller, it allowed her the freedom to live her dream and continue to write without the obstacle of a regular job.

"That's great that you get to follow your dream," Mike said, with a touch of envy in his voice.

"Yes, it is," she replied. "Now, let's talk about why you are here. Please tell me a little about your friend."

Mike smiled, "This is my friend, James. Everyone thinks he's Jesus, but he's Jesus's brother James. He only speaks Aramaic."

The mention of Jesus caused Ms. Sabar to twinge with apprehension. Being an expert in Aramaic sometimes brought unwelcome attention from some Christians. Although Ms. Sabar shared a common religion with Jesus, Judaism, some Christians sought her out to learn the secrets of Christianity. Aramaic, a Semitic subfamily of the Afroasiatic language, the tongue of both John the Baptist and Jesus, mystified so many people.

After the success of her first novel, an ever-growing stream of Christians wanted her to speak the verses of the New Testament. Some thought the vocal exercise would bring happiness. Others imagined that the words would cure sickness. Other nefarious individuals were certain that Aramaic might accelerate the "rapture" and the return of Christ to Earth.

"James, you say," Ms. Sabar, mumbled. She reached for her phone in case the conversation deteriorated.

The increasing flow of odd requests eroded her openness, resulting in a more reclusive existence. She relied on her public relations firm to completely filter out the undesirable individuals. So it annoyed Ms. Sabar when her publicist gave out her personal cell phone number to an individual named Paul. Ms. Sabar did not stay angry at her publicist, because Paul's charm quickly impressed her. Not only did Ms. Sabar speak to Paul for more than an hour, but she also agreed to meet with two individuals in her office.

"So you're friends with Paul?" Ms. Sabar asked.

"Yes, we have been friends since high school. He was the one I mentioned. He found you."

Paul's charm initiated her openness and his tale intrigued her. Of all of the Christians who approached with requests, none ever mentioned

Jesus's brother James. Most Christians were unaware of a sibling, assuming that Jesus was an only child. So when Paul called to tell her about a man impersonating the famous brother of Jesus, it sparked her interest. She had a natural affinity to the historical figure of James.

"So this is James," Ms. Sabar noted.

Her mind flowed with all the research she had done of the man. James, the brother of Jesus, mentioned several times in the New Testament, became a victim of history. After the crucifixion of Jesus, James led the church in Jerusalem, where the followers continued to obey Jewish laws. At this point, the Apostle Paul enters the story.

Paul and James struggled to shape the philosophy of the church. James held the opinion that Jesus's teachings were meant to be preached to Jews, while Paul believed that Jesus's message should be taken to Gentiles. In the end, Paul's philosophy won, while James has been forgotten by most Christians. Not only overlooked, but many Christian groups, to sustain Mary's perpetual virginity, argued that James was never a biological brother at all.

Ms. Sabar, perhaps possessing bias from her Jewish upbringing, felt a natural connection with James. In a college ancient history class, she had written a paper entitled, "What if Christianity Had Followed James?" In it, she argued that Christianity would have remained a non-distinct Jewish sect, never achieving world recognition.

Her professor, who normally loved all her writing, did not receive the paper well because he was a devout Christian. Not wanting to impact her grade point average, he dryly commented in the margin, "Beautifully written, but the large claims require large amounts of evidence."

Ms. Sabar never threw out that paper because of those comments. So when Paul described how a strange priest had introduced him to a shady individual posing as Jesus's brother James, she was hooked. Paul had assured her James and Mike were harmless. Now she wasn't too sure.

"Thank you so much for agreeing to see us," Mike said, interrupting her thoughts. "I know you're very busy."

"No problem; I was very intrigued by your story."

"You're older than I expected," Mike held up her book and showed her the photo on the back cover.

In a witty retort, she replied, "You're always older than you are in a photograph. Sometimes you're only a few seconds older and sometimes you're a few years older."

"It's a great picture," Mike stated, clearly smitten with the author.

"I'm glad you like it."

"Uhm, I mean you're still a striking woman."

"You're not here because of my photograph."

"No, I...I mean we are here because of your knowledge of Aramaic." Mike started to shake with nerves. "I'm sorry." Mike looked at photos of refugees on her shelves. "Did you take all these photos yourself?"

"Yes. These are Kurdish camps in Iraq. I volunteer in these camps. I speak various dialects that are useful to the aid groups. When I'm back in Iraq I'm going to help build a sanitation system."

"Sanitation system?"

"Yes. Do you know that unhealthy water is an underlying cause for the deaths of about twenty percent of children in some parts of the world?"

"Wow, that's so interesting," Mike said as he hung his head. "Did you study engineering?"

"Engineering, no. I just help translate, that's all."

"'That's all.' It's pretty impressive. You're so generous. You're so beautiful. You're so intelligent. I've read a lot of your work and it's quite fascinating."

Ms. Sabar squirmed in her chair, uncomfortable with all the compliments. "It's always nice to meet people interested in my work. You wanted to see me about Aramaic," she said, hoping to steer Mike to the point of the meeting.

"Yes, I'm sorry." Mike hesitated for a long moment. "I know we must seem strange to you."

"Actually, I get many requests from Christians wanting to connect with the language that Jesus spoke," she replied, glancing over to James, who had started to hum.

"Oh."

"But I must admit, this is the first time I've had a request for translating in connection with someone claiming to be the brother of Jesus." Ms. Sabar, sensing Mike's apprehension, leaned over to him.

"Yes, well, could we just focus on translation?"

"Do you believe he's actually the brother of Jesus?"

Shocked with the directness of the question, Mike's hesitation in answering showed he gave some validity to the possibility of James being heaven sent. Embarrassed to admit this, Mike tried to think of an answer that would not deter Ms. Sabar from helping him.

At that moment James tapped on Mike's shoulder and pointed to his own mouth. Mike handed James a small packet of hummus and pretzels. James clapped his hands, smiled, and started devouring the contents.

"Obviously, it's not likely that Jesus's brother could still be alive," Mike stated, never denying who he thought James might be.

"Yes, very unlikely," Ms. Sabar.

"He's helped me through a rough patch. And good things happen whenever he's around."

"How did you meet James?"

"Father Coady, the priest you saw earlier in here. He introduced me to him."

Ms. Sabar, sensing Mike's difficulty in the topic, paused like a chess player contemplating her next move. Paul had been more definitive in stating that this robed person was impersonating James. Fearing the conversation could turn into a dramatic train wreck, she studied a noodle sticking out of Mike's hair and wondered if it would be best to continue the conversation about James.

"I see," she stated, conveying her concerns with Mike's answers.

"Yes, I know this must seem strange to you," Mike explained. "I pal around with a guy who speaks Aramaic and dresses in a robe. But think of it this way. This is a kind of therapy to help me on my journey. It's like caring for an egg in a psychology class."

Mike's pathetic tone touched Ms. Sabar, "I will do what I can."

"Just spending time with him has been a great help."

"Okay. Well, let me talk to him a little bit."

Standing up, Ms. Sabar made her way over to James. Mike vacated his seat so she could sit next to James. She carefully surveyed his long beard, flowing robe, and various items stapled to the inside of the fabric. She noticed a small note. "Please contact Father Coady."

James, who had various pretzel crumbs on his cheek, smiled at her, so she returned it with a smile of her own. James opened a second pack of hummus.

In a soft and sweet voice, she uttered a few words in Aramaic. Mike did not understand the words, but the tone enchanted him. James stopped eating, gazed at Ms. Sabar, and put his index finger on her lips. Ms. Sabar said a few more lines. James giggled with excitement as her breath tickled his fingers as she spoke.

She said a few more phrases, generating a simple giggly response from James each time she spoke. Ms. Sabar reached for a pen and paper, jotting down a few words, and held them up for James to see. He did not acknowledge her written words.

Ms. Sabar leaned over to James and gently lifted his hair by the ear, where she could see a large scar running on the back of his skull. After a long moment, she let James's hair fall back on his head. She reached over to his shoulder and squeezed his hand.

"*Rahkama*," James finally uttered, responding to her touch. The words brought moisture to Ms. Sabar's eyes. James repeated, "*Rahkama.*"

"*Rahkama,*" Ms. Sabar repeated and reached over to hold his hands. She pulled back his robe to see burn scars all along on his forearm. "I know, James. I know," Ms. Sabar stated in English.

"He always repeats that one word. *Rah-ka-ma.*"

Ms. Sabar dabbed her eyes to make sure new tears had not formed and responded, "That word is Aramaic for love or mercy. I think he's trying to say 'mercy.'"

"So he is speaking Aramaic," Mike stated with enthusiasm, happy to hear that James had not been speaking gibberish. "Do you think you can translate for me?"

"No."

"I don't understand. I thought you spoke Aramaic."

"I do speak Aramaic. But this man is not speaking coherently. I think he might have sustained some type of brain damage."

"Brain damage?"

"Yes. He looks like a Kurd. Perhaps he was injured in the war. He has plenty of scars in different places." Ms. Sabar moved back to her desk and pulled out a stack of photos from her travels in Iraq. "I work with various refugee camps. There are so many victims from the years of conflict."

"Brain damage?" Mike repeated. She showed him photos of various war victims in the refugee camps. Pictures of women with large burns, others of men without limbs, and finally children deformed from the battles.

"These were taken in the hills of Northern Iraq," Ms. Sabar said as she handed Mike more photos displaying the devastation of war, bomb craters, demolished houses, and numerous people scarred in multiple areas of their bodies.

"Are you saying he doesn't understand anything at all?" Mike asked.

"No, I didn't say that. James would have to be examined by neurologist. I'm only saying that he does not appear to be able to communicate with me."

Mike moved closer to James. "I noticed the scars, but never knew how badly he was injured." Mike touched James's shoulder. "Why is life so brutal?"

"I wish I could answer that question," Ms. Sabar stated, collecting her photos. "Not everyone is as lucky as we are."

"I guess we are lucky. These people make my troubles seem so small," Mike concluded, glanced over to a smiling James. "You think James was hurt during the war?"

"I can't say for certain, but it is very possible. The number of people injured there is high. But whatever happened to him, he's no longer coherent."

"How can a brain-damaged man give me any type of real help?" Mike asked.

"I'm not sure I understand the question."

James smiled at Mike.

"But he did help me. I want to believe that."

"It's always important to have someone there with you in difficult times."

"And he has been there," Mike concluded. Mike peered at James and examined his scars.

Overwhelmed, as though a mad chemist had added every emotion to a melting pot, Mike felt an explosion of feelings. He felt pity for James. He felt anger at himself for not being able to help James. He felt confusion as to why Father Coady would bring James into his life. He felt a strong attraction to Ms. Sabar, who seemed to be a beacon of hope for struggling people.

As these thoughts swirled, he wanted order. As bewilderment seized control of his mind, he wanted structure. As confusion reigned, he wanted logic.

"Why?" Mike asked her.

"Why what?"

"Why for everything? Why?"

James, hearing the tone in Mike's voice, came over to him and put his large hands on Mike's cheeks. He placed his forehead on Mike's forehead, allowing for Mike's confusion and pain to dissipate.

Mike looked over to Ms. Sabar. "Can you come with me when I speak to this priest?"

Chapter 28
Dreams Don't Last

Allowing themselves a moment to forget their mission and enjoy New York, Amber and Father Coady sat at a table on the sidewalk outside the restaurant Taboon. Casually sampling wine and various small pâtés at this tapas restaurant until they received word to go back to Ms. Sabar's office.

Amber enjoyed spreading fig sauce on a saltwater cracker, topping it with a piece of gourmet cheese and slowly plopping it into Coady's mouth. Father Coady, at first distracted, relaxed after a few glasses of wine, and relished being pampered. People didn't normally cater to his needs. Instead, parishioners berated him with requests.

Coady also appreciated the parade of pedestrians, who could not help shooting surprised glances at him as he kissed Amber's cheek. Even Manhattanites could not hide their curiosity from the strange sight of a priest out in public on a date.

"I love the streets of Manhattan. I like to people-watch," Amber commented as she sipped her white wine.

"I completely agree. It's nice to be in a place where nobody knows your name," Father Coady replied before accepting another cracker.

"Definitely."

"No one will tell me their problems. No one wants me fix their life. No one wants anything from me. I can forget everything."

"I never realized how stressful being a priest could be. I guess you do hold the spiritual destiny of hundreds of people in your hands," Amber started with a sly smile.

"Are you mocking me?"

"No, I'm serious. I'm sure that everyone at church thinks you're going to save them."

"Maybe. I used to believe that it was my duty to protect peoples' souls. I used to think I held some special information. People would flock to me to get to this special knowledge. That all changed."

"Knowledge?"

"When I was a brother studying to become a priest, my main motivation was to save peoples' souls. When I grew tired, I imagined all the people I would be saving in my future. It gave me a boost to try harder and study more. I studied so hard and learned so much."

"That's admirable."

"At first, it was. The more I studied theology, the more complex things got. It made me feel special. I could name all the famous theologians and all the famous doctrines of the church. At dinner with the other brothers, I would sometimes bring up rare facts to show the benefits of my learning. I know it was vain, but it was also addictive."

"Addiction to knowledge is not a bad thing."

"I don't disagree. The knowledge has helped me in my growth. The problem arose after I graduated. Thinking all this knowledge would transform people, I eagerly set out to give it to everyone. Like a spiritual doctor, I thought people would want to follow my path and, through tremendous effort, heal their souls."

"Tremendous effort? I work as a pharmaceutical sales rep. The average person doesn't like tremendous effort. They want to pop a pill."

Father Coady's face stiffened with pain. "You're absolutely right," he sighed. "Most people were completely indifferent to what I had to say. Even the other priests. That's the worst part."

"Indifferent? In what way?"

"Everyone just wants to be saved without any effort. They think if they show up on Sunday and even if they sleep through mass, they will get an eternity in paradise."

"You sound a little bitter."

"I guess I am. We're spoiled; that's one of the reasons I enlisted in the military. I wanted to be there to help people in real need."

"What was different about being a chaplain?"

"It was so real. I didn't have to deal with all the petty day-to-day things. I felt such a surge of life being close to danger. The soldiers knew it. They knew life could be short. There was such a camaraderie with them. You don't get that here. Everyone here seems so much more isolated and self-absorbed in small things."

"You miss that time?" Amber asked, and Father Coady nodded his head "yes." Amber reached over and kissed him. "I can completely understand about being isolated. I've worked at my job for years and I'm lucky to have a few close friends. I spend my time obsessed with numbers that don't mean anything."

Father Coady shook his head in understanding. "What do you do when you can no longer fit into the normal routine of what other people expect from you?" he asked.

"Perhaps this is a good thing. When we realize we do not fit into the normal, we can search for something that is extraordinary."

Father Coady shot a sharp look at Amber as though she had uttered a parable more profound than any made by King Solomon. Feeling a special bond with Amber, he smiled as though his troubles were falling off him like leaves falling off a tree in late autumn. In a soft sweet voice, he stated, "Maybe you're right about this. Maybe God is trying to tell us both to look for something else."

"Someone is definitely trying to tell me something," she snickered. "I've spent all my energies on this job and I'm not happy. I spent twelve to fourteen hours a day working and I have no real friends."

"Why do you stay?"

"I've been chasing some false ideal. I've been working hard to get a big title."

"But you said you hate the people in the leadership positions."

"I make all this money."

"But you never really enjoy it."

Amber shook her head in disbelief, finally realizing what she had been denying about herself. "Are you saying that we both need a new occupation?" Amber firmly held his hands.

"Maybe." Father Coady squeezed her hands. "I care about you."

Amber kissed Father Coady until her lips went dry.

The food server, holding two more plates of food, coughed in hopes they would stop so she could deliver the food. Father Coady attempted to pull his arm away from Amber, but his shirt was caught on her blouse. As he pulled, her blouse opened. Flustered, Father Coady fumbled to detach himself from her clothing. Tired of waiting, the server left the two plates at the edge of the table and quickly retreated from the two lovebirds.

"That was awkward," Father Coady laughed.

While Amber and Father Coady alternated between kissing, sipping, and eating, Paul walked nearby, checking his phone for directions to Ms. Sabar's office. He carried the autographed photo of Rob Thomas and Pedro's blanket over his shoulder.

After discovering Coady's secrets at his apartment, Paul immediately booked a flight for JFK, arriving early in the morning, hoping to repair both relationships with his news. Looking up from Google Maps, Paul saw the shocking image of Father Coady putting his lips on Amber's neck, while at the same time putting his hand on her breast. Paul's mouth hung open.

"That sneaky fuck!" screamed Paul.

Sprinting down the sidewalk, Paul leapt over several bollards surrounding the tables as he rushed at Father Coady. Paul threw the framed Rob Thomas photo at Father Coady and jumped into his chest. The two men fell over a full table and landed down hard onto the pavement.

The force of the two men expelled dishes, glasses, and food from their places, causing them to crash on the ground. Customers scrambled to move back away from the men as the two rolled under a table, causing more dishware to cover the pavement. The female food server dashed inside to get help.

"I'm going to kill you!" Paul screamed and he started to swing wildly.

Father Coady, although affected by the alcohol, easily deflected the blows. He shoved Paul into the air and into a third table, where a several plates of food slid onto Paul. Father Coady searched for Amber to make sure she was okay.

Paul, taking advantage of Coady being distracted, scrambled to make another charge. The priest skillfully diverted the second charge with less effort than the first. Paul fell face-first into a plate of hummus. Two failed attempts did not dissuade Paul, who pushed his chest off the ground and made a third charge. Father Coady permanently stopped Paul when he delivered a short, powerful blow into Paul's midsection.

Unable to stand, Paul pushed himself to his knees and wiped blood from his lip as he struggled to pull air into his lungs. As though he was having a bout of dry heaves, Paul coughed and spat, trying to force oxygen back into his lungs. His frantic attempts failed, so he placed his palms on the ground and arched his back in a new effort to get his breath back. A small short-order cook entered the patio and stood between Paul and Father Coady.

"Paul, what the hell are you doing here?" Amber asked.

"What?" Paul croaked still not possessing enough air to form a complete sentence. "What am I doing?" he repeated as he still struggled to recover from Father Coady's single blow. "What the hell are *you* doing?"

"Eating lunch. You're the one assaulting a priest."

"Having lunch? Priest? Are you kidding me?" Paul spat on the ground. He rubbed blood from his nose. "It looked like you were snacking on his tongue to me!"

"Keep calm, my son," Father Coady interjected in a priestly-sounding tone. Father Coady tried to pat Paul on the shoulder.

Paul slapped his hands away from him, "Seriously? Don't give me that bullshit."

"I'm sure we can discuss this rationally."

Paul, enraged, but not willing to take another charge at Father Coady, vented through screams, "'Stay calm, my son?!' Kiss my ass!"

Amber, still in shock over Paul's sudden appearance, watched the normally calm Paul twitch with anger. For their entire two-year relationship, Paul had remained stoic. During a trip to Ocho Rios in

Jamaica, an armed gunman put a pistol in Paul's chest, but he did not panic. He calmly spoke to the man and offered him money as long as they could keep their wallets.

Now, Paul's cool exterior crumbled into an obsessive ex-boyfriend. Strangely enough, Amber found the transformation appealing. After all, she assumed she had triggered this response. He seemed far from indifferent to her now.

"You came all the way to New York to spy on me?" Amber asked.

"You're accusing me of something? Are you kidding me?" Paul screamed.

The short-order cook patted Paul on the shirt. "Come on, man, let's take a deep breath here try to stay calm."

Paul didn't want to listen. "Are you even a fucking priest?" Paul barked angrily at Father Coady.

"Come on, let's stay calm," the cook said.

"Calm? The fucking priest was assaulting her."

Amber growing impatient with Paul, snapped, "Trust me, it was not assault." Amber, with the help of the servers, tried to pick up their recently inverted table.

"I wouldn't trust this guy," Paul reached out for her, but she slapped his hand away from her.

"Don't touch me," Amber snapped.

"I've got to tell you something."

"It's going to have to wait," Amber screamed.

"Let's all calm down," Father Coady stated as he wiped blood from the corner of his eye.

"'Calm down.' I should cut that lying tongue of yours out," Paul yelled over the short-order cook at Father Coady. The cook attempted to block Paul from confronting Coady.

"I think you need to calm down," Father Coady snapped, finally losing patience with Paul.

Paul continued to stew over his failure to land a blow on Father Coady. Losing a fight to a priest, no matter how muscular, was emasculating. Paul watched as Amber scooped two ice cubes from a water pitcher, wrapped them in a discarded napkin, and delicately placed the ice on Father Coady's eye. While Amber's kindness cooled Father Coady's wound, her action fueled the fire of Paul's rage.

The short-order cook, thinking the fight over, retreated to the kitchen as the food staff cleaned up. A female manager instructed the three that she had called the police, which Amber applauded.

"Maybe they can talk come sense into you," she scolded Paul.

Amber's comment reignited Paul's hysteria. Feeling alone in his struggle, with Amber not listening to his discovery, Paul became more desperate. Knowing he did not possess Coady's physical attributes, he scanned the area for a possible weapon. He did not think he would need to use it, but felt he could compel everyone to listen.

Not taking any time for further contemplation, Paul grabbed a knife and held it out at Father Coady. Although Father Coady remained calm, Amber freaked. She waved her hands, pleading with Paul to drop the knife. As she was speaking, Mike and James approached them.

"Mike! Mike! Get over here and help us. Paul's gone friggin' nuts," Amber beckoned as she waved her hands feverishly.

Mike, still emotionally unwrapped, sprinted toward the conflict with no clear target. He felt irritation not only with both Paul and Father Coady, but with life in general. Like Jacob wrestling with an angel of

God, Mike wanted to lash out at whoever stood in his path. Not slowing as he approached, he leapt into the air at Father Coady, which caused a domino effect.

He fell into Coady, who then fell into Paul, and all three went down. Now punches flew from everyone.

Father Coady, the only one with real fighting skills, defended himself from the wild attacks and pushed the two to the side. Coady had spent hours perfecting his self-defense techniques during downtime in Iraq. Ironically, he never used the skill in the warzone, but it came in handy here on the streets of New York.

Father Coady delivered a second blow to Paul's soft midsection, which had the same result of reducing Paul to a pile of flesh on the pavement. Mike, who did not possess the same level of anger, gathered himself together and wandered over to James instead of reentering the fray. James took Mike by the bicep, signifying that the fight needed to stop. Amber bounded in front of Coady with the idea of trying to deter any more attacks on her new boyfriend.

"*Rahkama!*" screamed James at the group.

Father Coady, like a holy Bruce Banner, tried to keep his stress levels low, sensing the possible flood of war images. They started to pop up in his mind. He recalled the awfulness, the sounds of explosions, the smell of charring flesh, the taste of ash in his mouth, the sights of fights, and the touch of death.

Moving to back away from his attackers, he swung his arms, lashing out at the memories as though he were a man trapped in a spider's web. Amber dashed to him, cradling his head and whispering kind words until the moment had passed.

When the NYPD arrived minutes later, the combatants attended their scrapes and bruises in separate parts of the restaurant. The staff collected broken items, tallying the losses.

A police officer surveyed the damage with an exasperated restaurant manager, taking detailed notes on a small pad. After speaking with the manager and the combatants individually, the officer beckoned the three fighters to come sit at a table to face his interrogations.

With a sharp New York wit, the officer could barely hide a smile as he asked his first question. "So you're some kind of karate priest?"

"I've had some military training in the past," Father Coady sheepishly replied as Amber squeezed his hand.

Amber's affection did not go unnoticed by the officer. "You think you've seen it all. I mean, I live in New York and I've seen a lot of stuff, but I've never seen a Rambo priest."

"This is all a simple misunderstanding. I have no interest in pressing charges."

"No offense, Father, but it really isn't your choice about filing charges. After all, your little WrestleMania stunt caused quite a bit of damage. And I think the manager is not too happy."

"I'm really sorry."

"We can pay for the damage," Amber assured.

The officer turned to Paul and Mike. "Now why exactly did you two geniuses jump a priest over lunch?"

"I saw him making out with my girlfriend and I kind of snapped," Paul replied.

"Ex-girlfriend," Amber interjected.

"So you attacked the priest 'cause he stole your girlfriend, but didn't know he had Bruce Lee skills?"

"Yes, Officer," Paul nodded.

The officer turned to Mike. "And you ran in to help your buddy 'cause the priest was kicking his ass?"

"Not exactly. I didn't really mean to attack Father Coady. Even though he lied to me about James being Jesus's brother."

Mike motioned to James, who stood smiling at the small crowd gathered near the scene.

"Jesus?" the officer questioned. "The Jesus?"

"Yes," Mike replied.

"Jesus the Lord and Savior? And the priest told you that this guy was Jesus's brother?"

"That's the one."

"And you're upset because you figured out that the robed guy was not actually part of the Holy Family?" the officer asked with a tone of disbelief.

"It's kind of hard to explain," Mike started and then stopped, but the officer motioned for him to continue. "James is a good guy. Even though he had brain damage from the war, he has helped me through a desperate time."

"A brain-damaged guy helping the desperate," the officer repeated, not sure whether the whole thing was some form of prank. "Are you three for real? You guys affiliated with the NYU film school and doing some kind of spoof?" The three shook their heads no. The officer turned his attention back to Mike. "So what's this desperation all about?"

"I found out my wife was sleeping with my brother," Mike informed the officer. "And I've come to find out my kids are actually my brother's."

"Do you guys live here?"

"No, we're all from North Carolina."

"One guy loses his girl to a priest, and one guy loses his wife to his brother," the officer questioned. "Only down south." The officer turned to his partner. "I mean, this sounds like a *Jerry Springer* show: there's a womanizing priest, my kids' father is my brother, and this guy thinks he's part of the Holy Family. What the fuck?" The officer shook his head.

Paul spoke up. "We should stop referring to him as a priest."

"So now he's not a priest?" the officer asked.

Amber added, "Not a priest?"

"I can explain," Father Coady stammered.

"Amber, this guy is a fraud. I found this out when I broke into his place," Paul exclaimed.

"Broke into his apartment?" Amber asked.

"You broke into his apartment?" the officer repeated.

"That's not the issue. What I'm trying to say is this guy's a fraud. He's taking advantage of you," Paul became more animated.

"So are you a priest or not?" the officer asked Coady.

Everyone stared at Father Coady, anxiously awaiting his answer. Their eyes penetrated him. As Coady's mind fumbled for a response, the stress caused war images to flood back into his mind. Father Coady remembered a family he often saw.

The military had instructed him to avoid contact with locals, but he often watched families as he went from place to place. Beyond the obvious potential safety risk of interacting with unknown locals, the military command did not want chaplains attempting to convert Muslims to Christianity. Some soldiers distributed Bibles, which had caused local clerics to formally protest.

Jesus's Brother James

Father Coady did not interact with anyone, but this did not stop him from keenly observing people as they traveled from base to base. He had taken notice of a family who lived close to his main base of operations. He often observed the father with three children, kicking an old soccer ball on the side of the road.

The father, a strikingly large man, seemed like a gentle giant who laughed and called to his children as they played. One day, he watched as the three siblings leapt into his arms after one of these play sessions. The father hugged them and appeared to be in complete bliss as he enjoyed their affection.

That idyllic scene exploded when the boys accidentally stumbled across an IED moments later. Now, the man kneeled on the road with the bodies of his children. The father, covered in the blood of his children, called to the sky as tears streamed down his face. He kept screaming one word, "Allah," over and over again, until his voice collapsed and he could yell no longer. Father Coady, holding back tears, watched the man call for God.

"Where is God?" Father Coady asked, surprising everyone with the bizarre question.

"What?" the officer asked.

Father Coady did not hear the question as he flashed back to images of the children's bodies being ripped apart and it filled his mind. He recalled the screams of terror when they heard the awful click, nanoseconds before the bomb exploded.

Then, as though he were editing a film in his mind, Father Coady heard the voice-over of the children's father crying "Allah." The father's voice, which contained so much pain, rubbed against Coady's skin like nails on a chalkboard. Then came the awful sound of silence as the father waited for God to speak to him.

The officer, seeing signs of stress in Coady's face, said, "Please remain where you are."

"Where is Allah?" Father Coady barked at the officer.

The officer took out his Taser. "I think you need to stand still. Don't move."

"Why is Allah so quiet?" Father Coady yelled, not listening to the officer.

The officer tried a softer tone, "We're going to need you to calm down."

Father Coady wasn't listening because the flashbacks had pushed all the current reality from his mind. He continued to back away from the group, from the restaurant into the outdoor café area, while still talking to someone who wasn't there. "I need to hear something. Allah, talk to me!"

James rushed forward toward Father Coady, "*Shlama.*"

"Stand where you are, buddy."

Father Coady continued to move backwards into the busy street calling, "Allah!"

James screamed "*Shlama!*" but Coady did not react.

Father Coady did not hear James, he did not hear Amber, and he did not hear the officer. What he did hear were the sounds of car horns blowing as he drifted too far into the street. That sound brought him back from his flashback while James's hand kept him out of harm's way. As Coady fell safely to the sidewalk, the dreadful images from Iraq were replaced by the terrible sight of James being smashed by a large speeding car.

Chapter 29
Did James Have a Pentecost?

The group, including Amber, Mike, and Paul, silently sat in the waiting room for a surgeon to update them on James's condition. Father Coady flipped through a Bible, taking a mental note of each page that contained James's name. He stopped to read Galatians to himself. *I saw none of the other apostles—only James, the Lord's brother. I assure you before God that what I am writing to you is no lie.* He stopped reading at the word "lie." He contemplated his lies. He wondered if his lies had led to this.

Father Coady closed the holy book with a sigh and glanced over to Amber, who had kept her distance from him since the accident. Coady wanted to be near her. He wanted to put his face on her shoulder, with her whispering assurances to him.

He desired to go back hours earlier to be in that dark theater looking at the stars, with her holding his hand, with her lips touching against his. But he dared not approach her. Paul sat between them, still fermenting in his anger at Coady. The best course of action for Coady was to sit quietly.

Paul did not have the willpower to remain quiet. "Because we're going to have some time here, why don't you tell us who James really is."

Father Coady, not wanting to speak with anyone other than Amber, remained silent for a moment, but caved to all the eyes fixed on him. "His name is Yakov. He was a Kurdish refugee from the war."

"Not James," Paul emphasized in an attempt to illustrate the lie.

Father Coady scowled, irritated with Paul's tone. "Yakov is Aramaic for James."

"So why exactly did Jesus's brother become a Kurdish refugee?" Paul mocked.

Hoping that an admission of guilt might end the terse dialogue, Father Coady responded, "I figured you guys knew it was just symbolic." Father Coady turned to Mike.

"Of course," Mike agreed in a soft voice.

Father Coady bowed his head as though he were about to start a prayer and in a low steady voice stated, "James lost his family to an IED. The blast scarred him as well."

"So he's brain damaged," Paul commented.

"He said scarred, not brain damaged," Mike interjected pithily. The tone surprised Paul, who assumed Mike would join him in his vitriol toward Father Coady.

"And you brought this symbolic, scarred person to Mike because...?" Paul asked.

"Mike was so distraught, I thought James might have a positive effect on him," Father Coady explained. "I thought if Mike had some time to be with James, he would realize life is precious."

"Did you know all this bullshit was symbolic?" Paul snorted as he directed the question to Mike.

Mike shook his head "no," and then "yes," and then did something that was a mixture of "yes" and "no." He huffed, "I kind of knew it, but I liked hanging out with James."

"Kind of knew?"

"Hey, James was the only one with me. He always made me feel better," Mike snapped. "You know, a real friend sticks by someone."

Paul was stunned Mike could so easily overlook Coady's lie, and could still hold resentment against Paul. Moving over to his jacket, Paul retrieved several photos of their college trip to New York. He handed them to Mike with the note Mike had written.

"That was a great day," Mike commented. "Man, how things have changed."

"What do you mean?" Paul asked.

"When the photo on the Empire State Building was taken, I never wanted that day to end." Mike turned from Paul and looked up at the ceiling. "Now, I kind of wish I had jumped off the building that day."

"Why?"

"Wouldn't it be great to end life after a perfect day?"

Paul, not wanting to confront that comment, pivoted back to Father Coady. "Still, this guy is not who he says he is."

"What is he talking about?" Amber asked Coady.

Coady stood up and in a soft calm voice announced. "I was a priest. I ran into some trouble adjusting to life when I came back from Iraq."

"Was a priest?" Amber asked.

Father Coady turned to Amber, but in a reflex motion she turned her head away from him to avoid eye contact. "The bishop felt my techniques were unorthodox and I had received several complaints. And then one Sunday, there was an incident."

As the three listened, Coady told them about the "incident."

Father Coady, before giving mass, liked to survey the crowd from the vestibule—playing a game with himself, guessing on which people he might have the greatest otherworldly impact. On that particular Sunday, he noticed two elderly women in an animated conversation on the left side of the church. Curious, he slipped over to eavesdrop on their discussion.

"Can you believe this country is letting in those goddamn Muslim refugees?" the first elderly woman told her friend.

"It's these damn bleeding hearts. They're ruining this country," the second woman replied.

"We should ship all these idiots to a Muslim country," the first woman added. "We'll see how long their rulers would put up with them."

"We should ship them there," the second woman agreed. "Then build a wall around those countries and let all these barbarians murder each other."

"Problem solved," the first woman concluded.

The bitter conversation stayed with Coady as he put his final vestments on before mass. Being a strong advocate for welcoming refugees and having given several sermons on the topic, it surprised him that the women displayed such vitriol toward others, especially in church. Determined to combat such negative thoughts, Father Coady reviewed his homily, which provided another excellent chance to spread God's love.

When the time in the mass arrived, Father Coady stood, enthusiastic about giving his moving sermon. Surveying the parishioners, he noted sleepers, makeup-checkers, and many people doing to sneaky watch checks. Before beginning, Father Coady had the word of God on his side, so he felt optimistic about igniting warmth into the hearts of these followers of Christ.

Father Coady started his speech. "As the topic of accepting refugees is prevalent in the news, I would like to repeat a critical line in today's Gospel of Matthew."

The bitter, elderly woman who had insulted Muslims reacted by hiding a magazine in her hymn book. After a quick yawn, she flipped the pages until she found an interesting article.

Father Coady raised his voice, "'Truly I tell you, whatever you did for one of the least of these brothers and sisters of mine, you did for me.'" Father Coady held his hands in the air to emphasize its importance. "God is commanding us to help all people. Even the least."

The magazine reader in the front row rolled her eyes and let out a deep long sigh. She turned to her partner in anti-refugee feeling and mouthed, *Liberal priest.*

Father Coady moved from behind the altar, staggered to the top of the steps, and pulled at his thick black hair. Raising his voice even higher, he pleaded, "This is God speaking to us. Our Lord and Creator is telling us to help each other."

The parishioners gazed at him like students listening to a math teacher explaining a complex equation. Nothing existed but indifference throughout the church. Coady started to bang his fists on the nearest wooden pew, hoping to shock-and-awe a reaction out of some of them. He raised his voice a third time.

"'Whatever you did for one of the least of these brothers and sisters of mine, you did for me,'" Father Coady banged again on the pew and yelled, "'Whatever you did for one of the least of these brothers and sisters of mine, you did for me!'"

Taking a second to refill his lungs, Father Coady examined peoples' faces, but again was disappointed. Some expressed annoyance, while others looked at him with confusion and apprehension; no one was listening to the words he spoke.

He had persuaded no one closer to his perspective on the topic. His stress released all his emotion and he started convulsing like a man with an alien trying to break through his chest. Throwing hymn books, knocking over candles and dousing himself with the wine, he ranted about the love of God. From the side, a deacon and an usher rushed to the altar and dragged Coady away.

The group stared at Coady for a moment, and Mike commented, "You flunked out of the priesthood?"

"They recommended a transfer out of town and counseling for me. I did not want to transfer."

"Unbelievable—a priest on the lam," Paul snapped in a loud voice, but changed his tone when a nurse shot him a nasty glance.

"I'm not on the lam," Father Coady stated as he looked to Amber. "I just left the priesthood."

"I don't know whether to believe this story. Maybe you were never a priest."

"I'm telling the truth."

"Okay, if you're a former priest, tell me what's longer, a 'Hail Mary' or 'Our Father.'" Coady ignored him and turned and moved away.

"When you left the priesthood, why didn't you turn in the uniform?" Paul asked, pointing to the clerical clothing.

"Give him a break," Mike pleaded. "He only quit a job."

"You're on his side?"

"I'm just saying," Mike explained.

"He lied to you."

"I knew it wasn't Jesus's brother. Fuck, I'm not that stupid."

"Then why did you go along with it?"

"Because, I, uhm," Mike stumbled. "My wife didn't love me. My kids weren't mine. I was all alone." Mike tried to hold back his emotions. "He's got to be alright or I'll be alone again."

Coady hugged Mike. "He's going to be okay."

Paul, disgusted with the sympathy for Father Coady, stomped out of the waiting room. Amber, though not angry with Coady, left the room in the opposite direction. She needed a moment away alone to reflect on everything that had occurred.

Retreating to a hallway, Amber found a vending machine. Looking to satisfy her sweet tooth, she purchased a Mountain Dew and three candy bars, quickly opening both. The sugar load sent a rush of warmth through her body that calmed her. As she had her teeth sunk into a Reese's Peanut Butter Cup, Father Coady approached her.

"Caffeine and chocolate? Expecting a long night?" Father Coady asked, trying to find the proper angle to enter into a conversation.

"Old habits. It's what got me through long nights at work," Amber replied with a sigh, not ready for the serious conversation she knew was coming. As a person who loved structure and organized life, all these variables—Father Coady's lies, Paul's sudden change in personality, and James's condition—dazed her.

"I'm so sorry," Father Coady stated without elaborating.

Amber liked the simplicity of his apology. She sat down at a table and Coady followed. To her, it showed accountability. "I guess you're still adjusting."

"Yeah, it's only been a year."

"A year," Amber coughed. Now she worried that a man wearing his holy attire a year after a breakdown might still be struggling with an identity problem.

Father Coady, sensing her apprehension, reached out to hold her hand, but she hesitated. "You think it's a little weird that I still go out in public with my collar?"

Amber, although she agreed with his statement, felt it callous to condemn him for the action. Instead she tried to find a link with him. "No stranger than a grown woman seducing a priest."

"Technically, I was not a priest."

"But I didn't know that."

"Still, I should've told you that I was no longer a priest."

"I wonder if I would still have been interested in you," Amber stated with a bit of a chuckle. The laugh did not seem to fit the situation, but she could not help herself. After all, here she was sitting in a New York hospital, speaking to a new possible boyfriend who had impersonated a priest and been attacked by her ex-boyfriend. It all didn't seem real.

"Let me explain why I lied."

"I know why you lied. The question is, why are you still wearing the uniform?"

Coady sighed as though he were a teenager caught sneaking into his house on a Friday night. "What kind of guy do you think I am?"

"A very mixed-up guy."

"That's fair," Father Coady commented, saddened to hear her appraisal of his actions. "Susan Sontag once said, 'sanity is a cozy lie.'"

A few hours earlier, this witty quip would have impressed Amber, but it now annoyed her. She wanted Coady to return to his simple answers. She sighed and shook her head. She started to rise before Coady blocked her path.

"I'm a little mixed up," Father Coady admitted, which seemed to soften Amber. "The more I experience, the more confused I've become. It makes me question everything."

"You left the priesthood. It was your choice."

"Yes, I left on my own. I just didn't believe anymore. It made me feel like such a hypocrite."

"If you don't believe in the church anymore, why wear the collar so people think you are still part of it?"

"I believe that it can do good. People pay more attention to me with the collar," Coady stated, putting his head down from embarrassment. "I feel like this uniform gives me authority. I like helping people."

"So that's why you wore the uniform with me? You thought it would help you connect with me?"

Father Coady blushed and then stuttered, "I, well, I started out trying to help Mike. With you, I just kind of got caught up in everything."

"I guess I did too," Amber sighed with a subtle little blush, suddenly embarrassed. She looked over to Coady, examining how his confession transformed his mysterious, alluring appearance into a flawed character.

At the same time, he went from a fantasy person into a human being. Coady had not been transformed; instead, her own view had altered. Like a microbiologist looking through a microscope, she started seeing Coady more clearly. It was not better or worse to Amber; just different.

Coady, sensing Amber's heavy thoughts, moved closer to her, reaching out his hand to touch hers, but she retreated.

"I need a moment to process everything," Amber commented as she put her hand in front of him to stop his approach.

Coady complied, submission showing all over his face. "I understand."

The meekness in his voice caused Amber to feel guilt. Without turning her head, she slyly reexamined Coady's face. Hidden behind his strong, sharp features, a boyish demeanor that she found endearing peeked through. The expression articulated his bewilderment and uncertainty. Still annoyed and confused, she couldn't show him too much affection, but offered a token of possible reconciliation. "There's just a lot to take in."

Coady turned to her, "I wasn't honest with you. I can understand your apprehension."

His frank, terse self-assessment impressed her. He did not offer an excuse. He did not offer a promise of future behavior. He did not plead. She liked it. Not only did it improve his standing with her, but it unleashed a flood of recognition of her own flaws.

After all, she had been playing this romantic game, bordering on a lie with a man. She thought he had taken holy vows, but was willing to tempt him, while at the same time using him to exact an emotional toll on Paul. With his stock on the rise and her stock lowering, she felt she had more in common with him. She suddenly wanted to kiss him.

Her desire to kiss him stemmed not only from the recovery of her admiration for him, but also from a desire to escape the awfulness around her. James and Mike both swam in a pool of misery. Her future, normally clear, seemed murky and dark.

She felt empathy with the pain she saw in this former priest's face— pain that came from lying to her and Mike; pain that came from James's current state. Amber, who had her own pain, thought that perhaps if they kissed, their individual hurt might negate the other's pain. For a moment she hesitated, but then shook with want. Leaning forward she planted her lips firmly onto Coady's.

Coady, who first looked shocked, immediately wrapped his arms around Amber and returned her kiss.

"I will take mercy on you," Amber stated in a sly voice.

"Thank you," Coady replied with an enormous smile on his face. "What does this mean?"

"It means, let's worry about everything tomorrow," Amber replied.

They started kissing passionately. Their embrace, far from gentle, was frenzied. Heedless of their surroundings, they frantically pawed at each other. His hand first squeezing her breast and then moving down to clutch the curve of her hip.

She pulled on his hair with one hand and ground her lips into his; the other hand reached for his zipper and she felt his stomach tremble at her touch. His hand slid further down to grab the back of her knee, bringing her thigh up next to his hip. Their struggle took them off balance and they fell backwards into the vending machine. A nurse rounded the corner and jumped in surprise to see them.

"Oh, shit," the nurse called in a loud voice as she dropped her change.

"I'm terribly sorry," Coady stated as he attempted to retrieve his hand from Amber's blouse.

The nurse, who ran her eyes back and forth from Father Coady's collar to Amber's exposed Victoria's Secret bra, shook her head in disapproval, then commented, "You two realize this is a hospital?"

"I should probably explain what's happening here," Coady stated as he adjusted his collar.

The nurse snickered, "Explain 'what' is happening? I'm a nurse. I had to take biology."

"I meant, explain me being a priest."

The nurse shrugged. "Listen, I never knew how men could go their whole lives without women, so no need to explain. I'm just asking if you think this is the appropriate place and time for that kind of thing."

Amber's face turned stone cold as though she had peered into Medusa's eyes. "You're right. I'm very sorry."

"And what about you, mister? Can you control yourself?"

Coady blushed and promised, "I will behave." After a quick chuckle, he turned to see that Amber had left him.

Chapter 30
Fork in the Road

Amber felt comfortable sitting on a bench alone in the throng of people passing her. She watched pedestrians walk by as she enjoyed her Mountain Dew and Reese's Peanut Butter Cup. On the corner, a man dressed in a purple robe preached to the indifferent flow of people. It made her think of Coady's story about his meltdown about preaching to people not listening. She focused on the purple robe, the color of healing. She pondered the possibility that God sent this preacher to soothe her.

Eating the remainder of the candy, while simultaneously gulping down the soda, calmed her. She pondered the possible chemical reasons why sugar always seemed to relax her. Although spending more than a decade in the pharmaceutical industry, she had never liked chemistry.

Perhaps the candy, a minor temptation, allowed her a chance to indulge without major consequences. Part of her wished she had stayed with such trivial enticements, instead of such life-altering desires. The other part of her psyche wished she pushed harder toward her wants. Feeling her life's foundation shaking, Amber needed something stable to hold onto before everything changed underneath her.

The self-reflection brought her father, Peter, to mind. Strange—she had not thought about him for a long time. In her early years, the two were inseparable. Family members teased them for being so alike. Both loved structure. Both loved goals. Both loved working hard. When her age hit double digits, they started moving apart, little by little, until Amber put a permanent wedge between them.

I ended it, Amber huffed.

Her father, a moody guy, had been prone to sudden outbursts of frustration. For years, Amber only observed it when her father vented to her mother or brother about their lack of drive or ambition. He never scolded her because she had plenty of both. Then one day, while she and her brother played video games, her father ranted on the absurdity of bottled water.

Amber recalled her father coming into the den from his office, holding a stack of paperwork. Her father had accidentally knocked over some uncapped water bottles and stained his papers. Throwing the plastic water bottles at the television screen, Amber's father, like a deranged professor, lectured them on the stupidity of bottled water.

"Why did I install that expensive water filtering system?" Amber's father yelled. "For what?"

Amber did not want to answer, but finally felt obliged because she was eleven and older than her brother, "For water."

"That's right. But you and your brother spend all this money, wasting it on bottled water. You kids don't care. You don't have to pay for the water. You don't have to pay for the top-of-the-line filtering system. You don't have to pay for the video games or the television. You can just sit back and ride my back through life. You're just like your mother."

"I won't drink bottled water," Amber answered.

"That's not the point. You don't understand the financial stress involved in raising a family. Everything you guys need, I've got to figure how to get the money to pay for it."

Although the scolding seemed petty over such a minor issue, Amber reacted strongly. She went through her personal items, selling video

Jesus's Brother James

games, clothes, and books. She collected the proceeds into a small stack and placed them on her father's desk.

"What's this?"

"I'm taking some of the stress from you. I got a job, so I can buy my own things now."

"Amber, I'm sorry about the other day. I was just having an awful day at work. The pressure sometimes gets to me—that's all."

Amber, ever defiant, replied coolly, "No, you were right. I should start paying for my own things."

"Amber, I know this might seem strange to you, but I hate my job. I feel trapped. I only do this work for the money. Someone has to work to pay all the bills."

"Well, this will help take some of the pressure off you," Amber replied as she left the money on his desk and turned and left her father's office.

For years, Amber proudly told this story. Not only did Amber start paying for her high school activities, but she had won a full scholarship to college and never asked her father for any more money again.

Amber had taken pleasure in declining any of her father's offers. As keen as she was, she noticed the pain on her father's face each time she casually waved off his monetary offerings. This bold independence always had been a source of pride and now seemed to haunt her.

Amber peered at her phone and her inbox showed thousands of messages. She suddenly felt empathy for her father. Perhaps he had had a manager like Steve. Perhaps her father had poured all his energy into a job, but never won a promotion. Perhaps her father never had the ability to break free from the vortex of work. She felt pity for him. She quickly felt anger at herself. As though she had inherited a genetic condition, she endured the same fate as her father.

Amber's phone vibrated. It was her director Steve. "I can't speak on the phone. I'm at the hospital with a friend," she texted to him.

While she contemplated her new perspective on her dad's outbursts, Paul approached with a calm swagger.

"Getting some fresh air?" he asked.

"Fresh air? I'm not sure I would say that," Amber laughed as she waved her hand in front of her nose, while a passing truck spewed smoke from its exhaust.

"Still, you seem to be enjoying yourself."

"It's nice here. I like to people-watch."

"Can I join you?"

"Sure," Amber replied, noting Paul's somber and sorrowful face as he sat down next to her.

"Listen. I'm sorry for what happened at the restaurant. I just. I just... uhm..." Paul could not finish his sentence.

Paul's awkwardness pleasantly surprised Amber. "I was kind of flattered."

"Flattered?"

"Yeah, fighting for your woman," Amber snickered.

"Getting my ass kicked impressed you?" Paul asked. "Wow, I would never have thought."

"Getting your ass kicked is not the impressive part. It was that you cared."

They both laughed.

"It's kind of weird. I could have sworn that you and Mike would be pissed at Coady. But you're both okay with him."

Amber's smiled stiffened, sensing Paul was passive aggressively returning to the topic of Coady's deception. "Why did you come all the way to New York?" she asked.

Paul reached to his bag, pulled out photos of Mike, Pedro's blanket, and the photo of them in Mexico. "I found these and it made me think."

"Made you think?" Amber reached over and took the photo from Paul.

"Remember that trip to Mexico?" Paul asked.

Amber touched Pedro's blanket. "And you still have Pedro's blanket?" Paul nodded. "That was a great trip," Amber laughed, but turned somber. "Why did you come to New York?"

Paul shrugged his shoulders, "I didn't like the way everything was going between us."

Amber looked at the photograph, with all the thoughts about Coady, her father, and her career still swirling in her mind. Although flattered with Paul's attention, she didn't like his evasiveness. She coughed, "What are you trying to say?"

Although a simple question, it proved difficult to answer. "I'm sorry about how I've handled this whole situation."

"Situation?"

"You know."

"Paul, can we cut the shit here? You came to New York because you felt bad about the way you were breaking up with me?"

"Well, I'm sorry."

Amber looked at her phone. "Why be sorry? You're doing what you want." She started to delete all her unread messages. "Maybe I need to be a little more like you." She handed the photo back to Paul, but he didn't want to accept it. "There has to be more than just that."

"You're right." Paul ran his fingers over the coarse fabric of Pedro's blanket. "I was sitting in my empty apartment, alone, thinking what I had done to drive off both you and Mike."

"You came here because you were feeling left out?"

"A little," Paul admitted. "But that's not the only reason I came here. I know I might have appeared to be crazy, but I realized you and Mike mean something to me."

"What do we mean to you?"

"I know it might surprise you, but Mike and I used to be close."

"No, I'm not surprised at all. At first, I thought Mike was pathetic. First you see a guy who's middle-aged, bald, fat, and with no future. But I kept noticing how much he always tries to help others."

"Mike?" Paul asked, surprised.

Amber, noticing Paul's surprised expression, explained. "You're not the only one that's a little arrogant. I thought I had my shit together so much more than Mike, but I don't. I hate my job, but I've dedicated my whole life to it. Pathetic."

"I don't think you're pathetic."

"Yes, you do. That's why you treated me the way you did."

Paul started to say something, but stopped when he noticed Amber focused on her vibrating phone.

"Do you need to take that?"

"Yes, I do." Amber replied, noticing it was her director. She walked down the sidewalk away from Paul. "Didn't you get my message?" Amber snapped in an irritated voice.

"Amber, I've been trying to get a hold of you. I need the figures for the overall region's performance." Amber, although annoyed beyond

Jesus's Brother James

endurance, chuckled to herself at the fact that Steve had received these numbers a half a dozen times. Steve continued to ramble. "The Senior Director wants to review those numbers, but I was hoping I could review them with you first."

Amber deliberated on possible ways to vent her frustration. She decided to dangle Steve, "And when's this meeting?"

"In about an hour," Steve replied.

Amber burst into laughter at the ludicrousness of a man so incompetent and oblivious holding such a high-level corporate position. "An hour. You know I'm at the hospital, right? In New York City."

"Yes, yes. I know you're busy," he answered, but Amber did not believe he digested the information she just gave him. "This will only take a couple minutes."

Amber wanted to test Steve's listening skills. "I have a friend who might be dying."

"No, your connection is fine," Steve answered. "I have the numbers in front of me."

Amber moaned a melancholy chuckle, realizing Steve had never listened to her. "You want me to take time out of being at the hospital to review numbers with you again? The same numbers I reviewed at our last one-on-one."

"I don't recall that," Steve admitted.

"Well, I can send you the meeting minutes from that call." Amber stressed in a pointed fashion.

After a long pause, Steve responded, "I'm sorry I don't recall reviewing these, but I would greatly appreciate it if we could go over them now."

Amber, who felt a sudden surge of confidence, blurted. "Can I ask a question? Why have you been late to every one of our one-on-one meetings?"

Steve coughed with surprise. "I'm not sure what this is about."

"If you respected me as a valuable member of your team, you'd find a way to be on time."

"Amber, you know that I've always considered you a valuable member of the team."

"Then why aren't you ever on time for our meetings?"

"Amber, I think you're exaggerating."

"If you thought I was valuable, why didn't I get John's position?"

"Do you think this is the best time to have this conversation?"

"Yes, I think this is the best possible time to speak on this topic."

"Well, this isn't a good time for me. I'll put a meeting on the calendar for us to discuss this further."

"A meeting that you'll be late to?" Amber laughed. Her newly-discovered ability to openly express herself to this thick-headed asshole delighted her. She had so often held her tongue from a fear of possible reprisal. Steve had shown so much disrespect for her she now reveled in her chance to reciprocate.

"I don't think this is a good tone. You know I value you. You know I think you are an integral part of the team."

"I don't believe a word of it! I think you are obnoxious, incompetent, and disrespectful. Consider this my two-week notice."

"Wow," Steve replied. He turned on his corporate robotic voice. "I created such a great role for you. How can you be so ungrateful? I am shocked at this."

"You gave my promotion to a stranger." Amber looked at her phone in disbelief, wondered how this man could utter such a lie. "There's no way you can be this obtuse."

"Amber, you know I've always valued you," Steve stated in a panicked voice. The imminent meeting with his senior director was foremost in his thoughts.

"Please stop lying. You have my notice."

Steve hesitated and asked, "Will you be able to review those numbers with me?"

"Ask my new boss," Amber hung up the phone, pleased that she had caused such a hollow man some discomfort.

"Did you just quit?" Paul asked in shock. Amber nodded her head enthusiastically. "Are you going to be okay?"

"I don't know if I'm going to be okay, but I feel free all of a sudden."

"Free? Free from what?"

"Free from everything."

Mike sprinted out of the hospital. "It's James."

Jesus's Brother James

Chapter 31
Rahkama

Minutes before Mike rushed to find Amber and Paul, he had been dutifully waiting for news about James. Unlike the others, who were distracted with the complexity of their relationships, Mike devoted all of his attention on his friend. Blocking out his collapsing marriage, his undone fatherhood, and scary future, he implored God.

As common with desperate people, Mike was willing to deal. In exchange for James's recovery, he offered his own life. Then he retracted the offer, afraid God might find it an unfair exchange, because Mike had been so willing to part with his life multiple times. If not for the Chinese delivery person, God could have had Mike's life for nothing. Mike strained to think of a way to sweeten the deal.

I'll change my life, Mike promised. *But what kind of change?*

Mike took out his college acceptance letter and his photo with Paul. Mike then pondered various questions. *Why had he made so many bad decisions? Why didn't he have the discipline to change his own life? Why didn't things ever turn out well for him?*

"No, this is not about me. This is about James," Mike spoke aloud to God.

"What's that?" Coady asked as he reentered the waiting room.

Mike shot a look at Coady, noticing lipstick on his priest collar. "Nothing," snapped Mike. Coady's romancing angered Mike. The former priest should have been praying for James's recovery, not chasing Amber.

"I'm sure everything is going to be fine with James," Coady assured him.

"A few more prayers wouldn't hurt," Mike chided.

Mike retrieved his blood-stained college acceptance form his pocket and intensely peered at it. On the back of the page was the word, "*Rahkama.*" Mike could not remember when he had written it. He remembered Ms. Sabar had translated it as love and mercy. He pictured James insisting Mike have love and mercy now.

"I'm sorry. I shouldn't have snapped."

"That's fine," Coady answered. "I know you're worried. I know James means a lot to you."

Mike firmly nodded his head yes. "I'm not sure anyone means more to me."

"I understand," Coady replied in a sympathetic voice. Looking down at the paper in Mike's hand, Coady grew curious. "Is that something James gave to you?"

"No," Mike replied as he tucked the paper back into his pocket.

"What's the connection between the paper and James?"

"Connection with James?" Mike asked aloud. The question confused Mike. The paper had always served as self-flagellation device, which Mike used to punish himself over his decision to skip college. Like a holy man lashing himself with a rod, Mike chastised himself mentally with the paper. Then, in an incredible moment, Mike pondered over the word James had been uttering, *Rahkama*. Mike whispered, "Maybe he meant mercy."

Jesus's Brother James

"What's that?" Coady asked.

"Is it possible to show mercy to yourself?" Mike questioned.

"It is important to show yourself mercy," Coady said. He pondered the significance of the question. The question certainly applied to him. Coady stood up and paced.

Mike pulled out the paper again and peered at his acceptance letter. "Maybe Paul is right. Maybe it's not good to always look at the past."

"What's on the paper?"

"It's silly. This is my letter of acceptance to college."

"And why do you keep it?

"I didn't go away to college, but stayed near home went to Wake Tech after high school. And I never even finished there."

Mike could hear Paul's voice in his head. *Oh, my God, are you still replaying that? Get over it already.*

Mike continued his internal argument with Paul, *It was a big deal to me. I know you always make perfect choices.*

I might not make perfect choices, but I never revisit them, the imaginary Paul replied.

You mean like your decision to dump Amber, Mike yelled.

"Mike, are you okay?" a confused Coady asked.

Mike, so riveted with his argument with the imaginary Paul, did not acknowledge Coady.

You broke into a priest's apartment, drove all the way to New York, and fought for her, Mike continued.

What's your point? the imaginary Paul replied.

Mike took out the photo from the Empire State Building and started waving it around. *The point is, why didn't you ever do something dramatic to save our friendship? You just let time kill it. You never raised a finger to help.*

Uhm, the imaginary Paul stuttered, not able to generate an answer. Mike shook with anger.

Coady, shocked by Mike's behavior, put his hand on Mike's shoulder. "Mike, I'm here. And Paul is nearby."

Coady's touch snapped Mike from his unreal quarrel. "Yeah, you're here," Mike stated and tucked the photo into his pocket.

Before Coady could ask Mike what was wrong, the surgeon entered the waiting room and moved to Coady. Mike rushed over to join them. With a somber face, he informed them that they could go in to see James.

"Please only stay for a moment, James needs his rest," the surgeon instructed the two.

With that, Mike scurried down the hall and into the room. James, unconscious, lay silent, his body heavily bandaged, with tubes down his throat. The dramatic scene did not deter Mike's enthusiasm, who rushed over to his bedside and burst into tears of joy. Mike thought he saw James smiling back at him.

"It's so great to see you," Mike said. "Don't worry, you will be out of here in no time."

Coady moved over to Mike, placing his large hand on his shoulder. "Mike, the doctor told me that James's injuries are quite serious."

"I know. I know," Mike replied as he reached over for James's hand. "I'll be gentle."

Coady looked James's vitals on the monitor trying to make sense of all the numbers. Although he could not read the device, he sighed a long sigh of relief when the electrocardiogram line moved, signifying life. "We'll only stay a minute."

Mike nodded in agreement and noticed James's eyes slightly open. "Buddy, how many fingers am I holding up?" Mike asked James.

"*Rahkama*," he coughed from his dry throat.

Mike clapped his hands excitedly. "That's my buddy. Love and mercy," he exclaimed. "Everything is going to be okay."

Coady put his hand on Mike's shoulder. "I'm praying."

"Praying? Praying for what?"

"The doctor said it's very serious," Coady stated.

Mike started to cry and leaned over to hold James's hand. "I don't want to talk to you about this. Why don't you go find Amber?"

As Mike ignored Coady, but could not stop the memory of his first encounter with death. Mike's beloved seventy-six-year-old grandmother died suddenly of a heart attack. Mike, eight years old at the time, did not take the news well.

During the wake he sat stubbornly praying for a miracle to bring her back to life. With an unbendable belief, he knew God would return his beloved grandmother. Mike's prayers, however, went unanswered. Like a sentry sitting for hours, he waited for a divine signal. He did not see an angel. He did not hear the slightest whisper from God. He only saw death.

Mike left the funeral home without his grandmother and with the belief God did not answer prayers. Others might have been able to see God's fingerprints in the saving of a child from an apartment blaze, but Mike saw the unanswered prayers for the victim that did not make it. That realization made him sad now. He knew God would not answer his prayers or Coady's. His future rested on chance.

"God won't answer my prayers, will he?" Mike asked Coady.

Not wanting to lie, Coady admitted, "I am not able to answer that. I do not pretend to know why God takes the actions He does."

Mike hung his head, "You know, when I pray and there is no response, it makes me feel so alone."

"I know what you mean."

Mike took out the photo of the Empire State Building. "Alone."

Coady, peeking over his shoulder, gazed at the photo. Mike's smile jumped out of the picture. "That's a great photo."

"Yeah," Mike said. "If you would have told me that day that my next trip to New York would end up like this, I would have thought you were crazy."

"When James recovers, we'll take him up there. What do you say?"

"As long as God listens to our prayers," Mike said, hoping the sound of this statement would chase away his doubt that God might intervene.

Just then, the electrocardiogram's long steady hum and James's heart showed no electrical activity. James had flatlined.

Chapter 32
Empire State of Mind

The awful image of the flatline blurred Mike's vision as he ran into Amber and Paul.

"He's dead," Mike screamed. "Oh, dear God, he's dead."

"James?" Paul asked as he tried to clutch Mike's shirt, but Mike danced from him.

"He's dead. I saw the line," Mike yelled and looked up at the skyline.

"Mike, let's go back in together."

Mike, ignoring Paul, seemed to find something fascinating in the skyline. He muttered, "Paul, remember the pillows that you carried for that girl."

"What?"

"I helped with the pillows. It turned out great."

"Mike, you're in shock. Let's go back into the room together."

"No, no need for that. I'd be alone in there. I need some time. I need some time."

Mike stumbled down the street, ignoring impeccably dressed women, looking at the skyline. He did not notice the dog walker struggling to keep seven large breeds from bolting, but he looked at the skyline. He did not notice the limos pulling up to high-end restaurants; his eyes were above the horizon. He did not notice the two well-dressed women as he stepped on their new Coach shoes.

"You vile ape," snapped a large woman as she scolded Mike.

"What?" Mike questioned, not sure if she was speaking to him.

"You are a big, ugly, fat, sweaty fucking gorilla," she stated with a cocking of her head and wag of her finger.

"Gorilla?" Mike exclaimed. "Yes, I am a big gorilla. This must be a sign." Mike attempted to shake her hand, but she recoiled from his touch.

"Don't touch me, you pig," she scolded.

"No, gorilla. Yes, a big gorilla," Mike answered. Calmness overtook Mike. He proceeded to take off his button-down shirt, dropping it in the gutter. He had an "I LOVE NY" shirt on underneath, which was saturated with sweat.

"King Kong died on the streets of New York," Mike said out loud. *But which street? I guess it depends on the movie.*

Mike stopped for a moment, long enough to be flocked with men in yellow and red jackets selling expensive tours of New York. Being a tourist opened an individual to the dangers of being harassed by these relentless individuals.

"You can't come to New York and not take a tour," said one man as he pushed a pamphlet into Mike's face.

Mike took the brochure, read it, and then his face lit up. "There were three movies, right?"

"Three movies?" the salesman asked. "Listen, I'll give you a good price. Best tour of New York."

"The first and the third were different than the second, right?" Mike asked, surprised to be thinking about movies at such a time.

The red-shirted salesman gazed at Mike, concluding him odd, but still seeing a potential sale. "The tour covers spots of all kinds of movies. New York is the most filmed city in all the world."

"Yes," Mike said as he walked away leaving a disappointed salesperson as he moved past him.

While Mike wandered the Big Apple, Coady dashed straight into Amber and Paul as he exited the elevator. He was leaving the hospital as they were entering it. The collision caused Paul to stumble back, almost knocking him from his feet.

"Is Mike with you?" Coady asked, slightly out of breath.

"He walked off. He said he need a little time," Amber explained. "Is James—" she started, but Coady cut her off.

"I don't think we should leave Mike alone right now," Coady commented, motioning for them to follow him out of the hospital. "Where did he go?"

"I'm not sure. He headed up the street," Amber pointed at a crowded sidewalk. "It might be hard to find him."

"This is not good."

"What happened?"

"He freaked out when he saw James flatline," Coady replied, taking Mike's photo from his pocket.

"Flatline?" Amber gasped and covered her mouth with her hand. "Should we try his cell phone?"

"I'm calling him now," Paul commented as he called. After a moment, he updated Amber, "Went straight to voicemail." Paul looked at the skyline and noticed something.

"I know where he went," Coady announced.

"I do too," Paul added. He motioned for Coady to hand him the photo. "Let's get walking."

"I think we take the subway," Coady argued.

Amber, strutting to the curb, held out her hand, "We're taking a cab."

"We'll never get a cab," Paul insisted just as a cab pulled up.

"I've got good cab karma," she said and motioned for Paul to get in. She hopped into the middle, with Coady on the other side. The cab sped off with Amber squeezed in the back seat with her two boyfriends.

Arriving at the corner of 5th and 35th, Coady jumped from the cab and sprinted over to security guard at the entrance of the Empire State Building. Thinking his holy attire would expedite them past the line, he adjusted his collar. Clearing his throat, he delivered a well-crafted lie in a priestly tone.

"Excuse me, my son, one of my parishioners is inside and he's not well. Can you please help me?"

New York, famous not only for big buildings, but also for even bigger attitudes, contained security guards who were not easily impressed. "That collar don't impress me much. A priest is a title I think you want to live down to, not up to. Get to the back of the line," the security guard barked.

"But, sir, I feel the man is not well."

"If we stopped everyone that wasn't well, this place would be a ghost town."

Amber, lacking patience in Coady's approach, moved over to the loud security guard. She leaned over, whispered into the security guard's ear and within seconds the man escorted them to the elevator.

"What did you say to that guard?" Coady asked.

"Nothing. The weak-minded are easily persuaded."

Commotion greeted them as they reached the observation deck on 86th floor. Moving toward a ring of tourists, they saw Mike naked and hanging onto the 15-foot fence lining the perimeter used to prevent people from climbing out on the ledge.

Like a pale hairless Winnie the Pooh, he jiggled his soft frame in a futile attempt to free himself. Mike had his right leg stuck between the bars from slipping mid-climb. The stiff bar now pinched against his upper thigh.

Mike was now New York City's biggest live naked spectacle. His privates tangling on the bar provided an interesting image for everyone recording on their phones. With each screech erupting from a tourist, Mike wiggled faster to get free, but he only caused himself pain.

A large security guard arrived at the same time as Coady, moving over to help Mike. After lifting Mike's leg, he helped him down onto the ground and placed a jacket over Mike, who curled underneath the jacket to hide.

Coady timidly approached, not sure Mike wanted to speak to him, but Mike motioned for Coady to come closer.

"Is James," Mike started and then choked out, "you know, dead?"

"I don't know," Coady explained. "I left the room while they were still working on him."

"Do you know I finished that book on Jesus's brother James?" Mike informed Coady. "Everybody forgets about James. I mean, he was an original founder and everyone forgets him."

"But James served an important role. Just because everyone does not know him doesn't mean he did not live a fulfilling life."

"No, Paul changed everything and just threw away all James's ideas. Paul didn't care at all."

"I do care," Paul stepped forward, "Mike, I'm here."

"I wasn't talking about you. I was talking about the other Paul." Mike ran his eyes over Paul's features as though he had never met him.

"What did you think you were doing?"

Mike sheepishly looked at his leg and then around at the gaping crowd. "I wasn't really thinking. I figured I'd do a King Kong off the building."

"Butt naked?" asked Paul.

"Yeah, Kong was naked," said Mike with a sudden levity at his craziness.

"You're right, King Kong was naked," stated the calm security guard. Working in the famous building conditioned to him to bizarre behavior so Mike's little stunt did not bother him at all.

Paul, sounding like the imaginary Paul, offered advice. "Mike, you've got to let all this bitterness go. You've got to look forward and not back."

"Look forward? Like I'm going to jail soon."

"Oh, don't worry," the security guard assured him. "This happens all the time. You'll get a fine and be out in a few hours." The security guard turned to the tourists holding up their iPhones. "Now, the photos on Facebook are going to last a little longer."

Mike felt an immediate bond with the guard. He informed him, "My wife slept with my brother."

"Life sucks, doesn't it?" the guard commented. "My wife left me for my father."

"Your father?" Mike asked as he quickly tried to determine which was worse, losing a woman to a father or a brother.

"I mean, my dad was a Cuban singer, so he is charming as hell, but he is all wrinkly and shit."

"You don't sound upset."

"I was at first. Then I realized my wife was a pain in the ass. She was self-centered, always bitching about this and that. Now she's my dad's headache."

"You were able to overcome it and succeed."

"Succeed? I'm not the starting point guard for the Knicks, but my friends got me through it." The security guard stepped away from Mike so he could speak on the phone to the rescue team that was on its way.

"Friends," Mike sighed.

"We're here for you," Paul stated. Putting his arm under Mike's to support him, he took out the photo. "Remember that picture? It was a great time."

"That was a long time ago," Mike said.

"It was. But it was unforgettable."

"We did have some good times," commented Mike.

"Remember on the road trip, the head lights went out?"

Mike shook his head "yes." "You had that Ford Escort GT. The GT stood for 'got tricked' into buying an Escort."

"We couldn't afford a hotel, so we slept in the parking lot."

"I had so many mosquito bites 'cause I slept on the hood."

Paul laughed. "We saw all the sights that day though."

"But only because I met that girl. You got us lost and we spent fifty dollars in tolls driving back and forth between New York and Jersey."

"You're right. We parked the car in Hoboken and took the Path train. If it wasn't for you, we'd still be driving all over New York."

Mike laughed, then shoot his head as the humor leaked from his face. With a solemn gaze, he concluded. "You don't need my help anymore."

"If you were to have died without me...you know...without us being friends again, that would have sucked." Paul coughed back tears. "You know some people never get a chance to fix a mistake."

Mike, unclenched his hand, revealing the acceptance letter, "Why do you think things ended when you went away to school?"

"It doesn't matter. What matters is that I've got a chance to be friends with you again. I'm canceling my trip abroad. We can find a place together."

Mike smiled and held up the letter, "*Rahkama.*"

"Let it go, Mike. Let it go."

Mike put his hand through the bar and let the letter float off the observation deck and into the wind. Paul cheered loudly. Coady clapped and walked up to the bars, took off his white collar, and slipped it through.

"Yeah!" Amber yelled. She took out her corporate phone and tossed it over the edge.

"Damn, I hope it doesn't hit anyone," Mike exclaimed.

"Oh, my God," Amber cried.

"Don't worry; there's a net to catch anything that falls."

"It's a good thing I didn't jump. I would have been hanging naked in the net for hours. I would have died of fright."

The group laughed and hugged.

Chapter 33
Shwoqqan

Mike piled items in the back of a truck. "Because we're buying all the furniture from this apartment, would it be easier just to move in here furnished?"

"Probably," Paul laughed. "Perfect timing. We need furniture and she's selling everything."

"I hope you got a good deal."

"Ah, you know women, they're tough negotiators."

"Hey," Amber snapped. "I gave you a hell of a deal."

"I'm just kidding with you," Paul replied.

"I'm going to miss that sense of humor."

"You're always welcome at our place if you get tired of living with your dad," Paul said.

"Thanks, but he was pretty excited when I asked him if I could live at home while I go back to school."

"I have something for you," Paul told her and reached into the front seat to retrieve the infamous Rob Thomas birthday gift.

"Is this hot?" Amber asked.

"No, I paid for it, along with several hundred plates and glasses from that restaurant."

Just then James leaned his head out of the front of the moving van. "*Shwoqqan.*"

"Shit, James, you scared the hell out of me," Amber called. She leaned over to Mike, "He's made a speedy recovery."

"Well. He never did flatline. There was something wrong with the instrument."

"But he'll recover from the accident?"

"Oh yeah, he had a few broken bones. He has trouble walking around, but he likes to sit in the front seat when we drive around town."

"*Shwoqqan*," James repeated.

"What does that mean, Mike?"

"Oh, you've got to work a little harder to find that out," Mike answered.

"What's next?" Paul asked.

"Not sure. I've got so many things to think about. I'm going to spend some time with my parents for now. I think I'm looking for a whole new start."

"Does that mean you won't be hanging around Father Coady?" Paul asked.

"Can't let that go, can you?" Amber leaned over to Mike. "I have to thank you."

"For what?" Mike asked.

"You know, there are people I've known for years who have had no impact on me. In this short time with you and James, you have completely altered my life."

Paul nodded and leaned even closer to Amber. "So, you never answered my question about Coady."

"Nope," Amber picked up a bottle of water as she looked out onto the busy street. "I'm sure James had an impact on Coady too."

Coady stood outside a downtown bar smoking a cigarette, sipping whiskey from a glass, watching a prostitute applying a thick layer of red lipstick. Noticing Coady, she adjusted her tight mini-skirt, bouncing her butt cheeks back and forth for effect. Coady looked below her belly at a small cross piercing her belly button, which amused him. As Coady surveyed her appearance, he examined his black pants, black shirt, and black jacket. It felt strange to be missing his white collar.

"Would you have a cigarette?" she asked.

"For you. Sure."

Coady took out a cigarette and held it out to the woman. Without using her hands, the woman carefully took the cigarette with her lips. "And a light too?"

"Surely, my dear." Coady lit her cigarette.

The woman surveyed Coady, who stared at her with delight. She pondered a large number she might quote. She blew smoke from her mouth, making suggestive sucking motions on the cigarette as she stared at him.

"You're a good-looking guy," she commented.

"Thank you."

"The best-looking guy I've seen tonight," she added.

"Thank you, my dear."

"You're not a cop, are you?"

"No."

"You look like a priest."

Coady took a long drag as he considered her comment. He looked at the young woman with a stern glance. "No, I'm not a priest any more. I'm a war veteran."

"A veteran priest?"

Coady took a few deep drags from his cigarette and blew circles out. He chuckled. "You know, that has a very nice ring to it." He took out his wallet and counted its contents.

"Are you ready for some quality time?" the woman said with a smile.

"Yes. How much would it cost to talk to you for a little while?"

Acknowledgments

Thank you to my family, April, Annasofia, and Jacob, for enduring my pecking away at the keyboard for my books. I could not think of a better family.

Thank you, Chris Reinhardt, for your support; if it wasn't for you I would still be hanging out at Frank's in Esopus.

Thank you, Kirk Reinhardt, for your support; if it wasn't for your help I would never have graduated from Davis.

Thank you, Sue Reinhardt-Johnson, for all your support through the years, and for letting me leverage your theological background to improve my vocabulary.

Thank you, Mom, Kathryn Reinhardt, for reviewing early drafts of the book and providing such valuable feedback.

Thank you, Shane Reinhardt, for your support and driving long distances to see my film.

Thank you, Alice Osborn, for your wonderful support and encouragement from the early drafts to what this book is today. It is not an easy job being an editor for someone with my sense of humor.

Thank you, Tamara Farias and Steven Roten, for your help; there is nothing better for a writer than to have talented actors help you with dialogue.

Thank you, Greg Glazman, for all your support with the books, the film, and improving my Russian to what it is today.

Thank you, Roe Connor, for plodding through early rough drafts and providing such great feedback. Mary Howe, thank you for your support and reading my material; you made the corporate world bearable.

Thank you, John Mandy, for your thorough review and excellent feedback, as well as all the great trips we made around the world.

Thank you, Karl Larsen, for all your support with both with my books and films—not many people would bother people in Hollywood on behalf of a friend.

Thank you, Marcos Sanz, for all your support with both my books and films; not everyone would offer to put a poster on their car for you.

Thank you, Heidi Humpries, for your support and helping with the early drafts.

Don Vaughn, thank you for your support with my nonfiction writing.

Thank you, Alex Velasquez, for all your support of my writing and for always having such a positive attitude.

Thank you, Dennis Rojas, for bringing James to life, literally.

About the Author

 A veteran of the pharmaceutical industry, Tim Reinhardt has traveled the world extensively and studied many diverse cultures. His travels, coupled with an eventful childhood, shape his thought-provoking perspective on life. He enjoys writing comedies placed in dramatic settings most of all because he likes the contrast between genres. Tim knows life can be challenging and thinks stories like these make the tough times a little bit easier to handle.

Tim is the writer of the Academy-Award qualifying film *Crackers*, as well as the author of *Afaq: I'm Trapped in India*. He is currently working on a film adaptation for *Jesus's Brother James*.

When he's not busy writing, Tim enjoys making films, playing tennis, and learning about history. He currently resides in Holly Springs, North Carolina, with his wife April, daughter Annasofia, son Jacob, and rescue dog Faith.

Jesus's Brother James is Tim's second novel.